D eath looked annoyed. "I have people to kill, guys. An entire multiverse's worth in fact. You need to win the tournament in order to keep the Primal Orbs out of the hands of Entropicus. They are the physical manifestation of the Primals' power. Many times, mortals and gods have sought to acquire all seven for the purposes of being omnipotent within their own reality."

"It seems like a bad idea to keep those around," I said, pointing out the obvious risk in their existence. "You know, because of the fact they can give godlike power to people utterly undeserving of it, like me. Can't you password protect them or something?"

"No, Gary." Death shook her head. "This is why Entropicus wishes to win this tournament as he plans to use his wish to unmake reality."

I paused, blinking. "What kind of moron would want to do that?"

"I destroyed the universe," Diabloman muttered. "Once."

"Yeah, but we all agree that was a bad idea," I said, not really wanting to get into that. "What possible benefit could anyone derive from destroying everything?"

Death closed her eyes. "Entropicus was my champion at the beginning of this universe. He's the father of the seven children I presented Reaper's Cloaks in time-lost Acheron. He knows there's an afterlife waiting for mortals but despises the suffering needed to get there as well as the arbitrary nature of human suffering."

THE TOURNAMENT OF SUPERVILLAINY

By C. T. Phipps

Preface

By C. T. Phipps

MORTAL KOMBAT!
 techno music plays
Oh, sorry, I was briefly lost in the Nineties. You'll understand why I made that reference in a bit. When I completed the *Science of Supervillainy*, I briefly debated having Gary hang up his cloak for good. There's always the problem of dragging out a series too long. You don't want to overstay your welcome and it was a decent place to end the story. Gary had defeated Merciful, President Omega, and matured into a responsible adu…okay, I can't finish that sentence without laughing. Gary didn't mature in the slightest.

However, I didn't want the series to become nothing more than a series of constantly repeated jokes and pop culture references. I already had some people saying the formula was becoming stale. I will even share a secret with you: I wrote a good sixty thousand words of Supervillainy Saga #5 before realizing I just wasn't enjoying it. Thus, I scrapped the *Kingdom of Supervillainy* and decided to make the *Tournament of Supervillainy* instead. So what is this novel?

The Tournament of Supervillainy is an homage to all the dozens of fighting games I played during my teenage years ranging from *Street Fighter II* to *Tekken* to a few I don't think anyone remembers (*Virtual Fighter* anyone?). Gone are the days of the arcade and the replacement of fighting online in multiplayer matches just isn't the same. It's also an homage to *Enter the*

Dragon and other martial arts movies that inspired the fighting game genre.

Seriously, I must have spent thousands of dollars plugging quarters into arcade machines in order to try to win the various tournaments that countless villains had set up across the globe. I still have a poster of Chun Li on my wall even as I am torn between her and Sonya Blaze. Ahem, sorry, I made it weird. I loved the colorful collection of characters who, somehow, had to save the world by smacking each other around. The similarity to comic books is obvious and, even better, you have a reason why hero fought hero.

It's also a crossover story and fans of my other works will note Gary is going to be meeting the stars of *Agent G, I was a Teenage Weredeer, Lucifer's Star*, and a few other books of mine. Why is this? Well, I've always loved works like *Crisis on Infinite Earths* and it would lose a bit of its oomph if I just had Gary meeting analogues for other superheroes. You don't need to have read the other books to know what's what, though. All you need to know is Gary is very good at making friends even in other universes.

This book will also finally get to have Gary take a serious moment to examine just what he plans to do with the rest of his career as a supervillain. It also will give us some insight into how the Society of Superheroes is coping with losing its equivalent to Batman and Superman. *pause* I mean, the Nightwalker and Ultragod have no similarity to either! Honest!

shoos away DC Comics' lawyers

But is Gary going to continue? Yes, yes he is. Much like the comic book stories that inspired him and my idea for "What if Spiderman was a bad guy?", Merciless is a character who exists within the confines of a single story from beginning to middle to end. However, that doesn't mean there aren't plenty of stories left to tell about him. As long as there's evil to be fought and money to be made from it, Merciless will stand right there in the middle.

Until I get bored or maybe Gary does. Honestly, I'm not sure who is in charge of our relationship.

Foreword

By Jeffrey Kafer

*A*ction Comics #1000. Remember that number. Charles has lamented, on occasion, when he thinks Gary's saga should end. I've told him that so long as Gary keeps having adventures, I'll be there to narrate the audiobook version. But how many is too many? At what point do you end at the top? Is *The Tournament of Supervillainy* his *Judas Contract*? I don't think so.

See, that's the beauty of comics. There is a never-ending world of adventures and traumatic experiences he can subject his hero/villain to. If things get stale, just resurrect a character who died an emotionally devastating death and bring him back to life, thereby trivializing the emotional context of said death (I'm looking at you, Batman's *Death in the Family*). There are endless characters he can annoy with his pop culture references that come seemingly out of nowhere all to hide his insecurities. Gary's insecurities, that is. Not Charles's.

Although, maybe...

Anyway. *Action Comics* #1000. That's where Superman's adventures are numbered this year. One thousand issues of endless stories about the Mary-Suest of all superheroes. And we still don't have any logical reason why Kryptonite affects Superman. I mean, it's just a chunk of rock from the place he was born. Radiation blocking his abilities, blah blah blah. Still, makes little sense. I don't visit the place of my birth, Virginia, and suddenly break out in hives.

But I digress. What were we talking about?

Crap. I was talking about something super deep about why Charles should keep writing this Supervillainy Saga and not stop and consider this book his swan song. So long as there are stories to tell, keep telling them. Let Gary keep bumbling around. But whatever. Now I'm stuck on the whole Superman/ Kryptonite dynamic and I need to Google that to find out if there's really a canonical answer beyond fanboy justifications.

Because after 1000 issues, you'd think they would've fucking figured it out.

CHAPTER ONE

WHERE I START TO REVALUATE
MY LIFE CHOICES

So, I was getting my ass kicked. It was happening a lot lately. I was laying on the ground in the middle of the display room of W.I.Z.A.R.D labs with the Time Cube on display. It was a glowing little cube in the middle of spinning rings with a halo of blue white energy around it. What did it do? I had not the slightest idea, but the company that manufactured most of the super-technological devices of the world had made it their center display for their annual science expo, so I figured it would be a good idea to steal it.

Did I wait for nightfall when it was being packed up? Did I wait for it to be transferred from the heavily monitored display room to a less-observed armor car? Did I do it at any time other than broad daylight during the grand opening? No, of course not, because I'm a supervillain. I don't do things the easy way.

I was surrounded by the unconscious forms of Red Riding Hood a.k.a Cindy Wakowski-Karkofsky and Diabloman, who didn't have a civilian identity as far as I could tell. There was also the Teardrop Man, Mr. Stilts, the Ring-Tosser, and a bunch of other C-listers who had my exact same plan to rob the place. I swear to God, I'm not making this up, but *eight* different groups of supervillains had attacked the W.I.Z.A.R.D expo at once. That would have been a big enough disaster by itself, but no, there was also a single superheroine there.

Guinevere.

"Gary, we need to talk," the enchanting voice of the World's

Most Beautiful Ass-Kicker said, picking me up by the back of my hood and lifting me up to her face. Guinevere was a 6'2 woman who, in her natural form, basically looked like Pryanka Chopra if she was a buxom professional body-builder. Originally, Guinevere's appearance was just whatever the viewer thought was their ideal partner but she'd got herself shoved into a new body during a fight with Mr. Magick because weird stuff like that happened with superheroes more often than not. She'd also gained a boost in strength making her as strong as Ultragoddess.

Guinevere was dressed in a form-fitting suit of armor with a tabard on the front while Caliburn was sheathed beside her. A little crown rested on her forehead, marking her as Queen of Camelot. She wasn't the mythological Guinevere, but was Mordred Pendragon's sister and the daughter of Morgana Le Fey. She'd left the paradise of Otherworld in order to help regular humanity against the horrors of war. Guinevere was one of the two strongest superheroines in the world and well out of my weight class, even with the power of Death backing me up.

"Hi Gwen," I said, trying not to look at the dozen unconscious crooks surrounding me. My team had arrived late to the party and missed most of her massive beat-down of bad guys, but that didn't mean she hadn't had plenty more to share. "How's it hanging?"

I tried to turn insubstantial, in order to escape her grasp, but her magical gauntlets prevented me from doing so.

Crap.

"Do you know what it's like having to deal with you, Mr. Karkofsky?" Guinevere asked. She was using my real name, which was never a good sign with superheroes. It meant they felt they knew you personally and were inclined to take their beatings of you personally. If you were the Ice Cream Man or Big Ben, it was just a job, but if you were Gary Karkofsky then you were someone they felt connected to.

"That is a question my wife asks every day," I said, trying to figure a way out of this and seeing none. "Also, my girlfriend."

Guinevere wrinkled her nose in disgust. "You're vile."

"Hey, they know about each other," I said. "Don't be so prejudiced."

Mandy Karkofsky a.k.a Nighthuntress was a superheroine who'd died and returned as a vampire. That meant, according to Murray v. Harker, we weren't legally married and couldn't get married again unless she was returned to human form—which would never happen because there was no cure for vampirism. Cindy and I had gotten together when Mandy was soulless as well as evil. Cindy had given birth to my child, Leia. What did Mandy think of this? Well, she considered Cindy her mortal slave and servant, so she didn't mind. I had a *third* relationship happening that was complicating things with the other two. Yeah, I was a pig, but you try and deal with this kind of stuff.

Guinevere pulled me close to her face. "You. Are. An. Annoyance."

"This is also something they've said," I said, debating my options.

It wasn't that I couldn't fight Guinevere, it's the fact my options were limited to things that might seriously injure or kill the people around me. It also wouldn't work in terms of *winning* the fight. I could turn insubstantial (that hadn't worked), shoot fire or cold, and was a bit more durable than most people. It was times like this that I missed Cloak since he would have known how to handle a situation like this. Then again, the ghost of the Nightwalker would have objected to me trying to steal the Time Cube in the first place.

"Do you want to know what annoys me the most?" Guinevere asked, looming over me like a living statue.

"My acerbic wit?" I asked. "My diabolical genius? The fact I look like a model yet can recite every *Star Wars* movie from memory? Including the Prequels and *Rogue One*?"

Guinevere face planted me on the ground, breaking my nose then bringing me back up to her face. "The fact you've wasted the opportunities you've been given. You've saved the world twice. You don't kill innocents. You had a pardon from the government and Foundation for World Harmony after killing President Omega. Yet you threw it all away to become a petty criminal again?"

"I object to the word petty," I said, pushing my nose back

into place. "Also, the Gary who was pardoned was actually a version of me from an alternate universe and—"

Guinevere pulled out Caliburn and held it up against my throat. "Give me one good reason why I shouldn't kill you right now!"

I blinked. Caliburn, as one of the Great Artifacts, was one of the items that could kill me with no chance of resurrection or even undeath. I could maybe blast Guinevere with a full dose of hellfire or stygian ice, but that would probably just make her even madder. Even if I did get past her defenses, that would just kill her and I didn't want to do that. Instead, I relied on my words, as poorly chosen as they sometimes were. "Because you're one of the good guys?"

Guinevere stared directly at me before dropping me on the ground. She then put her boot around my neck, which seemed to work just as well as her gauntlets in penetrating my insubstantiality. "Yes, I suppose I am."

I stopped trying to escape and looked up at her. If I was going to get out of this then I was going to need to use my most dangerous superpower: my wits. "You know there are plenty of places where people would pay good money for this."

Guinevere's eyes blazed with fury.

"Okay, obviously not something you'd do," I said, grunting in pain. I'd taken plenty of poundings over the few years but this was particularly painful. Guinevere wasn't holding back nearly as much as she normally did. I had no idea why but she was furious at me. "However, I'm sensing some latent hostility. Is something wrong?"

Guinevere buried Caliburn in the ground beside my head before taking her boot off my neck. "Yes, Gary, there is."

I stood up, waving away what felt like a concussion. I'd probably be fine in an hour or two, the aforementioned tougher than normal power, but that didn't mean I wasn't feeling every one of my recent defeats. The Prismatic Commando, Splotch, the Bronze Medalist, and even Ultragoddess had all taken turns on the Merciless whack-a-mole.

At least Ultragoddess had taken the time to nurse me back to health afterward, but being defeated by her was no less humiliating. Gabrielle Anders was the third woman in my life but that was a whole other story.

Guinevere pulled her fist back to punch me again. "So I'm going to send you and the rest of these fools to New Alcatraz. Then I'm going to go to the next supervillain bash in what has become a three times a day occurrence."

I raised my hands in surrender as I slowly got to my feet. "Want to talk about it?"

"Excuse me?" Guinevere asked. "Gary, you're going to jail."

"From which I will promptly escape so while we're waiting for the police here in Atlas City to arrest me, why don't you tell me what's wrong?"

"You want to *chat*?" Guinevere asked.

"Versus getting thrown around like a ragdoll or used as a punching bag? Yes, yes I do."

"That's ridiculous." Guinevere looked intrigued, though.

"Not really," I said, sighing and going to check on Cindy then Diabloman. "I had a minor in superhuman psychology and I'm one of the few people who knows what it's like to be on both sides of the hero/villain divide. Besides, legally, you have to wait for the police."

"Technically, I can give a statement later."

I interrupted that train of thought as I went over to check Diabloman's eyes. "Hold up, checking bodies."

Hollywood made you believe that if you knocked someone out, they would be fine a little while after but if they weren't up after thirty minutes then they probably weren't getting up. As such, superheroes had quite a bigger body count than many people believed unless they were Society of Superheroes members who had Venusian equipment to stabilize them. The fact Guinevere *was* in the Society and hadn't bothered using it showed she didn't care. I cast some minor healing magic over my henchmen then went to the other villains to make sure nobody passed on. The Guinevere I knew wasn't the kind of person who killed. Not unless the victim was a monster and I meant that in the giant or dragon sense.

"Are they alright?" Guinevere asked.

"Nothing decades of medical debt won't cure."

"Good," Guinevere said, apparently missing the irony of my statement or not caring. "I didn't mean to go so harsh on them."

"So why did you?" I asked.

"The Time Cube cannot be allowed to fall into evil hands!"

I looked at her. "Do you even know what it does?"

"You don't?" Guinevere looked at me.

I raised an eyebrow.

"Things," Guinevere admitted, looking guilty. "Related to time."

"Uh-huh. You have my parole I will not attempt to escape while you're here. I wouldn't abandon Diabloman or Cindy anyway."

"Honor among thieves?" Guinevere asked, as if the concept was ludicrous. Which it was.

"They're my family."

Guinevere stared at me, looking around the scene then sighed. "Very well, I'll give it a shot. Gary, you and the rest of the supervillains you released from Merciful's jails are driving the Society of Superheroes to ruin."

Guinevere was referring to the fact, a year ago, I'd been one of the most famous super*heroes* in the world—except, for the fact it wasn't me. Merciful a.k.a Other Gary took my place after dumping me and Mandy in a secret prison of his own design. He'd proven a lot better at my life than I had, ending crime in Falconcrest City and becoming known as a world famous inventor despite the fact neither of us had an IQ above 135.

Other Gary turned my hometown of Falconcrest City into a police state. He locked away most of the world's supervillains in black sites along with a bunch of his political opponents. He even stuffed Gabrielle into a power plant, sucking on her energy for years. I'd ended up freeing her but it had required releasing all the other supervillains Merciful had locked away—many who had belonged in jail or in the morgue. It had destroyed all of the good will I'd garnered before my doppelganger had capitalized on it. Apparently, stopping World War 3 a few years earlier wasn't anything compared to the mild inconvenience of having to round up some goons I'd let loose.

I looked up at Guinevere. "The Society is being driven to

ruins? My frequently broken jaw says otherwise."

"You have a target on your back since you shut down your doppelganger," Guinevere said, revealing she knew it hadn't been me. "Just about every hero wants to punch you or blast you for destroying their lives."

"I think that's an exaggeration," I said, pausing to think about the implications. "Though I'm not sure which part is the exaggeration."

It did explain my massive amount of bad luck, though. Last year, I'd been ready to take over the world. Two worlds, in fact, only to have my fortune dissipate and virtually every heist I planned ended in complete disaster. I'd become a jobber and while I was one of those supervillains who treated every prison he was held in like Swiss cheese, that didn't keep me from experiencing the physical pain of every beat down. It had gotten to the point superheroes didn't even wait for me to commit crimes, they actually tracked me down in order to lay the smack down. That just wasn't kosher. Legal? Yes. Kosher? No.

"Gary, last year we were on the verge of winning the war against crime. Almost all supervillains were locked up and the major syndicates were all dismantled. P.H.A.N.T.O.M was destroyed along with SKULL and the Fraternity of Supervillains. We were finally able to work on things like clean energy, world poverty, hunger, and other social ills our powers were better suited to. Then you had to go reinvigorate the supervillain world, unite them, and lead them to free all their friends. Do you realize what you've done?"

I balled my fists. "Listen, *that wasn't a good thing*! Merciful was brainwashing people! He hurt Gabrielle! You let that happen."

"I'm sorry about that but one hundred twenty-two people died when you cut the power to the East Coast," Guinevere said, ignoring what I'd said.

I took a deep breath. I remembered when the news showed the faces of the people who'd been killed in the sudden blackout and the failure of the locals to be prepared for it. It was only one of the consequences of my taking down Merciful and his saccharine empire. "I'd do it again. That was sick and I love Gabrielle. By the way, don't tell Mandy or Cindy that."

"We know, Gary," Cindy said, getting up and feeling her head. She was dressed in an armored leather version of a 'sexy Red Riding Hood' outfit that was glamoured to be a lot more revealing than it was. "Would someone get me the number of the truck that hit me? It was shaped like a swimsuit model."

"You able to resist Guinevere's aura of peace?" I asked, surprised she was standing up.

"I think the concussion is helping," Cindy muttered, feeling her head.

"I've stopped my charm aura," Guinevere said. "It hasn't been working as well as it used to."

"Can't possibly be the changes to your personality," Cindy said, spitting out a tooth. "It's okay, it's a molar."

"Do you realize what you did by releasing all those monsters?" Guinevere looked at me with a condemnatory stare. "A lot of monsters were released by your incarnation of the Fraternity of Supervillains too. We're still trying to find Bloodbath and Killgore for murdering Lady Hollywood's family."

Okay, maybe what I'd done wasn't a mild inconvenience. "Hey, I killed those two, actually. They'd invited me to join in a job. It turned out to involve slaving—which I had only one response to."

"Turning it down?" Cindy asked. "Calling the cops?"

"Fire," I replied. "Lots and lots of fire."

"Ah," Cindy said. "That was my next guess."

Guinevere blinked. "What? You killed your fellow supervillains? Why?"

"Because they were psychos," I said, glad she understood I meant Bloodbath and Killgore. "There's two kinds of supervillains. The professional criminals and the monsters. I don't have any room for monsters in my vision of supervillainy. I also killed the Lakewood Slasher, Cannibal Hillbilly Redneck, and the Nightmare Fetishist."

"It's why the Fraternity of Supervillains blackballed him," Cindy said, trying to stand up before falling back on her ass. "It's technically illegal for any supervillain to work with him and I almost lost my membership card for it. However, I'm okay with them because they all think I'm willing to screw them."

"But you aren't, right?" I asked, half-joking.

"Of course not!" Cindy said. "I only have sex with you, Mister Inventor, the Florist, and three former nineties boy band leads."

I stared at her. "Yeah, that's fair."

I tried to put that image out of my mind and failed. Then I thought about it for a minute.

"Gary!" Guinevere said.

"Hmm?" I said, turning around. "Listen, I'm sorry about what happened but his tyranny couldn't be allowed to continue. The real Guinevere would know you can't sacrifice the freedom of seven people just to make sure one guilty person dies. I swear you were a lot nicer when you locked me up a few years ago."

"When I sentenced you to life imprisonment on the moon?"

"Yes, you smiled more then."

Guinevere didn't look impressed with my logic. "I don't want to sacrifice anyone's freedom, Gary, but this is a war that has stretched us to the limits. I've been fighting it since WW2 and I've lost more friends than you could count doing so. Nazi Basher, Captain Stalwart, Ms. Terri, and Two-Fisted Pulp-Hero. Ultragod and the Nightwalker kept us all together but the Society of Superheroes doesn't have them anymore. I've tried to carry the slack, but even I have trouble some days."

I frowned. "I miss them too. There's not a day goes by I wouldn't kill for Cloak's advice. He was my friend too."

The world had become a much darker place with the death of the Nightwalker and Ultragod. Lancel Warren and Moses Anders had been two of the three biggest heroes in the world. Their deaths had left a big hole in the ranks of the world's champions and Guinevere was obviously not dealing too well with the stress. Then again, maybe I was judging her too harshly, as Lady Hollywood was her goddaughter. Lord knew I'd gone crazy a few times in my career.

Guinevere narrowed her eyes. "Gary, do you know why we haven't just grabbed you and put you on an asteroid with robots to take care of you until you died like we did with Satan Man or Zull the World Destroyer?"

I stared at her. "Because that's horrifically immoral and against the law?"

"Ultragoddess said if we ever seriously hurt or, gods forbid, kill you then she would destroy the Society of Superheroes outright." Guinevere's voice was tired. "Her Shadow Society is made up of people who consider you to be a hero and hate us for abandoning her. There's also the argument you have saved the world a few times."

"Oh, really?" I asked, sarcastically. "Is that all?"

I'd saved the world from Tom Terror and two ancient Nephilim, Zul-Barbas (basically Cthulhu), and President Omega's attempt to commit genocide against all Supers. Hell, I'd even saved the world from my alternate universe doppelganger that the Society of Superheroes had given free rein to "solve" the supervillain issue.

"Ultragoddess wants nothing more to do with the Society or its laws. Mostly, she operates in the Third World nowadays, overthrowing dictators and ending civil wars."

"Gwen, have you considered you may not be on the right side of history here? A conflict between you and Gabrielle isn't helping anyone." Personally, I couldn't say who would win in a fight between Guinevere and Ultragoddess if they ever threw down but it would be a battle with no winners. They were the two strongest heroes left on Earth by my reckoning and should have been fighting together.

"That's on her, not me. I'm more worried about whether there will *be* a history," Guinevere said, shaking her head. "The Society of Superheroes has lost half its membership. People have retired, been crippled, died, or simply left. They just can't continue taking up the good fight anymore and the Age of Superheroes is about to end. I was hoping it would end in our victory but it may well end in our defeat. In that respect, I can't even bring myself to give a damn you've admitted to murder in front of me."

"Well, they had it coming," Cindy said, sticking her tongue out in disgust. "Especially the Nightmare Fetishist. He targeted children. I mean, you have to have some standards as a supervillain."

I didn't know how to respond because Guinevere being utterly exhausted from fighting evil was not something I'd ever expected to see. Combat fatigue affected a lot more heroes than anyone ever really acknowledged, often leading to those dramatic "I shall be a superhero no more!" or hero-on-hero fights you never stopped to examine the psychology of. Guinevere, like Ultragod and the Nightwalker, had always seemed above it all. Maybe I had screwed up. Police sirens echoed outside, signaling it was time to go to jail.

Guinevere's left gauntlet buzzed. She looked down at it then sighed. "Dammit, there's a volcano going off in Yellowstone National Park. All hands are needed on deck. I'm going to have to leave you here."

I stared at her. "Really?"

"Do me a favor and go with the police," Guinevere said, staring at me. "You are better than this, Gary. You could be so much more than you are."

"So my guidance counselor kept telling me," I said. "I promise I'll wait for the cops."

"Thank you," Guinevere said. "I'll put in a good word for you."

Guinevere aimed her sword at the Time Cube and caused a glowing bowl-shaped force-field to appear around it. With that, the Society of Superheroes teleported her away to the next crisis she had to deal with.

I didn't move for a second. Then I walked up to the display, blasted the bottom away beneath it, and let the Time Cube fall into my hands. Stuffing it in my pocket, I went over to help Diabloman to his feet.

"Are we staying for the cops?" Cindy asked.

I looked at her sideways. "What, are you kidding?"

CHAPTER TWO

IS IT STILL GOOD TO BE BAD?

The Atlas City Police Department was different from the Falconcrest City Police Department. For example, they actually attempted to do their jobs. Still, it wasn't that difficult to evade them when you had superpowers. I turned us insubstantial, walked us through the city's storm drain system, and brought us to an unmarked white van. It wasn't the most glamorous way to travel but was a lot easier to move around the city in. From there, the three of us drove to my hideout.

Atlas City was a shining monument of cleanliness, efficiency, and beautiful pristine towers. It was also a town with a rising homeless population, unemployment, and a growing set of slums. The heart of the city had been ripped out when Ultragod died. It made me sad just thinking about it and further proved Guinevere's point. Superheroes weren't just a bunch of interfering bastards preventing me from ruling the world, they were also people who inspired the public to be better.

"Man, I could go for a pizza now," Cindy said, uncaring about my existential crisis.

"Then you're in luck," I said, shaking it off. "How about you, D?"

"I prefer meat on my meat," Diabloman said.

My hideout was a small red and black building with a big M sign that read underneath SUPER PIZZA: OUR FLAVORS ARE ALL POWERFUL. I walked through the side door with Cindy and Diabloman without bothering to put on a disguise, passing numerous waiters and waitresses dressed like superhumans.

Fake artifacts of various superhero fights were scattered around the restaurant and the usual cosplay crowd was present. Even a couple of people dressed like me.

Cindy glared at one of the customers. "I'm honestly not sure how she made my outfit skimpier. I mean, I work hard on that."

"Yours has to be practical so it doesn't fall off during combat," I said, sitting down at one of the booths.

"It's all illusionary anyway," Cindy said, sitting down beside me. "Though I'm still waiting on you to get me that youth potion."

"Cindy, you're not even forty and look like you're twenty-eight."

"Because I *work hard at it*," Cindy reiterated. "The gym is my friend. Men don't have this sort of problem."

"That's because my cloak healing my injuries burns calories like a wildfire," I said, shrugging. "I do not recommend that as a weight loss plan."

My encounter with Guinevere weighed on me. I didn't like to think of myself as a bad-bad guy but Guinevere was right that I'd unleashed a lot of evil on the world when I'd liberated Gabrielle. I didn't regret it but I could have done more to contain the damage. What, really, was my legacy going to be with stuff like that on my record? I mean, what sort of example was I setting for my daughter?

Diabloman picked up the menu and looked it over. "You should not let Guinevere's words get to you."

"Yeah," Cindy said, sensing this was affecting my attitude. "She can go back to Camelot for all I care."

"No, it's a silly place," I said, leaning back in the booth. "I'm sorry, she hit a nerve. Honestly, I think it may be time to hang up my cloak."

There was an audible gasp throughout the restaurant and I looked around to see why everyone was reacting that way. Then I saw the cosplayer wearing a Red Riding Hood costume had slipped out of it and realized everyone was paying attention to that.

"Surely, you cannot be serious," Diabloman said, looking at me. "Look at all you've accomplished in the past—"

"Seven years," I said, pointing out the timeframe. "Five of which I spent in prison underground."

"You actually only spent one year imprisoned," a small feminine voice spoke. "The timeline has been compressed."

I turned to see a five-year-old, white-haired girl, with pigtails who popped herself up on the booth seat beside Diabloman. She wore a miniature set of blue jean overalls and a t-shirt with a cartoon cat holding a test tube. In her right hand was a modified cellphone that looked like it was from the 29th century. Mostly because it was. It was my daughter Leia Wachkowski-Karkofsky. Her superpowers were being hella smart, telepathic, uber-cuteness, and being able to invent anything. Leia already had her 'superhero' nickname of Gizmo, though I wasn't letting her anywhere near anything dangerous. Not until she was two hundred and fifty and I was dead from old age.

"Excuse me?" I asked, wondering what the heck she was talking about. "What now?"

"We're in an unstable temporal universe," Leia said, cheerfully. "This is due to the massive amount of time travel and divine intervention we have in our reality. As such, the timeline actually alters so events and years become merged. You only spent a year imprisoned underground now and I suspect it'll get smaller in the future. Your memories will change, too. I call it the Theory of External Retcons."

I blinked. "That is the most ridiculous thing I've ever—"

Weirdly, I remembered raising Leia for most of her childhood.

"Huh," I said, pausing. "Well, I'm not going to complain about it."

"Does this mean I'm older or younger?" Cindy asked, looking over at me. "I feel like this is an important question."

"It's not," Diabloman said, making a grumbling noise. "Gary, you have already left a positive legacy. You've stopped Tom Terror from escaping, killed a Great Beast, stopped World War 3, and saved Falconcrest City from an enlightened dictatorship."

"Plus, you made Opposite Earth," Cindy said, looking at the menu. "Not many supervillains can say they've one-upped God."

Opposite Earth was an exact replica of our planet that

existed on the other side our planetary rotation around the Sun. It had been created by Cloak sacrificing himself to turn all of Merciful's necromantic energy to a positive end. I swear, I couldn't make this stuff up if I tried.

"All true," I said, sighing. "But what do I have to show for it?"

"A beautiful family," Diabloman said.

"A chain of pizzerias that has walls stuffed with loot and equipment," Cindy said.

"A planet because if you hadn't done it, the world would be gone," Leia said.

"All true," I said, annoyed at their logic. "But the magic is gone. It's just not the same without Cloak. Worse, I don't really think I see the point of being a supervillain anymore. I'm not making any progress toward taking over the world and the majority of my fellow villains are scumbags."

"Who possibly could have seen that development?" Cindy muttered.

Diabloman shook his head.

"The heroes aren't much better," Leia said, surprising me. "Remember, I'm a telepath so I know that. A lot of them are burnt out or angry about past injustices. Only a few of them are motivated by the desire to do good."

I placed my right hand over my heart. "Which is why I'm considering becoming a hero."

Now there were gasps at the table.

"You can't do that, Gary!" Cindy said, her expression one of pure horror. "They'll really take away my v-card if you do that."

I stared at her. "Cindy, I think you lost that when you were fourteen. You helped me with mine not much later."

"I mean villain card!" Cindy said, wrinkling her cute little nose.

"Ew," Leia said, scrunching up her nose. "Parents referencing sex should be outlawed."

I pointed at her. "You're far too young to know sex exists, super intelligent telepathic girl or not. I forbid you to know anything about it until you're sixty."

"First, dad, biology means this won't be a problem for about nine more years. Boys are still icky to me." Leia stared at me. "Second, do you want me to drool and drink from a sippy cup? I'm almost six."

"Oh, I'm sorry, clearly you're an adult," I said before reaching into my pocket. "Oh, by the way, here's your present."

I plopped the Time Cube on the front of the table.

Leia's eyes lit up like Christmas before she grabbed it. "A Time Cube, sweet! With this, the power of the gods will be mine!"

"That's why we spent two weeks planning on stealing?" Cindy asked. "A present for your daughter."

"Our daughter," I corrected.

"Oh yeah," Cindy paused as if thinking. "I mean, seriously, children don't need presents. You just give them a box or sit them in front of the television. It's how I was raised."

I stared at her, opened my mouth then closed it. "Uh-huh."

Cindy shook her head. "You should be thinking of what's important about that Time Cube thingy."

"Which is?" I asked, uninterested.

"Selling it for money!" Cindy said, throwing her hands up in the air.

"I think becoming a superhero is a good idea," Diabloman said, ignoring Cindy. "Being a hero will help you achieve redemption for the many sins you have committed."

"Do not help him with this stupid plan." Cindy pointed at Diabloman. "Do you know what heroes do? They give away money! They do things without expectation of thanks! They heroically sacrifice themselves! I do not want Gary doing any of those things."

Cindy had done the hero thing herself, for a few years after Mandy's first death. It hadn't worked out in the long run because Mandy was back and because Cindy would rather be a rich bad person than a poor good one. There was also the fact she'd lost her license to practice medicine due to operating on a superhuman kid to save his life. You needed special permission to do that, apparently, because society was full of bigots. I regretted that whole series of events because not only did I like Good Cindy more than Bad Cindy but I think Cindy did too.

"Have you talked about this with Mandy yet?" Diabloman asked.

"No," I said, frowning. "She's been off in Karzakistan doing black ops missions for the Foundation since January."

"I don't think that's a real country," Cindy said.

"Well, neither is whatever nation she is in after she gets done with them," I said. "Personally, I preferred when she was a superhero instead of a spy. The two professions are mutually exclusive."

"What? Lying and murder aren't very good for superheroes to do?" Cindy said, faking shock. "You don't say. Next you'll tell me being a vampire is a bad thing."

"Funny," I said, deciding on getting the stuffed crust super-meat pizza with extra meat. "Except not."

Honestly, I was happy for Mandy because she'd finally managed to get the job she'd wanted since she was a child but on her terms. As a vampire, she had the ability to do things that normal people couldn't. The fact real-life vampires didn't have to worry about sunlight also contributed to her being the perfect undead operative. Unfortunately, she hadn't kept her pre-mortem sweetness and spent long periods away from home killing who knew who on behalf of the Foundation for World Harmony's Security Council. She also associated with arms dealers, secret police, and state-sponsored terrorists. Was it hypocritical that I disliked her hanging around those sorts of people when I was a self-styled supervillain? Yeah, it probably was, and maybe that was part of the reason why I wanted out.

There were other changes to her personality too. Weirdly, for whatever reason, Mandy refused to talk to Diabloman. Ever since she'd gotten her soul back and we'd dealt with Merciful, she'd avoided him like the plague. I had to ask him to take nights off to get some alone time with my life. Mandy's interests had changed too, becoming darker and more Gothic. She'd even shifted her religion and was less interested in Wicca than Mexican folk magic. In some ways, her darker more sensuous personality suited our lives better but in others I wondered if I'd really gotten my wife back. Wow, that was a dark thought.

"Second Mom is back," Leia said, piping up. "She arrived

about an hour ago."

"Really?" I said, smiling. "Well, that's good."

"Maybe she can talk you out of this nonsense," Cindy said, growling as she picked up the menu. "I need pineapple, small fishes, extra cheese, and other unhealthy things to help me cope with this."

"It's a good idea, Cindy."

"Of course, it isn't. I have to manage every single meal like... oh you mean becoming a superhero! Gary, have you forgotten why you became a supervillain?" Cindy asked, looking exasperated.

"To honor my dead brother?"

"Other than that!"

"Fame? Boredom? To strike at the corrupt institutions of society?" I asked.

"Money!" Cindy said.

"Which we have plenty of," I pointed out. "Really, I feel a lot less animus against the 1% since I became part of it."

"You can never have too much money," Cindy said, shaking her head. "Do I even know you anymore?"

"Right." I looked to my side and hoped Cindy would move. She didn't. "Hey, Cindy, do you mind if I get up to go see Mandy?"

"You can turn insubstantial," Cindy said, giving our order to a waitress dressed like Ultragoddess.

I sighed and did so, journeying through the various booths and passing through a number of customers who freaked out when I did so. "Don't mind me, I'm a ghost."

"Cool!" An eleven-year-old boy shouted as his father looked traumatized by the experience.

I arrived in the kitchen and passed by a number of masked criminals who were preparing the food. I made it a point of hiring nothing but prisoners at my business that, while it occasionally backfired, worked out well in the long run. Many of them were so grateful for their jobs, it made me feel guilty I'd originally hired them to have steady access to henchmen.

"Hey boss. Did you get your time doohickey?" Bill the Thirteenth Shark asked, waving. He was the Thirteenth Shark because he used to be one of a gang of twenty seven shark-suited criminals who served the Star Pirate. I hadn't been aware henchmen had their own themes but a whole subculture existed. I was thinking of promoting him to regional manager but wasn't sure he was crooked enough.

"I did!" I said, waving to him. "Soon, the entire world will bow before me."

"Keep thinking positive," Bill said.

"Do you know where my wife is?" I asked.

"Which one?" Bill said, ignoring the fact Cindy and I weren't married.

I really needed to get a handle on what language to use. "The one that drinks blood."

"Which one," Bill said, chuckling.

"Funny," I said, rolling my eyes.

"Out back," Bill said. "I was married once. How do you keep up with multiple women in your life? I'd be afraid they'd team up."

"I don't," I said, walking out the back door. "I'm probably going to die before the end of the year."

"Hell of a way to go out," Bill said.

He wasn't wrong. I called it the Rand Al'Thor method of suicide, which probably 5% of my autobiography's readership would get. Anyway, as soon as I stepped out the door, I found myself in a trash-filled alleyway where Mandy was standing in fight position surrounded by ninjas. I blinked a couple of seconds to properly assess what I was looking at before realizing, yes, I was watching my wife fighting a bunch of ninjas.

Mandy Karkofsky was a pale-skinned Eurasian woman in her perpetual early thirties with a short raven-colored bob, white shirt cut off at the middle, and a pair of black pants. Really, she looked a lot like Sonya Blade from *Mortal Kombat* as played by a Eurasian Kate Beckinsale. That should have clued me into what was going to be happening soon.

The ninjas were all wearing colorful sets of *shinobi shozuku* (what you called ninja costumes in Japanese—albeit, the translation is basically "ninja costume"). There were red, blue, orange, yellow, and black ones. All of the costumes also sported samurai vests and face guards that made them look even more conspicuous. A few of them had katana, others chains with sickles on the end, and even more were carrying shotguns or pistols that just seemed like cheating. There were about a dozen of them and two were on the ground where Mandy had managed to take them down. I then saw two Foundation for World Harmony agents on the ground nearby, a man and a woman, who had been killed by stab wounds.

Crap.

"Hey guys, Ninja Night is Thursdays," I said, staring at the group. "Remember, anyone who brings a turtle with them eats free."

"[There he is!]" One shouted in Japanese and pointed at me. "[Destroy him in the name of the Dark Lord!]"

Yes, I can understand Japanese. Blame it on years of obsessive subtitled anime watching.

None of the ninjas moved. It seemed like they were actually... afraid? Huh. It seemed like I was finally getting some respect for all the bad guys I'd killed. Plus some very-very jerkass good guys but I didn't know how they counted.

"Need any help?" I asked Mandy, cracking my knuckles. "Fighting ninjas is on my bucket list. I've already knocked off zombie apocalypses, kaiju, and killing non-Jewish gods."

"Given I was part of a group of three," Mandy said, staring around. "Yeah, I would really appreciate some help right now."

"Well, this will be a snap to take care of," I said, snapping my fingers and trying to set them on fire.

Accent on trying.

"Uh oh," I said, staring at them.

"[Fool!]" The head ninja said. "[We are protected by the power of Entropicus, Dark Lord of the Multiverse!]"

"Good for you," I said, elbowing a ninja beside me, grabbing his shotgun and shooting the head ninja in the chest.

That was when, I shit you not, Carl Douglas' "Kung Fu Fighting" started playing.

CHAPTER THREE

GO NINJITSU, GO NINJITSU GO

I wasn't the only one hearing Carl Douglas' voice as all of the ninjas looked up, confused too. That was when Cindy and Diabloman walked out of the door I'd just come through, the former holding up a cellphone.

"I just downloaded iThemeMusic as an app on my phone," Cindy said, cheerfully. "It automatically provides the best possible theme music for superhuman throw-downs!"

"[Kill them!]" Another ninja shouted.

That was when the fight actually broke out. Smashing another ninja over the head with the now-useless shotgun, I proceeded to kick another in the groin before punching another in the face. I wasn't what you'd call a master martial artist but having gotten my ass kicked repeatedly across the past year, I had picked up a decent amount of self-defense training through sheer survival. I also had been given several pointers by Mandy and Diabloman.

Specifically:

1. The object of the martial arts is to hurt the other guy.

2. There is no such thing as cheating.

Deprived of my fire and frost magic to directly affect them, I froze the ground underneath the ninjas and caused quite a few of them to slip or become unsteady on their feet. I grabbed a kukri knife from one of the fallen ones on the ground before stabbing one in the neck. I kicked that ninja's dying form into a group of the slipping ninjas, sending them falling to the ground like bowling pins.

One thing I noticed about these ninjas was the fact they disintegrated after they were killed. The ones on the ground at Mandy's feet faded away like shadows in the sunlight while the ones I killed burned up like flaming paper. I tried to think of any superhumans who had the ability to create temporary ninjas before I was shot in the head.

"Ow," I said, falling backwards on my ass and suffering from an enormous headache. "That's buried in my head. Ow. Just barely penetrated my super-tough skin but I am in a lot of pain. I can also taste sounds. Weird, a man screaming in pain is butterscotch."

"Die, Gaijin!" The ninja who shot me stood over me, raising his gun to my head for an even closer shot.

The bullet popped out of my head and I slashed across his femoral artery, causing him to bleed out black fluid before dropping his gun. The ninja disappeared again, burning up like so much dried paper set on fire.

"Okay, now these guys are just starting to piss me off," I muttered, trying not to deal with the fact I'd just been *shot in the head* and was getting up. I knew my powers were growing but it seemed they were doing so in a way that involved making it easier for me to survive getting my ass kicked.

Beside me, Cindy had taken out her enchanted ax and was slashing her way through the ninjas to the dance tune going on around us. Diabloman broke necks, tossed around ninjas like ragdolls, and even crushed the heads of two together. Mandy kicked, punched, and even broke the neck of one with her thighs—a move I was certain she was doing for me because that couldn't be an actual fighting move. A few of the remaining ninjas split in two to create more fodder to fight but they were taken out as well. Eventually, there was only one.

Mandy advanced on the guy, who was standing there with his arms raised, but I put my hand in front of her. "No, there's a narrative law about these things. It's easy to kick the ass of a bunch of ninjas but as soon as you're facing one, he's going to be all sorts of badass."

Mandy rolled her eyes. "God, Gary, will you give the genre logic a rest! Not everything works like a movie."

Cindy and Diabloman charged at him before both came flying backwards, landing on the ground beside us.

Mandy looked down then puckered her lips. "Why does the universe continue to prove you right when everything you say is stupid?"

"Because the world is a stupid place," I said, holding out my hands. "Duh."

"Silence!" the remaining ninja said in a thick Japanese accent.

"Ah, so you do speak English," I said, crossing my arms. "Okay, who the hell are you and what the hell are you doing attacking my wife?"

"I am Multi-Ninja!" the man spoke, his voice booming throughout the alleyway. "Interdimensional assassin! I am a one man army who is able to distribute his strength over many individuals at once."

I blinked. "Okay, that is both cool and silly. I will say, however, the guns were not cool. Real ninja should always stick to the katana, shuriken, sai, and quarterstaff theme. Female ninja, or *kunoichi* as they're called, can use needle-tipped fans."

Multi-Ninja didn't seem interested in my advice, though. "I have been hired by Entropicus to eliminate Earths' greatest warriors in order to prepare the way for his victory in the Eternity Tournament."

"The what in the who now?" I asked, blinking.

"Why go after Gary, then?" Cindy asked.

"Hey!" I said, snapping at her. "I am on that list! Just not at the top of it. Maybe even close to the bottom but I am on the list of Earth's greatest warriors."

"He is," Multi-Ninja said.

"Which is sad," Cindy said. "We've lost so many to be so reduced."

I'd argue but she was right. Still, I was more concerned with the implications of Multi-Ninja's statement than my place on any hypothetical list. Entropicus was, in simple terms, the most dangerous supervillain in the universe. Past, present, or future. In fact, supervillain was probably not a good term for a guy who went around conquering galaxies and trying to unmake the universe. He was the God-Emperor of an undead technopolis called Abaddon that existed at the end of time. It had taken the entirety of the Society of Superheroes to stop Entropicus' three major plots across the past three decades with Ultragod having challenged the space god a dozen more times on his own. The thing was, Ultragod had *lost* a few of those battles, which was something Tom Terror couldn't say he'd ever achieved. He was so out of my league it wasn't even funny.

"You want to eliminate Mandy? Shame on you!" Cindy said, shaking her head as she tried and failed to lift Diabloman off herself again.

"Actually, I was sent here to eliminate Merciless," Multi-Ninja said.

I blinked. "Really? I qualify as one of the greatest warriors on Earth?"

"I didn't believe it either," Multi-Ninja said, sighing. "But a job is a job."

I nodded. "Yeah, I understand that."

"Your wife is also on the list and I was going to kill her too," Multi-Ninja interjected. "Two for one!"

I was starting to dislike this guy. I probably wouldn't offer him a place in my organization after this was over as was typical with supervillains I fought. "What's the Eternity Tournament?"

Multi-Ninja snorted. "You really have no idea, do you? So much for the *Book of Midnight*'s vaunted keeper."

The Book of Midnight was the book of all black magic in the universe. It was alive and had the personality of a small dog. I couldn't make this up if I tried. If there was an occult secret in the universe then it was inside *The Book of Midnight* somewhere. Death had entrusted it to me and I kept it watered, fed, and played with it whenever I could.

"Hey man," I said, trying to think of a defense for the fact I hadn't gotten as much out of it as I could have. "A lot of that book is in Latin, Greek, Linear A, and other foreign languages! Do you expect me to learn how to read another tongue just to gain more power?"

"Yes?" Diabloman asked.

"Then clearly you don't know me very well," I said.

Mandy rolled her eyes. "Agents Steve Caldwell and Thomas Machin died getting the information about Hell Island to me. There's been kidnappings across the galaxy and signs of the dimensional barriers between the closest parallel universes weakening. Hell Island is the epicenter of it all and where this tournament is going to take place?"

"Hell Island, really?" I asked.

"I didn't name the damn thing!" Mandy snapped.

"Sorry," I said, shrugging.

"It doesn't matter," Multi-Ninja said, chuckling. "Both of you will die and your universe will be swallowed whole. Time will be compressed and it will be as a single moment stretched out for all eternity under the law of He Who Is Eternal."

"That's like five or six *Final Fantasy* plots together," I said, wondering why anyone would want to compress time. Isn't that just reversing the Big Bang? There wasn't much interesting back then. I mean they hadn't even invented alcohol. "I feel like we're wandering from our topic. Like, for instance, if you're so confident about your heightened ninja powers—why haven't you attacked yet?"

"Because he was expecting to only fight one of Earth's greatest warriors," Mandy said, chuckling. "Not two."

I was glad she had confidence in my role since I'd just spent my morning getting curb stomped by Guinevere. Still, by the way Multi-Ninja was fidgeting, I was under the impression she was right.

Multi-Ninja was about to say more when the backdoor to my restaurant opened again, this time Leia popping her head out the door to look at us. "Hey, mom, dad, what's going on? There's a weird static keeping me from reading....oh hey, a ninja."

Multi-Ninja backflipped over Mandy and me before running like lightning toward Leia, picking her up, and holding her tightly against his chest. He then lifted a finger up under her neck, popping out a glowing laser nail underneath my daughter's throat. "Entropicus provides. If you come a step closer, either of you, I will slit her throat."

I stared at him. "Pal, you do not know who you are screwing with."

Mandy trembled with rage. "If you think for a moment I'm going to let you leave with my child, you've got another thing coming."

"Leave?" Multi-Ninja said, splitting into three forms. "Hardly? I know your histories. Entropicus does not reward failure so I will complete my mission. You're going to allow me to kill you both. Only then will I allow your child to go free."

"That sounds like a bad plan," Cindy said, not able to look back. "Gary, I recommend against that. We can get Leia brought back to life."

"You suck, mom!" Leia shouted.

"Obviously, I'd like you to survive!" Cindy called back.

"That makes it so much better!" Leia shouted back.

"Doesn't it?" Cindy asked.

Mandy knelt on the ground. "Fine, I'll do it. Better I die than the only light in my life other than my husband."

I blinked and seeing the two bad guys, I looked at Leia. "Honey, close your eyes."

I proceeded to concentrate and pull Gizmo from Multi-Ninja's hands with magic at a huge rate of speed, catching her like a football before turning insubstantial before the ninjas charged at me. Mandy intercepted them, broke both their necks, and charged at Multi-Ninja who screamed before she tore him into two separate pieces.

Multi-Ninja screamed before dissolving into nothing while Mandy stared down with red eyes. "Fatality."

"You didn't close your eyes, Leia," I said, turning substantial again.

"Yeah, that was awesome!" Leia said, clapping her hands. "Do it again!"

Mandy took a needless breath, looking around for any other ninjas. So far, none of us saw anything. "That was an awful risk you took with Leia's life, Gary."

"Yeah, well, I was playing the odds a guy willing to slit a five-year-old's neck wasn't the sort of guy who could be trusted to let her go afterward," I said, staring at her. "I'm also not going to let my wife sacrifice her life when I'm there either."

Mandy grunted, clearly not happy with my decision but

willing to go along with it. "We have to go find out what this Eternity Tournament is and how it relates to us?"

"Gee, I hadn't figured," I said, sarcastically. Laying down Leia, I looked at her. "Leia, remember what we said?"

"I am not going to be a Maguffin supervillains kidnap to make you do things," Leia repeated. "Dad, I can build a giant robot out of Legos. One that works and breathes fire. You don't need to protect me."

"That's cute," I said, patting her on the head. "What do you want on your pizza?"

"Pineapple please," Leia said. "Also, ultraniun. I want to slowly dose myself with radiation until I become a godlike being."

"No, dear, that will give you cancer," I said.

"Who is the super genius here?" Leia asked.

"Clearly the person who doesn't want to eat radioactive material," I said.

"Boo," Leia said, yawning. "After I take a nap, I'll do a board proving you wrong. Stupid superpowers taking up so much of my energy."

I loved my daughter. She was the one shining beacon of light in my life after having devoted myself to filling it with darkness. I'd wanted to be a supervillain since before I hit puberty but the fact was, I was a father now, and I didn't want her to follow in my footsteps. I wanted to inspire her to be a better person and live a life free of danger as well as despair.

"Our daughter," I said, looking over at Mandy and Cindy. Mandy was picking Diabloman up off Cindy with one hand and slapping him awake.

"Why the hell would Entropicus be worried about us?" Mandy muttered. "I mean, he's a little out of our genre. He's the sort of guy the Cosmic Surfer or the Sixth World Giants deal with."

"I dunno," Cindy muttered, standing up. "Maybe the fact we've killed a bunch of gods and demons over the past few years?"

"Yeah, we have been punching above our weight class," I said, remembering their earlier description of my legacy.

"He is also the Chosen of Death," Diabloman pointed out.

"One of the Primals of the Universe believes he's worth using as a pawn."

"Did you have to mention the pawn part?" I said, frowning. "I prefer chosen agent of doom."

"Of course you would," Diabloman said. "However, she's not about to show up and talk to us about what's going on."

There was a huge crash of thunder. I looked up toward the sky and saw storm clouds had gathered, blotting out the sun over Atlas City as the temperature dropped rapidly enough I could see my breath. Given Atlas City was in central Florida that was damn impressive.

Cindy rubbed her hands. "You see? This is why global warming is a real thing. I don't care what the Omega-ists say. We need to build an enormous freeze ray and reverse all the problems at both poles."

"Death's here," I said, turning around.

"Oh," Cindy said, pausing. "I knew that."

"No one wants you to get political," Diabloman said. "Politicians aren't supervillains."

"Except the one that actually was," Cindy said, referring to the late President Omega. Well, sorta late. He was a time traveler and a living temporal paradox so you could never be certain whether they were really most sincerely dead.

"Hush you."

Mandy ignored Cindy as well, turning around to join me as we waited for the arrival of my otherworldly boss. Seconds later, an unearthly beautiful woman with pale white skin and black hair appeared before us. She was wearing a black tactical vest with nothing underneath and a pair of camouflage pants with two smudges of black paint across her face. Goth soldier girl was an eclectic outfit choice even for her but one I approved of. Death's resemblance to Mandy was considerable and I'd often found myself greatly attracted to her. I wasn't sure I'd survive the experience if I ever made a move, though—not that I didn't have more than enough problems with the three dangerous but beautiful women in my life.

"Hey, Boss," I said, waving my hand. "What's happening?"

"The end of the multiverse," Death said.

CHAPTER FOUR

WHERE WE TOTALLY DON'T RIP OFF NINETIES FIGHTING GAMES

I pointed at Death. "You see? That's the problem with media franchises these days. The entire multiverse is at stake? You couldn't just say the city or the planet or even the universe? No, it's the entire multiverse. How is that even possible? According to the late great Stephen Hawking, you'd have a bunch of people succeeding where other people don't. Which would require infinite multiverses and that's just silly."

"It's like what happened to *Supernatural*," Cindy said, checking Leia to see if she was all right, even pulling out a tongue depressor to check her mouth. It was the most motherly thing she'd done for her since her birth. "Five seasons built up to the apocalypse and they defeat the Devil. Do they go back to all the wonderful low-level road monsters? No, it's every season against more angels or demon gods so it becomes ridiculous."

"Cindy, don't help," Mandy said, keeping her eyes focused on Death as if she was afraid the Primal would reveal something horrible about her.

"I'm just saying, I only watch it for the eye candy now," Cindy said, smiling cheekily. "Also the fanfic potential."

"The multiverse is a little more complicated than any single scientist can speculate on from Earth, even one as talented as him," Death said, smiling. "The Eternity Tournament takes advantages of universal constants and the fact certain beings exist outside space-time to make its existence possible."

"What is the Eternity Tournament?" I asked, wanting some damn answers.

"It is a gathering that occurs once every ten thousand years," Death said.

"Earth years or another planet's?" I asked, still trying to process everything everywhere was at stake. "Because, again, when you get to string theory levels of discussion, all logic breaks down."

Death narrowed her eyes. They became like portals to hell and could stun even a strong willed man to silence. "Just shut up and go with it, Gary."

"I'm just saying that year length varies from planet to planet," I said, taking a deep breath and deciding to let her tell her story.

"When you're the Primals of the Universe, you get bored with what the universe has to offer. It requires a shakeup. A chance to stretch the limits of omniscience," Death said, staring at me. It was as if she was daring me to point out omniscience, by necessity, would not work that way.

"Uh huh," I said, not taking the bait. "Please go on."

"The Eternity Tournament gathers the seven champions from seven universes for each of the seven Primals and has them compete against one another. There are very few rules other than each champions must have a chance of winning, no matter how miniscule. In the end, the winner is given the Primal Orbs for a single moment and granted a wish."

"A wish," I repeated. "Like an *Aladdin* wish?"

"Yes," Death said. "One with no limitations."

"Even wishing for more wishes?" I asked.

Death glared. "No, Gary."

"Then there's a limitation," I said.

"Why are you my champion again?" Death asked, looking annoyed.

"I often ask myself that. You'd think you'd have been smarter," I said, having no apparent self-preservation instinct.

Death, however, just smiled. "Yes, you'd think."

"What are the Primal Orbs?" Cindy asked. "You know, since we need to get exposition out of the way for the audience."

"What audience?" I asked.

"My online followers," Cindy said, pulling out her cellphone. "I put up all of our adventures to go with my selfies."

I stared at her. "And I wondered why the cops and superheroes were always waiting for us at our heist sites."

"Way more publicity this way," Cindy said, giving a wink. "You're welcome."

"She doesn't actually post before the crimes," Diabloman said, stepping between us. "We leave that for Mr. Puzzles."

"What a relief," I said, sarcastically. "How many crimes did he get away with?"

"None," Diabloman said. "He's currently serving thirty-seven life sentences."

Death looked annoyed. "I have people to kill, guys. An entire multiverse's worth in fact. You need to win the tournament in order to keep the Primal Orbs out of the hands of Entropicus. They are the physical manifestation of the Primals' power. Many times, mortals and gods have sought to acquire all seven for the purposes of being omnipotent within their own reality."

"It seems like a bad idea to keep those around," I said, pointing out the obvious risk in their existence. "You know, because of the fact they can give godlike power to people utterly undeserving of it, like me. Can't you password protect them or something?"

"No, Gary." Death shook her head. "This is why Entropicus wishes to win this tournament as he plans to use his wish to unmake reality."

I paused, blinking. "What kind of moron would want to do that?"

"I destroyed the universe," Diabloman muttered. "Once."

"Yeah, but we all agree that was a bad idea," I said, not really wanting to get into that. "What possible benefit could anyone derive from destroying everything?"

Death closed her eyes. "Entropicus was my champion at the beginning of this universe. He's the father of the seven children I presented Reaper's Cloaks in time-lost Acheron. He knows there's an afterlife waiting for mortals but despises the suffering needed to get there as well as the arbitrary nature of human suffering."

"Yeah, what's up with that?" Cindy asked, stepping in front of me. "I'd like to register a complaint."

"All systems have bugs," Death said, opening her eyes. "Chaos and Order are as much a part of it as Good or Evil."

"That's a shitty answer," Cindy said.

Death refrained from smiting her but I could see she was debating it. "Entropicus will use his power over the dead to set himself up as the God-Emperor of all the dead universes and create paradises for those he considers the worthy while creating hells for those he considers unworthy."

"Who does he consider worthy?" I asked.

"No one," Death said, her voice bitter. "His is a hatred formed across epochs to all humans, aliens, and spirits. No being is perfect in his eyes and anything less is trash. All of life's pleasures are ash in his mouth so only pain can be enjoyed."

I let that sink in. Then I shook my fist in the air triumphantly. "Well, it's a good thing no Primal is insane enough to make him their champion then!"

Death didn't say anything.

"Oh come on!" I said, staring at her. "Who would do that?"

"Is it you?" Cindy asked. "Because that would be bad."

"No," Death said.

"Who then?" I asked, wondering if we were now going against one of the beings behind the Big Bang.

"Destruction," Death said, her voice low. "He is the part of the All-God who regrets the pain and suffering that comes from existence. He has chosen Entropicus as part of a larger plan to bring oblivion to all things. Destruction is a sadistic little troll who enjoys high stakes games and tormenting mortals. If he wins, then all of us will have to make a new universe for him to play with."

"Well fuck," I said, sighing. "Just when you think things can't get any worse, you find out God has an immature mean streak."

"That explains so much," Cindy paused. "We totally need to get him some planet-sized meds and therapy."

Death actually looked amused. "In any case, I need you to go to the tournament as my champions for this universe and win against Entropicus. We are forbidden from interfering with each other's champions until the battle but the champions, themselves, can attack one another or fight through proxies."

"Real great system you've got here," I said, shaking my head in disbelief. "This tournament might end the universe and you can take out the other competitors before the competition. Don't worry, though, we have rules!"

Death looked between us. "I remind you, Gary, all of you have things you could do with that wish. You want to rule the Earth? With the Primal Orbs, you'll be able to rule over the planet and establish an order that is lasting as well as peaceful. The Age of Superheroes will end not with a whimper but a bang with no more tyranny or injustice. People will bow before you and the Pax Merciless."

"Or the Pax Nighthuntress," Mandy muttered, narrowing her eyes.

"That doesn't actually make sense in Latin," I said, surprised she was actually encouraging my dark side. "Also, fuck the Romans. They're awful people who did terrible things to my ancestors. After I run out of Hitlers to kill, I'm going back in time to work on Emperor Titus."

Death didn't speak for a moment. "Aren't you sick of it all, Gary?"

"Yes, I'm sick of it," I said, pausing. "I hate the way the world is and how things are continually going in endless cycles of pain versus pleasure. I don't need to rule the world for more than a minute to fix all of the horrible crap that has been left behind by everyone else. I wouldn't want it to be just Earth, though. I'd want the entire Solar System. We can work on conquering or fixing the rest later."

"Isn't that similar to what Merciful did, dad?" Leia asked, looking up at me. "I mean, he enslaved much of the world for the interests of—"

"This is completely different," I said, cutting her off. "Because *I'm* doing it."

"Do I have your agreement to fight on my behalf?" Death asked.

"Are we all in this?" Diabloman asked. "Cindy, myself, Mandy, and Gary?"

"Yes," Death said. "I have other champions selected as well. Though Entropicus is doing his best to eliminate them."

"You had my curiosity," I said, pausing. "Now you have my attention. I want a guarantee you'll make sure nothing happens to Leia while we're gone, though."

"You want Death to be our daughter's babysitter?" Cindy asked, incredulous.

"It's like the Dresden Files," I said, breaking my rule about making constant pop culture references. I was trying to dial down. "God protects Michael Carpenter's family in exchange for Satan not constantly going after them like he would normally."

"Gary—" Cindy started to speak, as if I'd said something incredibly stupid. Which I had.

"Alright," Death said. "I will see to her safety by entrusting her to people Entropicus cannot trust then return her to you when the tournament is done."

"Alright?" I asked. I hadn't actually expected her to do that. I mean, when God asked Moses to free his people, he didn't negotiate.

"I want you to win this tournament," Death said, her voice low and threatening. "There's no place in the universe for Life or Death in the world that Entropicus wants to create. I have other champions but I have my faith in you."

"How will I know the others?" I asked, wondering what sort of other heroes or villains she'd gathered into her service. "Assuming any of them manage to get to the tournament alive or undead."

"Grrr," Mandy growled, staring at me. Apparently, undead qualified as hate speech in her opinion.

"Just assume anyone with incredibly bad attitudes and constant snark is one of mine," Death said, smiling, "They're sort of my signature."

"That *also* explains much about the universe," Cindy said, crossing her arms.

"I question how anything good can come from being the Champions of Death," Diabloman said. "I have the suspicion you have long been manipulating Gary to your own ends and this is part of a long term plot to destroy everything."

"Mmm-hmm," Death said, not denying it. "This is why I don't normally talk to you. Is there anything else?"

"Can you stop being so hot?" Cindy asked, raising her hand as if she was in kindergarten. "I hate being in the presence of anyone who makes me feel like I'm not the hottest woman in the room. It's why I hate missions with Mandy, Guinevere, or Ultragoddess."

"Cindy, stop setting our gender back decades," Mandy muttered.

"No promises," Cindy said.

"I'll take that as a no," Death said, gazing over us.

"So, where are we going?" Leia asked.

"The future," Death said. "A utopian one full of heroes and no villains."

"Does it have replicators?" Leia asked. "Also, would it be against the rules if I copied their technology and sold it in the present?"

"Not my rules," Death said.

I was so proud of my daughter. "My little temporal criminal slash entrepreneur."

I walked over to her and gave her a hug. She hugged back. Cindy, reluctantly, approached and hugged us both. Mandy didn't come anywhere near the three of us but just stood off to the side, looking on in disgust.

Death snapped her fingers. "It's time to go."

A swirling portal appeared that had an image of a tropical island on the other side. The island was covered with a beautiful Chinese castle that incorporated elements of Western architecture. There were a few futuristic elements as well, including strange towers that looked like something out of *Star Wars*.

"You know, if I were running a *Tomb of Horrors*-esque slaughterfest, I'd have a portal open up to like a black hole or something," I said.

Death raised an eyebrow. "Really, Gary?"

"Not that you wouldn't be able to obliterate out of hand," I said, reluctantly letting go and heading through the portal. Seconds later, I was on the shores of Hell Island that didn't look like any infernal dimension I'd seen. It was beautiful with warm sea air flowing in from the oceans surrounding us and bright sunlight coming from above. There was also a sense of power to the island and while my mystical senses were about as attuned as a dairy cow's, I could feel it surging through everyone and everything.

I wasn't the only person present on the beach, either, which looked to have a couple of hundred individuals gathered in groups of seven. Some of them were costumed heroes, some of them villains, others aliens, and a few of them looking like quote-unquote "normal" people. I recognized a few of them from not only my world but also people who were dressed like fictional characters. No, seriously, I swore I saw people who were straight from fantasy and science fiction novels I'd read. It was weird even by my standards.

"Pardon me, but are you Gary Karkofsky? Merciless?" A woman beside me asked.

"Who wants to know?" I asked, suspecting she wasn't a bill collector but always wanting to know who I was talking to before I admitted who I was.

"A fellow Death champion," the woman replied.

I turned my head to see a 5'4 brown haired woman who resembled Jenna Coleman dressed in a pair of tight workout pants that said JUST DOE IT along the side and a t-shirt that said, DEER IN THE HEADLIGHTS in black letters. She was wearing a pair of sneakers and had a headband tied around her forehead. It looked like she'd just arrived from a workout or was filming a fitness commercial despite her petite size.

Standing beside her was a tall dyed blond-haired man in a black business suit with mirror shades. He had a heavy coat on despite the environment and had an aura that reeked of both technology as well as death. If you somehow managed to combine Ryan Gosling with the Terminator, you probably would get this guy. Which, now that I thought about it, was just describing *Blade Runner 2049*. I noted he had several guns hidden on his form as well as a couple of knives—well-hidden but I could sense the lives they'd been used to take. I was going to be really disappointed if this competition allowed firearms.

"Do I know you?" I asked, looking over at the pair.

"Probably not," the woman said. "Jane Doe."

"Nice pseudonym," I said.

"I wish it was," the woman said, shrugging. "My parents hate me. However, what else are you going to name a weredeer?"

I needed a second to process that. "A were...deer?"

"I know," the handsome secret agent said. "Blew me away."

Jane closed one eye and squinted at me. "Coming from the guy straight out of a comic book."

"Comic book?" I asked. "Wait, Jane Doe, like from The United States of Monsters series?"

Cindy loved those books. Personally, I wasn't sure they were the best work of their author. I'd preferred C.T. Phipps' *Cthulhu Armageddon* books.

"Maybe?" Jane said, blinking. "How the hell is fiction in one reality true in the next?"

"Lady, that is the least weird element about this place," I said, looking around. "Did you get the whole spiel about this being the end of the multiverse?"

"Yep," Jane said, looking about. "I'm privately hoping I've just lost my mind and not living in a bad video game plot."

I blinked. "Wow, that is exactly how I feel about this whole thing."

"I wonder if we'll see a certain spider-themed superhero around here," Jane muttered.

"Who?" I asked. It sounded like a supervillain. Everyone knew spiders were evil. "Oh and could you introduce me to your friend? The guy who looks like he's a model pretending to be from the Secret Service."

Jane shook her head. "This is Agent G."

"Agent G?" I asked.

"I didn't pick it," G said, shrugging. "Sadly, it came with being grown in a lab."

"What's your thing?" I asked.

"Cyborg assassin," G said.

"Sweet!" I said, always glad to have one of those around. "Wait, are you a brooding assassin who has a heart or just a jerkass one who kills for money?"

"Well, you can be both," G said, looking to one side. "I only kill bad people now. It's a lot easier on the conscience and still profitable."

"Then you're fine by me," Jane said, patting him on the shoulder. "I say that, in large part because you're stupidly good looking."

He was, too. Not quite Adonis levels but definitely in the upper tier of human beauty ranges. It kind of made me self-conscious and I lived in a comic book world where almost everyone could make money modeling athletic wear.

"Thank you," G said.

"You need a better codename," I said, pointing at them with finger guns. "Weredeer and....Assassin in Black."

"Those are terrible names," Jane said. "Do I call you Nerdy Jewish Guy?"

"I almost had that codename," I said, disregarding the obvious jibe. "But it was taken."

Mandy, Cindy, and Diabloman arrived through the portal behind me. "Good, I was starting to get worried I'd have to master the fine art of small talk with these two."

Cindy pulled out her phone and took a picture. "Cool Jane Doe costume! You're wearing my favorite skin from Urban Legends vs. Capcom."

Jane blinked. "Excuse me?"

"Are you the rest of our team?" Diabloman asked, looking at them.

Mandy moved a few feet away from Diabloman, keeping her distance. I really needed to talk to her about what bugged her about him so much. I mean, yes, he'd once murdered the universe but that was in the past.

"No," I said, shaking my head. "They're from an alternate reality. There's also only two of them. So, that means we've got three people from our reality."

"Ultragod?" Jane asked. "Is he coming?"

"No," I said, taking a deep breath. "He's dead."

Jane grimaced. "That sucks. Usually, you guys come back from the dead a lot."

I stared at her. "Uh, right."

"Which is probably not something to say to you," Jane said, looking embarrassed.

"Sokay," I said, remembering how Ultragod had died because he'd mistaken my doppelganger for me. "So, you are all up to date on what's going on?"

Jane shrugged. "I'm pretty sure I'm hallucinating this in a sweat lodge back home. Spirit World journeys to comic book land aren't unbelievable among my people, though. All things exist in the Great Forest. My grandfather once visited Middle Earth and boned an elf."

"A remarkably sensible attitude to have. How about you, G?" I asked.

"I'm ninety percent sure this is all a hack of my cyberbrain or I've been stuffed into a virtual reality simulation designed to keep me incapacitated," G replied. "On the other hand, my normal life is full of nothing but murder and betrayal so I'm all for actually being the hero for once. Plus, I have a beautiful companion in saving the world."

"Thank you," I said.

"Not you," G said.

I smirked. "It's funny because you're really good looking and I say that in a mostly heterosexual way."

Jane chuckled. "Be sure to take the red pill not the blue one when you want to leave the Matrix."

"Men's Rights Activists have ruined that metaphor," I said, grumbling. "In any case, I'm happy to work with you both as you both seem to be snarky but good hearted souls."

"Yeah, let's go with that," Jane muttered.

"I spent years learning how to pretend to be trustworthy," G said, giving the kind of smile that only movie stars did. "Glad it's working."

Usually, superheroes fought each other when they first met as part of some weird gangland initiation. Supervillains were much easier in that we just exchanged information, figured out who was going to be the leader, and focused on making money. I wasn't sure about what the general cordiality here meant regarding my companions but I was determined to take advantage of it.

"Thanks," Jane said. "I'll pretend I don't know intimate details of your life from reading your comic book."

"I wonder if I can sue for royalties across universes," I muttered. "In any case, I think Team Merciless is off to a great start!"

"Team Merciless?" G asked. "Why are we Team Merciless?"

"Seniority!" I snapped. "Also, I call the right of naming the team due to the ancient right of dibs."

"Ah," G said. "Well, that makes perfect sense. Nothing can go wrong now."

Jane covered her face. "Great. You both jinxed it."

"Eh, what's the worst that could happen?" I said, daring fate to intervene. Seriously, we were working for death. I couldn't actually think of anything going wrong that wasn't already built into our situation.

"You!" I heard Guinevere shout at me. Death's timing was impeccable. "Criminal!"

I turned around to see her, the armored form of the Prismatic Commando, and a very ticked off looking Ultragoddess ready to punch them.

Great Fantasy Superhero League, Death. Really awesome choices.

CHAPTER FIVE

WHERE THE GOOD GUYS AND BAD(DER) GUY SHOWS UP

"You should behave like an adult, Gabby," Guinevere said, lifting her fists to Ultragoddess. Guinevere looked at me, a disdainful look on her face. "If you'll hold still, Merciless, I'll arrest you in a minute."

"The only way you're getting to him is over my dead body," Gabrielle said.

"Your relationship to your father is the only reason I'm not—" Guinevere started to say.

"Do not speak my father's name! You've lost the right to talk about him when you betrayed everything he stood for!" Gabrielle shouted.

"Ladies, please. We have more important things to talk about," the Prismatic Commando said, trying to interject. He sounded like a man in his twenties despite being the oldest living superhero of the Modern Age. Like Ultragod and the Nightwalker, he was a WW2 veteran. Stephen Soldiers was formerly known as the Star Spangled Commando but he'd traded in that name during the Vietnam War when he'd tried to become a soldier for justice in all nations.

Stephen now worked for an intergalactic police force that seemed to consider its laws to supersede the rest of the universe's governments. Honestly, I think he could have chosen a slightly more dignified name. Someone also needed to talk about his red, white, and green color scheme that made him look Captain Mexico instead. Not that there was anything wrong with that.

"Yeah, I agree with Grandpa Patriotic," I said, walking over toward them and conjuring a pair of sunglasses from my cloak's extra-dimensional pockets. Putting them on, I made the quip, "Reality is at stake and I live there!"

Guinevere reached over and grabbed my sunglasses before crushing them in her fist and dropping them on the ground. "If I'd known you were going to be here, Karkofsky, I wouldn't have come. You humiliated me by breaking your parole."

I stared at her. "This from the woman who actually believed a supervillain when he gave it. Also, those were $500 dollar sunglasses, ass—"

Mandy cleared her throat. "Death chose all of us for the purposes of saving the multiverse. I don't agree with all of her choices but I think her judgment should be trusted. Surely, everyone can agree Entropicus is a bigger threat than Gary?"

"Evil is evil. It must be opposed wherever it appears," Guinevere said, speaking with all the fury of a true believer.

"Says the woman who allied with Gary's tyrant doppelganger," Gabrielle said, surprising me by siding with me on the Society of Superheroes' hypocrisy. "Every one of Merciful's crimes is on your head because you let him get away with them. You deserve to be locked away in the darkest dungeon the Foundation for World Harmony can build."

Guinevere looked genuinely hurt by Gabrielle's statements and I couldn't blame her. Gabrielle had been effectively raised by the Society of Superheroes with Guinevere being her *de facto* aunt if not second mom. It was painful to watch how deep the rift from the Society's failure to find her was. In a way, I think I blamed the Society of Superheroes less for beating up on me than she did for their negligence.

"I can never apologize enough—" Guinevere stared to say.

"You're right, you can't," Gabrielle said, her fists glowing. "I don't want your apologies either."

"Can you conjure me some popcorn, Gary?" Jane said, as Weredeer looked to her companion.

"Sure," I said, snapping my fingers and giving her a bag.

"This is what superhero comics are all about," Jane said, taking a few handfuls and eating them. "Cheap melodrama and excuses for fights."

"If you ever have a fair fight, you're doing it wrong," G said, taking some of the popcorn.

"So, no fighter levels, only rogue, huh?" I asked, crunching.

"Well, I take some of those too," G said, shrugging. "No plan survives first contact with the enemy."

"I better intervene before they team up to fight a villain—like me." I put two fingers in my mouth and whistled. "Listen, guys, how about I promise to turn myself into the Society of Superheroes after this is over?"

"You'd do that?" Guinevere asked, confused and her hand on her sword.

"No," I said, snorting in derision. "Not in the slightest. In fact, it's doubly funny because you fell for that just a few hours ago. However, I will *act* like I'm going to do it and you can consider me under house or island arrest until the multiverse is saved."

Guinevere did not look at all amused. "You mock my code of honor."

"Frequently," I admitted.

"That sounds like a reasonable suggestion," Stephen said.

"It does?" Guinevere said, turning around to face Stephen.

Stephen removed his helmet to expose the African American man in his thirties underneath. Alien cybernetics mixed with Society of Superheroes future technology meant there wasn't much left of the original soldier but he sure didn't look it. He was also one of the few heroes I genuinely respected.

"As a soldier I learned you have to choose your battles," Stephen said, his voice soft and reassuring. "Also, Merciful was a tyrant who used a combination of fear, war, and information control to make himself a second Augustus Caesar. No matter the consequences to us, personally, overthrowing him was the right thing to do."

Guinevere shook her head. "I don't believe that."

"I think you do and I believe in you," Stephen said. "You are the best of us."

Cindy grabbed Jane's popcorn bag and ate some. "You're right, this is quality melodrama."

Guinevere seemed chastened then took a deep breath.

"Alright, I'll put aside my anger for the time being. There is no such thing as a lesser evil but I also know there is such a thing as a greater good."

I wasn't sure how that made sense but I was too busy being hugged by Gabrielle to notice. "Gary, it's so good to see you again. I've been so worried about you."

"Back off, sister," Mandy grunted.

"Sorry," Gabrielle said, taking a deep breath. "I thought—"

"You thought wrong," Mandy muttered.

Yeah, Gabrielle's relationship with me was *complex*. It was doubly so because Mandy had encouraged me to comfort her after the events at the prison. Apparently, there had been some misinterpretation over what exactly comforting meant. We'd rekindled our relationship only for Mandy to be furious about it. This despite the fact she was drinking from a small army of willing worshipers and didn't mind Cindy in the slightest. When I asked her about the distinction, she just said it was a vampire thing. I wasn't the cheating type but, bluntly, I wasn't sure where I stood with my wife anymore. In many ways, she seemed further away than ever since getting her soul back.

"I searched everywhere in Falconcrest City for you," Gabrielle said. "I was worried the Society of Superheroes finally murdered you."

Guinevere said, "We don't murder—"

Gabrielle glared at her.

I sighed. "Falconcrest City just isn't the same since Merciful did his number on the place. Crime rates are down, the economy is up, and you can actually walk two blocks without passing a strip club or liquor store. I mean, who wants to live in a place like that?"

Gabrielle laughed, thinking I was joking. "Well, I'm glad to see you and I think we'll be able to save the day just like my father would have. Who are your friends?"

I looked over at Jane and G. "Oh, this is Weredeer and Super Handsome Assassin Dude."

"We're not calling ourselves that," Jane said.

"I like my codename," G said.

"You do not," Jane said.

"When in Rome," G said, shrugging then looked at Jane as she checked her top. "Is something wrong?"

Jane looked down at her bust. "I think they provided me with a wondeer bra. I've also put on a crap ton of muscle. If everyone looks like MMA fighting supermodels in this reality, I might have to move here."

"Welcome to my world," I said, smiling. "It's not enough we have powers but we have to be sexy as hell too. Oh what a terrible curse we bear."

"Are you any different?" Jane asked G.

"Nope," G said. "I was stupidly handsome back home. One of the benefits of genetic engineering combined with cybernetic face-sculpting."

"Oh doe," Jane said. "Well I just better buck up and accept the fawning this outfit is going to get me."

"Deerlightful," G said.

"Puns are punishable by death on my world," I said, looking at them. "Just a fair warning."

"You doe say," Jane said.

"These two are fictional characters brought to life!" Cindy said, cheerfully. "I've read both their series!"

Given the multiverse was an infinite number of infinite universes, it meant there was a reality mirroring every work of fiction ever created. It's why a universe with evil goatee-wearing versions of you and your friends existed even if it made no logical sense. As a result, I was fascinated by the possibilities of who might be participating. I could end up beating up Ramsay Bolton or meeting with Eowyn and Aragorn. However, I had a question to ask Jane about something she'd said earlier.

"Seriously?" I asked. "I have comics?"

"Yeah," Jane said. "I mean, they're kind of derivative but everything is in the industry. The jokes are pretty forced at times and the recent relationship stuff has been ridiculous."

"Says the pun girl."

"Sorry about your dad and Cloak dying," Jane said, turning serious. "I always felt they were a good balance for you."

Okay, that was weird. "Yeah, me too."

We didn't get to talk about much more because a pair of

horns blew from the top of the island's central mountain. Going up it was a massive spiraling staircase lined with flags along its side. At the top of the staircase, coming from a cavern entrance underneath the castle on top of the island was a presence that made my blood run cold. While Death chilled the air and summoned storms, there was a palpable evil around the arrival of Entropicus' party.

Entropicus was difficult to describe but if I had to try, I'd go with Skeletor crossed with a pro-wrestler. He was eight feet tall with bleached white skin, his facial features seemingly carved off until it resembled a skull, and a body that was muscles on top of muscles. He wore a cloth skirt that only came down to his knees, sandals, and had a pair of belts forming an X across said chest. His eyes glowed with entropic energy, having a weird trail of blue energy rising from them into air above his head.

Surrounding Entropicus was the colorful collection of killers (try saying that three times fast) that served as his favorite minions. There was Cackler the morbidly obese cannibal clown, Magnifisense the Chaos Witch who looked like someone's Disney villainess cosplay, and a guy in a diving suit I couldn't make out.

"I feel like we've stepped out of *Mortal Kombat* and into *Masters of the Universe*," I said, looking up next to them.

"I used to write naughty *She-Ra* fanfic," Jane said.

"You too?" Cindy asked.

"Welcome, champions of the Primals!" Entropicus said, his voice echoing through the entire island as he spoke. It was akin to an audio incarnation of hate. "I am Entropicus, Emperor of the End of Time and Lord of the Nega-Force. I have been chosen to serve as master of ceremonies for this occasion."

"Why him?" Jane whispered. "Isn't he competing?"

"Because I challenged the previous champion of this tournament and killed him," Entropicus said, apparently able to hear Jane. He conjured the severed head of a red-bearded man that he tossed down the steps. "Thor Odinson's mantle has passed to me. Thus, I do not need to fight until the final battle of this tournament."

"There goes the next *Avengers* movie," Jane muttered.

"I'm more worried about Ragnarok," I replied. "The Midgard Serpent isn't going to slay itself."

"We each compete for the opportunity to have our greatest ambitions and dreams come true," Entropicus said, addressing the crowds. "Take note that violence between participants is encouraged but must all be taken in the form of a challenge. Those who are defeated in battle will have their fates decided by the victor. Interference will broaden the challenge but only one person will walk away victorious."

"Two men enter, one man leaves," I muttered. "Except if a third guy enters and still one man leaves. Yeah, this is sounding very much like he's making the rules up as he goes."

Entropicus turned his attention to me and I immediately regretted not learning from Jane's examples. "Rules are made to be broken, Merciless. As such, the first challenge this evening will be you versus Diabloman."

I blinked, rapidly. "Excuse me? You can't do that! We're on the same team."

"There can be only one master of the Primal Orbs," Entropicus said, sounding very much like I imagined Sauron would sound. "However, if you wish to compete in a dual contest then I agree to it. You will fight against the Cackler and Magnifisense."

The Cackler and Magnifisense were two of Entropicus' children and Ultragod villains in their own right. While Entropicus was a world-ending threat, they were more monsters who routinely showed up to murder the innocent and wreck mayhem. They were always driven back but no one had ever managed to put them down for good either. Some of the Brotherhood of Infamy, your one-stop evil cult that worshiped all things vile and nasty, counted them and their father among their gods.

Diabloman frowned. "Gary, did you just get us in a tag team match against two gods?"

I paused. "Yes, yes I did."

Diabloman facepalmed.

"Don't worry, Gary," Gabrielle said, putting her hand on my arm. "My father fought them all the time and won more than half of their battles."

"Which means the most powerful superhero in history lost almost half?" Mandy asked, looking over her. There was a disturbing amount of satisfaction when she said that particular observation.

Gabrielle blinked. "Well, we didn't advertise those moments but they never succeeded in killing him either! Mostly because he could reconstitute himself if he wasn't killed by Ultranium and—"

I put my hand on her arm. "Please, Gabrielle, stop helping."

"You should note Magnifisense casts her spells off from her life force so she's got a limited amount despite being immortal," Jane said.

"How do you know that?" I asked.

"It's in the comics," Jane said.

I stared at her, blinked, then shrugged. "Okay, works for me."

Guinevere surprised me by pulling out Caliburn and handing it over toward me. "You should take this weapon. It is capable of piercing the hides of even gods."

"Thanks," I said, taking the sword and immediately dropping it. I had to pick it up with two hands due to the weight. "Hey, Diabloman, are you up for this?"

"I am unworthy to fight in a battle alongside the holy blade of King Arthur," Diabloman said.

"Arthur murdered a bunch of babies to try and kill Mordred," I said, pointing out a little known passage from *The Once and Future King*. "He also tried to have his wife burned alive for adultery when he was shacking up with his sister."

"Oh right," Diabloman said, taking the sword.

"The execution of the innocent is a vicious lie about my father," Guinevere said, not denying the incest or trying to kill his wife. Seriously, the Arthur myth sometimes went further than *Game of Thrones*. Instead, Guinevere turned to Diabloman. "I also intend to make sure you pay for your crimes."

"I do that every day," Diabloman said, lifting the sword.

"Just focus on us killing the demon-god," I said, trying to reassure Guinevere her sword was in good hands.

Guinevere grumbled a few words in Welsh I didn't

understand but I took to be acceptance.

"Try not to die and remember back, back, forward, punch," Cindy said. "That's the code to throw a fireball."

"You got it," I said, casting several protection spells around Diabloman while also working a few incantations to allow him to use his tattoo magic to channel Death's power. Diabloman originally drew his strength-enhancing energies from the Great Beasts and they'd almost killed him. Since he'd gotten a new body, long story, I'd done my best to ingratiate him with my boss. As such, Diabloman could fight longer and harder than he ever could as a universe-destroying bad guy. I wasn't sure that would be able to do anything against a being like the Cackler, though.

"Abra cadabra, make Diabloman stronger?" Jane asked, looking at me. "That's your spell?"

I shrugged. "Magic is in the will not the words."

"What's next, Presto Chango?" Jane asked.

"Maybe," I said. "It's better than saying everything in Latin like some urban fantasy heroes."

"There's nothing wrong with Latin," G said. "It gave us French, Italian, and all the other languages that I use to get laid."

"Yeah, because the handsome spy needs help there," Jane muttered.

"Every bit helps," G said, smiling. "Also, we're not supposed to mention we're spies."

"But that'd help with the sex!" Jane said, shocked.

Diabloman touched a tattoo on his shoulder of a man wearing glowing armor and a suit of futuristic Medieval armor with glowing lines over plate mail appeared around him. It also had a pair of metal wings sticking out of the back.

"You ready, D?" I asked.

"Not in the slightest," Diabloman said. "The Cackler helped me destroy the universe. It was really a plot of Entropicus I was manipulated into."

"You could have told me that earlier. At least we're going to die on a tropical island paradise," I muttered. "Okay, Entropicus, we're ready!"

The two of us were teleported to a disgusting green

slime-filled sewer underneath the island where skeletons hung off of meat hooks. The place was barely illuminated and had a lengthy stone bridge between two flowing rivers of acidic muck. This was going to be the arena for our battle with Entropicus' minions.

"When will I learn to keep my big mouth shut?" I muttered.

Diabloman looked down on me. "We have long debated that question and my ten pesos is on never."

"Ten pesos? Really? You couldn't afford to go a little higher?" I asked.

That was when our opponents teleported in. The Cackler had a small resemblance to the Ice Cream Man with the same sharpened jagged teeth but his eyes were like a reptile's. He was dressed in a dirty foul-smelling Renaissance clown outfit even as his hands were like skeleton's. At the risk of saying the Cackler was ripping off Stephen King more than the Pennywise look, I could see the form of a giant oozing multi-eyed orb hiding behind the clown that I recognized as the monster's true form. The Cackler was just the big toe of a far greater cosmic being that liked to slum with us mortals.

Magnifisense had the pointed hat of the aforementioned Disney villainess but a black tank top that exposed her midriff and a long spider-silk covered dress that didn't quite reach the floor. Underneath it, I saw cloven hooves that caused green balefire to leap off the ground where she stepped as well as the top of a clubbed tail. Her fingers glowed with the green balefire that accompanied her hooves and I could hear the sound of screams coming from it. She was a beautiful woman besides it, but her face lacked anything resembling warmth or hope. It was the face of a thing every bit as inhuman as the Cackler but better at hiding it.

I leaned over to Diabloman. "You know, maybe we should ask if we could draw from some other fighting games. Like ones with succubi, fighting schoolgirls, or Chinese teenagers who ride pandas."

"Begin!" Entropicus' voice echoed through the chamber.

Ah hell.

CHAPTER SIX

WHERE I THROW DOWN WITH GODS

Magnifisense created a swarm of flesh-eating scarabs I burned away with a blast of flame. She blasted me with black lightning before I conjured a wall of Stygian ice that was instantly reduced to steam by it. Fighting with magic was a bit like Paper, Rock, Scissors when you got down to it. You had to come up with the right thing to overcome the wrong thing trying to kill you since an all-purpose, "Dispel Magic" spell didn't exist.

Fireballs, once conjured, weren't magic and could only be removed by methods to deal with actual fire. I'd learned all this from the Trench Coat Magician's online magic class I'd taken for $2000. I was next blasted with a lightning bolt and sent spiraling across the ground. Yeah, I hadn't gotten my money's worth.

"It is foolish of you, Lord Merciless to try to tangle with gods," Magnifisense said in a voice that sounded like chattering insects. "You might have survived to see the rebirth of the universe had you pledged fealty to the God Emperor of Abaddon."

She conjured a glowing ball of balefire above her head as I knelt down before her, my chest sizzling. "First of all, Lady, I am no one's Lord. I'm a Jewish kid from the suburbs. Second of all... Ed Boon taught me everything I needed to know about surviving this battle."

"Who?" Magnifisense asked.

"Google it!" I shouted, giving her a magic enhanced uppercut to the jaw and sending her flying into the acidic green goop beside me. "Merciless wins. Fatali—"

That was when Magnifisense, her skin melted off to reveal an insect-like carapace underneath burst out of the goop with a pair of giant dragonfly wings buzzing behind her. She also had an enormous bee-like stinger.

"Ah hell," I said.

"The power of the immortals flows through me!" Magnifisense hissed.

I promptly froze her in a block of ice that went crashing down into the goop once more. I didn't think it would hold her for long but I wanted to give myself some breathing room for figuring out how to finish her off. I had one weapon that I knew could kill gods but it wasn't a very practical device since I'd gotten it back from death: the Reaper's Scythe. Man, did I long for the days when I had two guns.

"Prepare to die, traitor!" the Cackler said, letting loose a peal of loopy insane sounding laughs.

I turned around to see the Cackler had already managed to rip off large portions of Diabloman's magical armor and was presently trying to strangle him. Diabloman had struck him numerous times with Caliburn but the Abaddon demigod was healing every blow almost as quickly as they'd been struck.

"Yo, Krusty!" I shouted, throwing a fireball at his face. "Pick on someone your own size!"

The Cackler growled and opened his mouth before a torrent of inky-blackness shot forth. If darkness could be said to have a physical substance, it would take this form. I turned insubstantial and disappeared under the floor before grabbing his feet then pulling him halfway down giving Diabloman a moment to swing and decapitate the deity in one blow. Diabloman then kicked the Cackler's head into the goop beside us.

I came up behind the now headless Cackler. "Flawless victory!"

The now-headless Cackler's form broke through the stone he'd been entrapped in and ripped up a slab of the floor before swinging at Diabloman's head. Diabloman managed to duck, only for the Cackler to kick him in the hand and send Caliburn flying into the acidic goop beyond.

"Oh yeah, Guinevere is going to be pissed about that," I muttered then remembered whose property I just lost. "Eh, I can live with that."

Diabloman proceeded to punch, kick, and grapple with the monster even as I knew it was a pointless gesture. The headless thing attacking him was nothing more than the big toe of the real monster inhabiting a corpse.

"I really hope this is a good idea," I muttered, walking over to the headless monster and reaching into the insubstantial place before worlds before pulling out the gigantic multi-eyed orb thing that came out and landed behind me. It splattered on the ground before turning into an oozing tree-stalk with a thousand mouths, so I decided the creature's true form was less from Stephen King's imagination than H.P. Lovecraft's crossed with H.R. Giger's. It extended outward hundreds of tentacles that seemed to bend reality around them while my vision struggled to comprehend its true form.

"You will be dead by dawn!" the Cackler's true form howled with a thousand slit-like mouths.

"Yeah," I said, gesturing toward him. "I don't think so."

I proceeded to blast the Cackler with every ounce of fire inside me, drawing on the raw necromantic power of the island that was greater here than anywhere else on Earth (if we even were still on Earth). The Cackler's mouths let out a scream that threatened to shatter my ear drums but only encouraged me to blast the monster harder. The monster's true form wasn't the size of a person, it turned out, but a small city. It just existed in five or six different dimensions simultaneously that were all closing in around me. Too bad for it I had more than enough flame for a state. The Cackler's last words were some sort of incantation but it wasn't able to finish because I eradicated it body, mind, and soul. "Hail to the King, baby."

"Is it dead?" Diabloman asked, coughing behind me.

I stared at the dark stain on the ground where the Cackler had once been. His headless body had dropped to the ground like its puppet strings had been cut. "Yeah, I think it is dead. It's not the first god I've killed and probably won't be the last."

Seriously, I'd faced a surprisingly large amount of hellish

deities in my short time as a supervillain. Magog, Adonis, Zul-Barbas, and these two. It was enough to give a man a complex until I reminded myself it was actually Death's power that had defeated them rather than my own. Also, it had been the Nightwalker's job to keep reality clear of the multiverse's various eldritch abominations. That was a job that still needed a replacement and I was wholly unqualified to take up. I should get on finding someone for that—maybe start by seeking teenagers with attitudes.

Diabloman laughed only to stop in mid speech. I saw his body turn to stone before my eyes. Where once my friend stood I only saw a fossilized statue. Behind him, having broken free from the ice was Magnifisense. She was covered in a bit of frost but had managed to shake herself free of the frozen tomb I'd imprisoned her in.

I stared at her. "Turn him back."

"Foolish human," Magnifisense said. "It is not like fairy tale. Turning person to stone is like turning them to ash. Easy to do but impossible to reverse."

I screamed at her and tried to blast her but only a tiny bit of flame shot forth that she easily deflected. She then turned insubstantial herself and passed through the statue before I found myself frozen in the same sort of icy block I'd imprisoned others in. I couldn't breathe, see, or move.

Until I turned insubstantial and reached into Magnifisense's head then popped the pen on the Reaper's Scythe. She exploded as the six foot long weapon detonated inside her. The glowing weapon then sucked up her soul, taking it to whatever dimension my master imprisoned evil bee women. Vengeance was a poor substitute for Diabloman's loss.

"I am sorry, Merciless," Diabloman said.

I turned around and saw the ghost of my friend, standing there, without his mask on. He was a tall Hispanic man with a goatee and a shaved head. A tattoo of a red devil was on his scalp and he was wearing his wrestling attire.

"No," I said, staring at him. "It's my fault. Don't worry, I've got a wish coming my way and I'll get you restored."

"No," Diabloman said, his voice low.

"What?" I asked staring at him.

"I died fighting to save this world," Diabloman said, raising his hand. "I have been searching for a good death since I met you. I do not know if this is sufficient atonement for what I have done. I do not know if there is anything I could do that is sufficient atonement for what I have done but I have done my best."

"What about your family?" I asked, looking at him. "They need you."

Diabloman looked down. "They do not. I spent less and less time with them as the years passed because I was afraid I would ruin them. My wife and I have not spoken in six months."

"Oh, Merciful Moses, I'm sorry," I said, taking a deep breath. "I didn't know."

"Look after my daughter when she comes to you to become a hero, Gary," Diabloman said.

"I will," I said, noting he called me by my regular name. "You were my best—"

Diabloman screamed as his ghost swirled around before retreating into the hand of Entropicus the God Emperor of Abaddon. The seven foot tall warlord was standing over the Cackler's ashes with his hand extended.

"I think Diabloman is making a mistake," Entropicus said, curtly. "Thankfully, he will not need to make any decisions ever again. His spirit will join the ranks of my legions and help me administrate the new order."

I assumed a fighting stance. "Okay, Space Satan, fuck you! You want to throw down? Let's throw down!"

"Ha ha!" Entropicus laughed. "Not until the end of the tournament, boy."

He vanished.

"Mother puss bucket," I said, getting up off the ground.

"I'm sorry, Gary," Death said behind me.

I didn't turn around. "Why did you let him take away Diabloman?"

"My power is still his until he renounces me and the souls of the dead are his to claim just like they are yours," Death said, her voice low. "It is also a matter of judgment. Diabloman's murders are in the hundreds of trillions thanks to his destruction of the previous universe. While most of those souls were reincarnated, he is still responsible for the greatest karmic debt in history. Nothing he has done, or could do, can make up for the horrors he has committed."

"So, he's damned no matter what," I said.

"That has yet to be determined," Death said, her voice soft. "I know he was your friend—"

"Can it," I said, risking the wrath of my patron. "What's his punishment?"

"That has yet to be determined but Entropicus can devise whatever tortures he wants," Death said. "It is within his purview to punish the souls of the guilty. They were given unto him to bring about a sense of justice to the treatment of souls. That a mortal would be the one determining their fate."

I had been less than pleased to find out hell was a real thing. I'd never been inclined to believe eternal punishment was something a good god could contribute to. Death wasn't a good god but she was better than most. Finding out she'd given souls to a monster like Entropicus, who certainly didn't qualify as mortal in my opinion, lowered my opinion of her tremendously.

"I'll get D back."

"We've done this dance before, Gary," Death said.

"Yeah and it got me Mandy back," I said, trying not to remember it had been Merciful, not me, who had restored her. To this day, I still didn't know why he did it and Death had been tight lipped.

"As you wish," Death said. "You have, of course, free will to do as you like."

That was a cop-out answer if I'd ever heard one. "Okay, you're going to have to tell me why I'm actually here because I know it can't be here to win the tournament. I've pulled off some stunning upsets over the years but this is like playing Dan Hibiki in tournament mode. Which, if you have no idea about fighting games, is a crappy character. Fun but crappy."

"This is an intervention," Death said, surprising me with a straight answer.

I paused. "An intervention?"

"For Destruction," Death said, her voice low. "Our brother is willing to abide by the rules of the Eternity Tournament but pressing him too far is likely to result in him lashing out."

I finally turned around, looking at Death who didn't remotely look like Mandy now. Instead, she looked like a goth version of the weredeer girl.

"New look?" I asked.

"I like to mix it up," Death said, her eyes completely black with no irises. "Destruction has the potential to reduce all of creation to ruins and force us to begin again, assuming it doesn't lead to our ends as well. You are here not to be a weapon but as part of my efforts to convince him reality is worth fighting for."

"My best friend dying and being sent to hell is not filling me with *joie de vivre*." I tried not to think about what Entropicus might be doing to him now. Soul-theft was one of the grossest and vilest abuses of magic anyone could engage in. I was a real son of a bitch but there was no way I would touch it with a ten-foot pole.

"No," Death replied. "I imagine it is not. Nevertheless, I have faith you will be able to make things entertaining for our brother."

"So, the universe's survival is dependent on whether or not a god finds my misery amusing?"

"Yes."

"I regret Cindy got the chance to be the one to say that explains a lot about the universe." I stood up. "On a scale of one to one billion, just what are my chances of doing whatever is needed to save everything?"

"I won't tell you the odds," Death said.

"That bad, huh?" I asked.

Death nodded. "Entropicus has managed to persuade Destruction he can end all of the problems of the multiverse and make things perpetually interesting. It is the only thing keeping our brother from doing something unspeakable. However, I believe there are other ways of shaking him from his madness."

"Like?"

"Love."

I closed my eyes. "Mine or yours?"

But she was gone when I opened my eyes.

CHAPTER SEVEN

WHERE I THINK ABOUT MY LOSSES

I sat on the edge of one of the castle's ramparts while staring at the sunset. The tournament was continuing below, dozens of fighters having been eliminated one by one. Two of Entropicus' champions were gone but that was a hollow victory since it had cost me my best friend. I'd lost people before, Cloak was always on my mind, but Diabloman's loss was worse. I'd brought him to this place and now he was gone. It was the inevitable result of the life I'd chosen to live where every battle was another chance to die. I'd stupidly ignored that for years and the odds had finally caught up with me.

Mandy, Cindy, and Gabrielle had all tried to talk to me, but I couldn't say anything to them because they had their own battles to fight. I sat there, watching them, and wondered if Entropicus would rig the fights to get more of my loved one's killed.

Weirdly, Mandy seemed the most affected by Diabloman's death despite their recent estrangement. She'd gone full vamp, smashing up her room, and then channeling her energy into fighting her next opponent. She ended up winning against a hulking behemoth version of Frankenstein's Creature, despite him being much-much stronger. It was like a super-fast version of Bambi beat up Godzilla, except Jane wasn't involved.

Cindy ended up fighting a sadistic serial killer dressed like a clown (what was with monster clowns here?). Gabrielle punched down a flying brick of a woman who sported a weird diamond shaped crest with a letter in it. Everyone had won on my team. Which meant they had another chance to die.

"Yo, Merciless," Jane said, coming up behind you. "You got a moment of time?"

I looked over my shoulder. "You win?"

Jane nodded. "Yeah, I won against a legally distinct and completely not copyright violating version of Freddy Krueger."

I blinked. "Like Robert Englund or the new guy?"

"There's only Robert Englund," Jane said, climbing on top of the parapet beside me. "G managed to win against a man called Mechani-Cal."

"You mean Mechani-Carl," I corrected her. "The C-List Supervillain guy."

"Whatever," Jane said. "Guinevere and Prismatic Commando fought a tag team bout against the Darden Valley Guardian and a witch named Coven."

"Anyone die?" I asked.

"No," Jane said, looking uncomfortable with the reminder the winners had the option of murdering the losers. "Though I've seen plenty of blood spilled by the bad guys this tournament. Five or six heroes killed and another half-dozen villains."

"Great," I muttered. "This is not going to help the realities they come from."

"Yeah," Jane said. "Honestly, if they'd taken anyone else other than me from my world then losing them would have been a good thing. My world is full of superpowered assholes who do evil but has no one to fight them."

"Really?" I asked, thinking I might need to find some new digs. I wasn't sure I could return to my world after this. I couldn't face Diabloman's daughter and tell her I'd gotten her father killed and damned. "No superheroes on your world?"

Jane took a deep breath and stared up at the sky. "No."

"Must be nice," I said, only half-joking.

Jane snorted. "Not in the slightest. It's a world of vampires, demons, warlocks, and witches with almost everyone using their powers for selfish gain. The only people who fight them are hunters and they don't care if you are a good supernatural or a bad supernatural. They just kill you because you are. Shamans like me are among the few people who straddle the fence, trying to bring peace between the various factions."

"Is it worth it?" I asked. "Trying to bring peace, I mean?"

I often felt like that was my role. I wanted to live in a colorful world of supervillains and heroes but not the one I was currently living in. I wanted to live in a place where superheroes were good but not zealots and supervillains were dastardly but not evil. Killing the worst on both sides had made things slightly better for a time but it seemed the balance was totally screwed now. Hell, Guinevere was *mean* now. What did that say about the world?

"No idea," Jane said, shrugging. "It's who I am, though, and who he is. I also like living and that's why I'm here trying to save everything."

I grunted, acknowledging her words. "Ever wonder if the afterlife is better?"

"I'm a witch as well as a shapechanger so I know it exists," Jane said. "But I'm not eager to explore the other side."

"I've sent tens of thousands of ghosts to the other side," I said, thinking about my side job as a psychopomp. "So many millions of spirits clinging to life on this side because they're afraid of the other world. It makes me wonder what's so great about this one."

"Familiarity breeds contentment," Jane said, turning around the old phrase. "But this side has stuff like sex, chocolate, and video games."

I nodded. "I suppose it does."

I wanted to hear more about her reality because the multiverse was looking like a good place to explore after this was done. I'd visited other worlds as well as other times in my career as a supervillain, however I'd never contemplated leaving my current one. The constant battles between good and evil were starting to wear on my soul. A reality where none of the local superhumans gave a shit about helping the world was appealing, even if it did sound like my old World of Darkness tabletop roleplaying-game campaigns.

"May I ask you a question?" Jane asked. "Assuming you aren't weirded out by a woman who used to read your comics from the time she was eight until her high school years?"

"I am, in fact, very weirded out," I said, having not actually given the matter much thought. It was a little strange to think about the possibility what was fiction in one reality was fact in another but I'd encountered weirder things. In an infinite multiverse, everything was bound to be real somewhere, though. "Still, I'm anxious for something to take my mind off my friend's death. This seems as good anything. How accurate are those, anyway? I mean, do they have everyone's secret identity and all that?"

"You're Gary Karkofsky in them so I guess. Did you really once own a flying pirate ship?" Jane asked.

"I did, actually," I said, proudly. "Sadly, I crashed it into Wall Street."

"I wonder how many people got that was a riff on a Monty Python sketch."

"Among geeks? Quite a few."

Down below, Andy Johnson aka The Amazing Andy, was getting blasted by the Shadowmaster. Amazing Andy could regenerate but that was just causing him to get spammed by the black cloaked figure's fire magic. The Shadowmaster was an evil wizard who'd shot me during one of my 'Murder Hitler' time-jumps (I got better) and ran a villainous consultation agency. Personally, I thought the guy's advice was overrated. I was surprised to see him here, multiverse at stake or not, and suspected he'd bail the moment he could.

"May I ask a question?"

"You just did," I said.

"Point taken." Jane asked. "Why call yourself a villain?"

"I beg your pardon?" I asked, turning to her.

"The whole card-carrying villain thing," Jane said, wrinkling her brow in a fashion that reminded me of my sister, Kerri. "I mean, no one in the real world thinks they're villains. Everyone is the hero of their own story. They don't grow up wanting to put on costumes and hold the world ransom."

"Maybe not in your world," I said, shrugging. "To paraphrase Henry Hill, I always wanted to be a supervillain."

"*Goodfellas* was about how the mob lifestyle was destructive and self-defeating."

I shrugged. "Yeah, but it also showed Ray Liotta having a lot of fun first. It's like the Bond movies. Yes, the villains all die in the end but damn they have nice pads and hot girlfriends. Talk about a life well lived."

Jane rolled her eyes. "Gary, you forget I've read your comics. You only kill bad guys."

"Heroes don't kill," I said.

"Tell that to World War 2 veterans."

Jane had a point there. "Do the comics tell why I became a supervillain in the first place?"

"Your brother got killed by a superhero," Jane said, reciting it as if it was a fact of a fictional character rather than something that had happened to the person across from her. "Some gun crazy wannabe vigilante broke in your house and gunned him down."

"Yeah," I said, taking a deep breath. I still had nightmares about that night, decades later. "He was a superhero who people cheered for murdering the dangerous Stingray despite the fact my brother, Keith, was out on parole. If he's the kind of guy who people consider to be a superhero, then I don't want any part of it. Being a supervillain means I'm accountable to myself and myself alone."

I wondered if the Merciless comic books on Jane's world talked about how I'd eventually tracked down Shoot-Em-Up when I was fourteen. He'd been visiting Falconcrest City's worst establishments, carrying out his brand of justice, and taking time to have sex with underage prostitutes. I'd killed him when he'd answered the door and the authorities never found out I was responsible. The only person who knew the truth on my world was Cindy. I hadn't even told Mandy.

"There's a difference between a dirty cop who murders a guy at a traffic site because he looks different versus a guy who takes a bullet trying to stop an armed robbery," Jane said, her voice low. "I know real life heroes and they have to make hard choices sometimes. You remind me more of them than the alternative."

I felt a headache coming on before I leaned my head against the stone wall beside me. "Did you know I actually got to speak with my brother's ghost?"

"Merciless: The Supervillain Without Mercy #113, yeah."

I paused. "You know you're an urban fantasy series in this world, right? I'm totally going to read those now to find embarrassing stuff about you. In fact, if we survive this, I'm going to your world to give you samples of your fanfic."

"I've actually written Merciless fanfic. My hard drive is full of Cindy/Gabrielle and Gary/Diabloman fanfic." Jane then realized what she said. "Oh Jesus, I didn't mean—"

"It's okay," I said, sighing. "Our relationship wasn't like that but I understand. In any case, I got to talk to my brother and he told me I was wasting my life being a supervillain. That I had so much potential to be anything I wanted, I'd served myself and my family poorly by imitating his mistakes. My father said about the same thing when he passed away."

"I don't think so," Jane said. "I think you are a hero and the only person who you need to convince of that is yourself."

"I was thinking about that earlier," I said, pausing. "There's no way Guinevere or the other Society of Superheroes folk would ever accept me, though. I don't know if it was because of what I did last year or something more personal but she hates me."

I'd been hoping to turn over a new leaf and be accepted like the proverbial prodigal son but that didn't seem to be the kind of reaction that the Society of Superheroes was likely to give. They'd already welcomed "me" into their ranks once and it had turned into an epic disaster. Worse, Guinevere's reaction meant I had the dislike of the person reputed to be the most compassionate as well as fundamentally "good" in the organization.

Frankly, if they ever found out Ultragod was dead because he'd thought Merciful was worth keeping on the street then they'd find the deepest hole in the world to toss me into—which they probably owned. Merciful had used Ultragod's trust to close and put an Ultranium bullet in his chest. I still had nightmares about that. I was responsible for the world's greatest hero's death, however indirectly.

"Yeah, I expected Guinevere to be a lot nicer," Jane said, looking back out to the fight going on below. "I mean, I feel like I should turn in my throwing tiara and net of justice from

Halloween 2007."

"We've all been wounded these past few years," I said, thinking back to when we first met. Guinevere had been putting me in jails but there hadn't been any of the anger or resentment she'd felt earlier. She'd been happy. The sum of her losses had worn that person away, especially Lady Hollywood's death. A wound even an immortal like her couldn't heal.

"Maybe that justifies some of it but not all of it," Jane said. "I've got quite a few broken pedestals of my own. The thing about being a hero is it's about trying to do better, even if you don't succeed."

"Who said that?" I asked.

"Ultragod," Jane said. "*Amazing!* comics Issue #600. I have the foil and hologram cover that was supposed to be worth big bucks in twenty years but costs less than my brother paid for it now."

"God, I hate when that happens," I said, grinning despite myself. "Still, I don't have any idea where I'd even begin trying to be a hero."

"Just keep doing what you've been doing," Jane said, smiling. "Just with less theft and mayhem. You can also try the no-killing thing if you really want to. I'm not going to hold it against you if you don't."

"Yeah, well, I don't think I'm becoming a hero anytime soon. Entropicus needs to be killed."

"Well, you don't have to be an idiot about it either," Jane replied. "If a guy is an inter-dimensional dictator who wants to enslave or murder billions then go ahead and kill him. The same goes for a mass murdering supervillain who escapes constantly because prisons are apparently made of cardboard in your world. Just don't do it for repentant criminals, drug dealers, or robbers. Hell, just focus on murderers and people who are threatening the world if you have to."

I paused. "A lot of my friends are criminals so it'll be difficult but I suppose I could use Gabrielle as an example and work from there."

"Yeah, I suppose that would make you Merciless: The Hero with Some Mercy™."

"That makes no damn sense," I said, chuckling at the very

idea "Too bad my doppelganger already took Merciful."

"Yeah, but he was an asshole," Jane said. I was really starting to like the walking talking slab of venison.

"He was," I said, pausing. "However, I may have to hold off on becoming a hero until after I've conquered the world. I'm sorry, but that's been on my bucket list for a long time and I'm not about to give that up just yet."

"Whatever Gary," Jane said, finishing her drink and putting the plastic bottle to one side before standing up. "In any case, I think I spotted Robin Hood down there. I'm going to ask him if he's up for a go."

I snorted. "Aren't you with someone back home?"

"Hey, what happens on Hell Island stays on Hell Island," Jane said. "I'll make it up to him when I get back."

"Good luck, Jane," I said, smiling. "You've got this sociopathic hero's friendship."

"Gary, you're not a sociopath."

"Why's that?"

"If you were then you wouldn't have friends," Jane said, jumping on the parapet and walking off.

She had a point. There went my insanity plea. I wasn't sure if I was cut out for the life of a superhero but I wanted to do right by Keith and Diabloman. I wasn't worried about Keith's soul and I had a better track record than Orpheus for rescuing souls from the Underworld. If I had to contact the Trenchcoat Magician and transfer all of Diabloman's karmic debt to myself or some other way to get him a "Get out of Hell Free" card, I would.

Hell, I could probably take it on since as a Chosen of Death I wasn't ever going to Heaven or Hell. I was effectively doomed to become an Elohim postmortem. Like Samael with a place in the 5th Heavens as well as real estate in Hell. I tried not to think about that.

Getting up, I proceeded to head down the rampart's top floor toward the snack bar. Hell Castle, despite its name, was actually a decent vacation spot. It had ghostly servitors who provided everything from snacks to magazines to more sensual desires if you were up for that. It really was like Han's island from

Enter the Dragon. Personally, I never slept with anything from hell as you never knew where they'd been. Also, I was pretty sure succubi wouldn't fall under Mandy's rules of 'expanded monogamy.'

I didn't get to sleep with anyone she didn't get to sleep with, which opened quite a few doors while closing others. I hope that didn't change when I became a hero. Who knew what kind of weird rules they operated under. Anyway, I went down to the bar and got myself several vodka martinis that I hoped my enhanced metabolism would deal with. Walking back with an extra-large one in tow, I decided to take a nap until my next battle.

"Psst!" A voice spoke from an alcove I was passing.

I stopped and turned to see Gabrielle had ditched her normal costume for a one-piece cleavage-exposing blue bathing suit with a V-neck tied together by string, kinky boots, and ninja mask. She had a pair of sais in her hands.

"Gabrielle, why are you dressed like a ninja stripper?" I paused. "Not that I'm complaining, mind you but—"

"It's a disguise!" Gabrielle snapped.

I paused. "Shouldn't a disguise not draw the attention of every red-blooded heterosexual male and queer female in the area?"

Gabrielle rolled her eyes. "Gary, please."

"No, seriously. It's only disguising your face and there are not that many stunningly gorgeous Afro Hispanic women on the island. Well, if there are, then Cindy is going to be all—"

Gabrielle gave me an Ultra-Force dope slap to the side of the head. "Focus."

I stared at her. "Gotcha."

"Eyes up here," Gabrielle said.

"Again, the downside to your outfit," I said, blinking.

"I need your help," Gabrielle said.

I nodded. "Always. Except, well, if my wife gets mad about it. Honestly, I think it may not be so much the fact I'm spending time with other women but spending time with you, specifically. Have you two had any superhero fights recently I've not been aware of? I can barely keep up with my own continuity these days. Did you know I only spent six months in Merciful's underground prison?"

"Gary, have you been drinking?"

I paused. "Yes. Water. Also, whiskey. Diabloman died today."

"I'm sorry," Gabrielle said, looking behind me then both ways down the rampart. "This may be bigger than all of us, though."

"How?" I asked. Gabrielle knew how important Diabloman was to me.

"Someone is trying to steal the Primal Orbs!"

CHAPTER EIGHT

THE RULES OF THIS TOURNAMENT SUCK

I stared at Gabrielle and blinked. "Umm, I know this is probably not the answer you're expecting but isn't that a good thing?"

"What?" Gabrielle asked, an appalled look on her face.

"I mean, we're all here because these damned orbs represent an existential threat to everything. Skullface McWizardton only wins if he wins the tournament and uses the orbs to kill everyone."

I neglected to mention I was also here because I wanted a wish to conquer the solar system. I didn't know if Gabrielle would overthrow me afterward, probably, but I was comfortable with her defeating me. If destiny hadn't made it so the two of us could be together, I loved my wife and Cindy after all, I was comfortable being her archnemesis. How screwed up was that?

Gabrielle shook her head. "It's not that easy, Gary."

I sighed. "Of course, it isn't. The universe is set up to keep its audience of violence and joke-hungry masses amused."

I turned to my left.

"Gary, what are you doing?" Gabrielle asked, looking at me sideways.

"Staring at the fourth wall. I assume the Primals can see me glaring at them," I said, making the most annoyed face I could.

"Uh huh," Gabrielle said, annoyed.

"So," I said, going back to what she said. "What happens if they get away with them?"

I had no idea who 'they' were but I figured we could get

to that in time. It wasn't like this was a place that lacked for potential suspects. As far as I could tell, it could be anyone from Professor Moriarty to Arsène Lupin.

"If they succeed in stealing the orbs then the tournament is cancelled," Gabrielle explained, a fearful look on her face. "All participants forfeit their matches and the tournament's host wins by default."

I blinked. "The tournament host being Mumm-Ra."

Gabrielle blinked. "You shouldn't call Entropicus that."

"The tournament host being Jack Skellington."

Gabrielle rolled her eyes. "Yes, Gary, the tournament host being him."

"Which will result in the end of the world," I said.

Gabrielle nodded. "Every world everywhere."

"Which means he actually has a vested interest in letting these yokels get away with the orbs," I said.

Gabrielle nodded again. "Is there like a rulebook I didn't get a copy of? I feel like there should have been one to let us know about these things. It should have been passed out at the start."

"There was a four-hour orientation by the priests of the All-Knowing on the beach at the start," Gabrielle said, frowning. "You didn't attend?"

I stared at her, trying not to be snide. "No, I was too busy mourning my best friend."

It was hard to believe Diabloman was gone. I kept expecting him to come back but the return of heroes (or villains) to the land of the living was greatly overstated. There had been a few times it had happened, Ultragod coming back from the dead once in the nineties as well as Mandy of course, but the vast majority of heroes stayed dead. Sunlight, Ultragod for the second time, the Nightwalker, and others were beyond this life now.

Ironically, I'd faced many of my enemies multiple times before. The Ice Cream Man, Big Ben, the Typewriter, and others had come back repeatedly. I'd faced them as zombies, ghosts, and even demons only to send them right back to hell after I was done with them. It seemed the damned spirits had the least to trouble crossing back over into this world.

For a moment, it actually made me hope there was no peace

for my best friend since that would make it easier to summon him back with necromancy. But I wasn't a very good wizard. I didn't know the dozens of languages necessary to translate spells, possess the mathematical genius to coordinate the stars properly, or even simply have the right spells. I hadn't just been joking back at the pizzeria that I wasn't smart enough to get all the bonus spells your typical D&D wizard needed to dominate the world. I did have the approval of a very powerful patron but she was a spirit who was fickle in her patronage.

"I'm sorry, Gary," Gabrielle said, placing her arm on my shoulder. "Diabloman was a… complicated individual but I knew you and he were close. You made him a better person."

Gabrielle was suppressing her anger at Diabloman, I could tell. Being imprisoned for years (months?) at the hands of Merciful had shredded her formerly calm demeanor. Gabrielle had been a member of the Texas Guardians with the Guitarist and Spellbinder, only for Diabloman to kill both of her friends. He'd also tried to kill her on numerous occasions. That's not including the time he destroyed the universe. So, yeah, I understood why she couldn't bring herself to mourn him like me.

"Did I?" I asked. "Did I really? If so, what does that make me?"

I was Diabloman's Luke and Gabrielle was his Leia. One sibling was willing to forgive and the other not.

Gabrielle looked confused. "Pardon?"

"I was just thinking of *Star Wars*," I said, pausing.

"Of course you are," Gabrielle said, sighing. "Why am I not surprised?"

"Because you know me so well," I said. "Real life redemption isn't like Darth Vader in *Return of the Jedi*. If Anakin Skywalker had managed to survive the Second Death Star then he would have found himself spending the rest of his short life on trial for war crimes. Luke would have been vilified for trying to defend his father, Leia for being his daughter, and the Rebellion for employing them both. He would have ended up executed and the galaxy would cheer. The fact he got into Jedi heaven would also strike all of his victims as a cop out."

Gabrielle blinked. "The Force or God has to be greater than man. I don't want Diabloman to suffer for what he did but, no, I don't think I'll ever forgive him."

"He'd never forgive himself either," I said, pausing. "So, who are the idiots who are trying to steal the orbs?"

"I only know one of them," Gabrielle said. "He's a warrior from Universe-LS."

"Universe-LS?" I asked.

Gabrielle paused. "Basically, it's like..."

"What?" I asked, wondering why she trailed off.

"*Star Wars*," Gabrielle muttered. "It's a universe where humanity has traveled the stars and become an interplanetary power."

"So it's the future?" I asked, trying not to hide my excitement. I was half sure mankind was going to destroy itself before it got outside of the Sol system. I had a spaceship with an FTL drive, a gift, but I'd never used it. Humans had been to other space empires but we hadn't adapted the technology and there was no sign Earth's governments had any interest in spreading beyond. They were too terrified of the other powers coming to wipe us out despite all the previous alien invasions being unmotivated.

Gabrielle said. "Not really. Universe-LS never had a past with superpowers."

"That doesn't make a damn bit of sense to me," I said. "How do you have a universe without superpowers?"

Gabrielle shrugged. "All I know is he's one of Death's champions and I thought you'd be able to talk to him."

"I don't know Death's champions beyond my group. Can't you just punch them into submission?"

"Then Entropicus might make it a fight and eliminate them," Gabrielle said. "Or me."

"He's got every angle covered, doesn't he?" I said.

"Maybe," Gabrielle said. "I think he's afraid of you."

"Pfft!" I snorted in derision. "How do you figure that?"

"Because if he kills you, Death will never forgive him," Gabrielle said.

That actually might be right. "Alright, let's go try to talk these thieves down."

Gabrielle nodded then directed her hand down the hallways toward the interior of the island's mountain. The two of us headed down a long string of steps and torches illuminated all around us, glowing with green fire. There was no noise except for the sounds of fires crackling as well as the dripping of water into puddles on the ground.

"So, can I ask you a question?" I asked.

"You can ask me anything, Gary," Gabrielle said. "You know that."

I paused. "Perhaps. I was just curious—"

"What?" Gabrielle asked.

"How are you?" I asked.

Gabrielle stopped in mid-step then looked back at me. "Do you really want to know?"

"Well, I freed you from a technological prison built by my evil twin and we've seen each other like, what, three times?" I asked. "One being a booty call."

"I didn't think your...uh wife and lover would mind," Gabrielle muttered.

"Well Mandy did," I said, frowning. "But no matter what, I'm your friend and worried about you."

"Friend?" Gabrielle asked, the word carrying a lot of pain.

"I love you and always will but you made your choice," I said, remembering how she'd ended our engagement because she was worried I'd get killed by a supervillain if we continued to date. Then she took my memories of our time together for years. The pain was still fresh even though I remember everything we lost. "I also made mine. I'm glad to have to have the life I have,"

"And me?" Gabrielle asked.

I blinked. "I...do I have you?"

I needed to tell her to stop and not say her next words because if she said them, I wasn't sure I'd be able to tell her to stay away.

"I love you Gary," Gabrielle said, admitting it. "I never want to give you up."

Dammit.

"But I'm not sure I like sharing," Gabrielle said.

I looked down. "That could be a problem."

"I know," Gabrielle said, taking in a deep breath. "There's also something else I need to tell you."

I took a deep breath. "Could we put a pin in that while we're on a mission? I mean, you know, until I've had a chance to cope with the first revelation? Plus, you know, my best friend dying and being in hell? Not sure I have room for anything else right now."

Gabrielle looked troubled and given she routinely moved asteroids out of the way of Earth, that meant the news was probably devastating. Given she'd just proclaimed her undying love for me and wanting to be exclusive, I wasn't sure what could be that troublesome. "Alright, Gary, let's talk about something less troubling. Are you going to wish Diabloman back?"

I hadn't thought of that. I was also bothered by the fact resurrecting my dead friend was less troubling than her news. "That would be a convenient solution to my problems, wouldn't it? I could restore things to the status quo and everything would go back to the way it was."

"It's never that easy," Gabrielle said. "We're not like the characters in the comic books made after us. There's no returning to the status quo at the end of the issue."

"It sure feels that way sometimes," I said, considering my options. "I suppose I might wish him back but I might as well wish hell to not exist or the magic to bring him back."

"Wishing big never helps," Gabrielle said.

"It never helps to wish small either," I said, taking a deep breath. "Certainly, I can take over the world on my own if I want."

Gabrielle snorted. "Yes, the mid-level magic user who doesn't want to kill anyone is going to take over the world. You don't need to give me the same false bravado you give everyone else, Gary."

"False bravado?" I asked. "There's nothing false about it. I've killed three figures worth of assholes."

"But not innocents," Gabrielle said, sighing. "If you're going to take over the world then you're going to have a body count of good people who don't want to be conquered. You're not the kind of person who hurts innocents."

Gabrielle had me wrong, though not by much. "That used to be the case but it seems I got a lot of innocent people killed when I broke out everyone from Merciful's prisons. Perhaps I should have been more discriminating."

"You've been talking with Guinevere," Gabrielle said, her voice lowering. "That's her interpretation of events."

"Is there another one?"

"That people make their own mistakes and trying to pass them off on the self-styled supervillain is an unworthy path for so-called heroes," Gabrielle said.

I felt the bridge of my nose and took a deep breath. "Gabrielle, I'm going to go out on a limb here and say you're not doing well."

Gabrielle started walking down the stairway again. "No, I'm not. Guinevere was like a second mother to me. She and my father had been close friends since before WW2. She was there at my side from the beginning, trained me when I wanted to be a hero, and fought for my membership in the Society of Superheroes when I was thought too young."

"I saw the articles in *TIME* and *People*," I said, frowning. "It must have hurt you beyond measure to have her give up on finding you."

"Yes," Gabrielle said, her voice quivering with rage. "But that's not the worst part. It's not even the fact she tried to shift the blame on you when you saved me. It was the fact she dishonored everything my father stood for by siding with Merciful. Worse, she did it in his name. Without the Nightwalker and Ultragod, she turned the Society of Superheroes into a tyranny."

I was really going to regret saying my next words, I just knew it. "Have you tried talking to her?"

"About as much as she's tried talking to me," Gabrielle said, gritting her teeth. "Specifically, to let her know how much she disappoints me."

I took a deep breath. "Maybe you should both try to talk like people who have saved the world repeatedly as well as being two of the most famous role models for girls across the globe. People who should be focused on making the world a better place than fighting each other. I know a lot of people speculate on who would win in a fight: Sherlock Holmes or Captain Nemo but the truth is nobody really wants to see heroes trying to kill one another. We want to see our heroes team up and beat up the real bad guys."

"Are you seriously defending her?" Gabrielle asked. "After all she pulled. After all she's done to you? She's smeared your reputation across the globe."

"You mean my reputation as a supervillain?" I asked. "Yeah, I think that's fine."

"You know what I meant."

"I know," I said, following her down the steps. "The truth is, though, Guinevere lost her two best friends five years... a year... goddammit, this time compression thing is ridiculous, a while ago. The burden of leadership for the Society of Superheroes falling on her shoulders when it used to be shared with three. Maybe I'm not fond of her and she's never going to be my friend but if I'm able to forgive the worst then why not forgive the best?"

A gust of wind shot forth from the base of the dungeon, blowing me a foot back. I stepped forward and shook my head. "I think we're getting close."

"Yeah," Gabrielle said. "What's your angle?"

"Excuse me?"

"Gary, you're a man of many qualities I admire. However, I don't think of you as the soft sensitive type. Why are you trying to get me and my godmother to make up?"

I paused. "I want to be a superhero."

Gabrielle stopped dead in her tracks before bursting out laughing.

"Gabby—" I started to say.

Gabrielle continued laughing.

"Gabby," I said, frowning.

Gabrielle started to calm down then ended up giggling a little more. "Okay, we really shouldn't be stopping to talk about this but are you serious? That is the worst plan I have ever heard in my entire life."

I stared at her, not at all amused. "You know, I've saved the world a couple time. I've stopped a bunch of bad guys. Maybe

I did a little thieving and killing along the way but I didn't think the idea of my being a hero was something so incredibly ridiculous."

Gabrielle looked guilty. "I'm sorry, I really am. It's just you've never cared about what people think before. It was one of those aforementioned admirable qualities."

"Well, maybe I don't want to spend my adult life being chased down by people I admire," I said. "I don't want my daughter growing up with the same cloud hanging over her head that my parents had."

"Leia has no reason to be anything but proud of you," Gabrielle said, looking at me. "She is the thing I am most jealous of."

I looked at her and said nothing then walked past her.

CHAPTER NINE

WHERE THE THIEVES ARE US

The Primal Orbs were kept in an enormous seven-sided chamber in the heart of the mountain. The seven orbs formed a circle in the air, glowing each with a different color of the rainbow, as they moved in a circle with an eerie soft music generated from their motion. The chamber was illuminated by hundreds of wax candles in each corner while the seven corners of the chamber each contained a robed statue of a human male or female of differing ethnicities.

Notably, one of the statues looked vaguely similar to me , and another to Entropicus. I didn't recognize any of the others, which bothered me to an extent, as you'd think I would have met the other Chosen Ones. Merciful wasn't up there either, which surprised me since he'd been the Chosen of Life. Apparently, he'd either been a temp in the position or the Primal of Life had chosen someone to replace him.

It didn't take long to see who was the party going to steal the Primal Orbs since there were only two other individuals in the chamber. The first of them looked a bit like a male model had stolen Captain Malcolm Reynolds wardrobe and added a sheath for a *Warhammer 40K* chainsword to it. He wasn't quite as good looking as Agent G, not that I paid attention to that sort of thing *cough* but definitely had a kind of messy gorgeousness. The second person was holding the *Book of Midnight,* the cursed book of everything, and apparently trying some sort of incantation.

Mandy.

"God dammit," I said, walking down the steps. "Gabrielle

did you know my wife was behind this?"

"Maybe," Gabrielle said, pausing. "Actually, yes, that would be why I knew what was going to happen."

I rolled my eyes. "Mandy, you can't steal the magic orbs because that will cause Entropicus to automatically win. Also, who is the space dude?"

The man pulled out his sword and rather than a chainsaw blade, it produced a crackle of blue white electricity around its blade. "I am Cassius Mass, Count of the Archduchy of Crius. Who are you?"

"What? No *you killed my father, prepare to die*?" I asked.

Mandy felt her face.

Cassius shrugged. "Eh, if you killed my father, I'd be thanking you."

"Ah, daddy issues," I said, nodding. "That's always the thing with space opera heroes."

Cassius looked back at Mandy. "Who is he and what is he talking about?"

"Gary Karkofsky a.k.a Merciless," Mandy said, not putting down the *Book of Midnight*. "He's my husband and I wouldn't recommend trying to make sense of anything he says. He's basically what the internet would be like if it was intelligent with less porn."

"I resent that remark," I said, frowning. "I have plenty of porn."

Mandy shut the book and pointed at Gabrielle. "Gabrielle is wrong. There is a way we can win this contest by stealing the orbs."

"How's that?" I asked, wondering what I'd stepped into and whether I should automatically be supporting my wife in this.

"We can use the Primal Orbs to kill Entropicus and the worst of his lieutenants, preventing us from needing to go through this tournament," Mandy said, brimming with confidence. "We can end this now and not have to play by the villain's rules."

"And you decided to break the rules, my forte, with Captain Tightpants here instead of me?" I asked, offended.

"Gary!" Gabrielle said. "We need to stop—"

"Hold up," I said, raising a hand.

"I'm standing right here," Cassius said. "As for how she recruited me, it was at the bar."

"There's a bar here?" I asked, appalled. "No one told me that!"

"I recognized him from *Lucifer's Star*," Mandy said, shrugging. "I love that movie."

"The crappy SyFy channel original picture?" I asked. "You couldn't go with Luke Skywalker or Captain Kirk?"

"I feel insulted for multiple reasons," Cassius said, pausing. "Either way, I refuse to be a champion of any cause I believe to be unjust. I did it once before and it shall not happen again."

"Okay, Ned Stark, that's great," I said, walking forward to him. "But let's point out the obvious fact that there's no security here. No ancient Chinese curses, giant golems, or multicolored ninjas."

"There's some pretty hefty magic around here," Mandy said, now looking suspicious. "What do you think, Cass?"

"I don't know, I don't have magic in my world," Cassius said. "Just extremely advanced science."

"Really, none whatsoever?" I asked, shaking my head. "That's terrible! We need to cross pollinate your world and G-man's with Jane's. Get you some vampires, werewolves, demons, and other stuff."

"I'll pass," Cassius said.

Gabrielle stepped in front of me, raising a glowing fist. "I have to stop you from endangering the world!"

"Gary, have you been egging her on?" Mandy asked.

"I swear, I haven't" I said, raising my hands. "I've just been asking if she's been happy!"

"That's egging her on!" Mandy asked. "She's a superhero! They don't do anything by halves!"

"You're a superhero!" I said, turning to Gabrielle.

Gabrielle had started glowing a brilliant shade of gold as she prepared an Ultra-Force blast that would knock Mandy cold. I had to make a choice now whether to go against her or my wife who was possibly doing something really stupid.

That was when Cassius took the choice out of my hands. "Forget this hero vs. hero crap! I'm going after the plunder!"

He then turned his sword against the orbs and swung at the circle they were floating it. He struck an invisible force shield that shattered in every direction, sending out a glowing rainbow of light.

"No!" I shouted, covering my face in my cloak. "Prismatic Spray is the most deceptively dangerous of all *Dungeons and Dragons* spells!"

The glowing blasts of red, green, blue, purple, orange, black, and gold went in every direction. The blasts bounced against the walls and statues, Cassius slicing through the red blast with his sword while the black disappeared into my cloak. The orange blast struck Gabrielle in the chest, sending her spiraling backward against the stairs while Mandy dodged the blue blast only to be hit in the chest by the white one. The remaining balls of light proceeded to vanish in midair, as if some hidden agenda was accomplished.

I looked up from my cloak. "Anybody dead?"

Gabrielle was moaning behind me while Mandy was scrambling to her feet, her hair stringy and covering her face while she growled. Cassius, the only person in the room I didn't actually give a crap about, was uninjured.

"No," Cassius said.

"That was a stupid plan," I said, glaring at him.

"I have a general belief that whenever people get bogged down in talking, it's best to dramatically act," Cassius said, sheathing his sword.

"That is the dumbest thing I've ever heard in my life!" I said, staring at him. "Who are you, Anakin Skywalker?"

"The future Darth Vader?" Cassius asked, looking like he was trying to parse out the reference. "An odd choice."

"Wait, you have *Star Wars* in the future?" I asked, deciding this guy might be alright after all.

"Well, it is a classic of Old Earth mythology, even in the thirty-first century," Cassius said.

"Yes!" I shook my fist. "Reality has some hope after all! I hadn't had any hope for Star Wars' future since *The Last Jedi* came out."

Mandy growled some more.

"Oh hell, she's going to be evil or berserk now. I just know it," I muttered turning to my wife.

Mandy's face had twisted and contorted into something grossly inhuman with shark-like teeth instead of fangs and glowing white eyes. Her fingernails had turned black and extended outward like velociraptor-esque claws. Her skin had also become sallow and corpse-like with none of the vibrancy that differed her from other vampires.

"Gabrielle, could you—" I started to say before turning around and seeing Gabrielle was staring at me with pure hate in her eyes. Her golden aura had turned a darker shade with orange flames flickering against it every few seconds.

"That doesn't look good," Cassius said, drawing his pistol.

"You could say that," I said. "I don't suppose you have any planet punching powers?"

"No," Cassius said. "Just an energy shield, a sword, and fusion pistol."

"Well, we are boned."

That was when Entropicus' gravelly voice spoke throughout the room. "Double-elimination match! Two on two battle!"

"Wait, what?" I said, looking up.

"FIGHT!" Entropicus shouted.

I barely managed to maneuver before Gabrielle jumped forward and punched me across the face with a glowing fist. She had to be holding back since, as the inheritor of the Ultra-Force, she could have easily taken my head off in one blow. Mandy, by contrast, went after Cassius who blasted her with a blue energy wave that I assumed to be stun. Sadly, as anyone who knew anything about the undead could tell you, they weren't creatures easily subdued.

Gabrielle conjured a glowing orange-yellow scythe, which I felt was ripping me off then swung it in my general direction. I turned insubstantial and went down below her. Normally, this was when I went behind my opponent, but I stayed put and Gabrielle swung around in that direction. Coming up behind her by not moving in the slightest, I mentally apologized to her, and unleashed a torrent of Sith-like lightning.

I'd expanded my power's variety to include the equivalent

of third-level spells but with significantly more wallop when I drew from Death. I was terrified of accidentally killing her but didn't want to die either so I gradually turned up the electricity in hopes of using the minimum amount to disable her. A minimum amount which, it turned out, didn't seem to exist.

Ultragoddess screamed but it was more a roar of rage than a cry of pain. The Ultragod Family was vulnerable to magic, one of their few vulnerabilities, but it was more in the context of not having any extra defenses against it versus being invulnerable to anything else. Watching her all but shrug off the power plant I was throwing at her and start marching toward me, I wondered if they'd made up that vulnerability to sucker wizards like me into thinking they had a chance.

"Must...destroy...you," Gabrielle said, making a glowing chainsaw out of her powers. "You are Merciful! Betrayer!"

Oh, great, she was convinced I was my doppelganger. Before I could react, a glowing cage appeared around me of the Ultra-Force. Gabrielle stepped through the bars as if they weren't there. I proceeded then to blast hellfire outward that disintegrated the cage and her chainsaw. I checked on her the moment the blast was done and saw aside from some singing to her hair, she didn't even look injured.

"Roargh!" Ultragoddess cried out, conjuring a suit of armor straight from Dark Souls and aiming her sword at me before fireball after fireball shot forth. I once more hid in the floor, only for her to start smashing through the area above me to get at me. This was not a fight I could win hand-to-hand, magic-to-magic. I was both underleveled and under-geared.

"Gabrielle, it's me!" I shouted, trying to think of something special. "Your favorite literary character is Katniss Everdeen, you love coffee ice cream, and you have the highest score of anyone on the planet with *Tekken*. A game you know I hate because I'm a *Street Fighter* and *Mortal Kombat* man. Plus, you hate the fact they consistently nerfed Ultragoddess whenever she's a guest fighter!"

"Argh!" Ultragoddess hissed, ripping away all the rock between us. "You lie!"

So, there was something of her left over. It required me to

say something that was so shocking and terrible that it would break her away. "Gabrielle, I really think you should find a relationship with someone else. I love you and always will but our lives have just moved in opposite directions. You're too wonderful a person to not find someone else who is going to make you happy."

Gabrielle momentarily broke free. "Wait, what? You think I've been mooning over you for, what, a decade? Or maybe a few years? Time has been pretty wonky lately. I've had dozens of relationships since then and just because I still like you and I recently had a night of pity sex—"

"Distraction-fu attack!" I said, blasting her with my ice powers.

Gabrielle was trapped in a huge block of ice and looked decidedly cross with me. I didn't blame her. That was a cheap shot. She could, of course, easily break free but what was the point when we had no reason to fight? It turned out there was a very good reason as a gong resounded through the temple, signifying an elimination. Entropicus had decided, apparently, this qualified as Gabrielle being defeated.

"Awesome, I won!" I said, glad at winning on a technicality before the weight of that fell on my shoulders. "Which means, oh crap, I've just removed the single most powerful hero from the tournament and made it that much easier for Entropicus to destroy the multiverse."

I didn't get a chance to contemplate the monumental nature of my screw up because Mandy leapt on my back and started going for my throat. Nearby, I could see Cassius lying on the ground, trying to hold the blood back in his neck as he used a future laser of some kind to treat a bite wound. He hadn't been eliminated yet but that was only because Entropicus hadn't called a stop to the contest yet.

"Dammit, Mandy!" I said, spinning around and trying to avoid getting my head ripped off. "I do not want to hurt you!"

"Too bad!" Mandy said, her voice having a shrill Evil Dead witch-esque quality. "I will swallow your heart!"

"Must not do any double-entendres," I muttered, before turning insubstantial and letting her fall through me onto the ground. "I will not say she wants inside me, that she's inside me, that she loves sucking, she wants my fluid, that she's naturally cold but I warm her up—"

Mandy shook her head, a moment of lucidity appearing on her face. "Oh Gary, shut up!"

"Sorry, Mandy," I said, grabbing the *Book of Midnight* off the ground and smacking her across the face with the leather-bound Bible-sized tome. It sent her spiraling backward against Gabrielle's ice block where I proceeded to freeze her over. Unlike Gabrielle, I was pretty sure Mandy didn't have the ability to break free. Sure enough, a second gong sounded and I had the dubious satisfaction of having eliminated the smartest most dangerous woman alive from the tournament. Yay me! God, Death chose a crappy champion.

"*That's the plan,*" Death whispered in my mind.

Wait, what?

"No ice puns?" Cassius asked, standing up, a big scar on his neck and some blood on his outfit but otherwise unharmed.

"Please, I have some standards," I said, huffing. "Though I'm glad I got both women to chill."

"Oh for hell's sake," Cassius muttered, covering his face with his right hand.

I was about to make a few more when Gabrielle shattered her icy prison as the orange fire returned to her eyes and she clocked me in the jaw, sending me flying, and landing in the middle of the orbs.

The orbs glowed, and everything went white.

CHAPTER TEN

A GLIMPSE OF THE FUTURE

I found myself, face down, in the middle of some truly epic carpet. I mean, I've fought kaiju and something legally distinct but pretty damn similar to Cthulhu but this was some truly magnificent carpet. It was thick, furry, and felt like I was face down on top of a panda. Which, as any poacher will tell you, is the cuddliest of all animals. I don't deal with poachers by the way and have killed more than a few over the years, FYI, I'd just like to make that clear. All panda fur products in my home are completely artificial or cloned.

Ahem.

Lifting my head up from the panda fur carpet, I found myself in an enormous palace's throne room. It was a kind of neo-classical Rome crossed with corporate executive. The floors reflective black marble, the columns holding up the ceiling were white stone, and the walls were covered in red tapestries marked with the Merciless Symbol. The Merciless symbol was a double-A anarchy symbol combined to make an M. Light was provided by modern lights above but also hellfire braziers.

The carpet I was lying on was a single long straight rectangle stretching back to the throne room's entrance about a football field behind me up the steps in front of me to an elevated dais. There, with the throne's back to me, was an enormous electronic throne chair that was facing a wall-window that showed a futuristic Falconcrest City. The skyline had all been replaced with metal buildings reaching miles into the sky and flying cars zipped around the airways.

It was also raining with a steady downpour of greenish-brown water that clung to the transparent steel finish. It was like someone had combined *Blade Runner* and Coruscant. Oddly, despite the fact it was an archvillain's lair, the place smelled like Red Dust combined with marijuana and I could hear the sounds of an Xbox being played.

"Goddamn zombie Nazis!" my voice, except much older said, followed by the sound of electronic gunfire. "Screw you ten year olds in Korea! Do you know who I am!? I swear, I am outlawing multiplayer tomorrow!"

"Uh, hello?" I asked.

The sounds of yet another installment of *Call of Duty* stopped being heard before I saw a smoke ring blow in the air. The throne slowly turned around with a grinding noise before I found myself facing yet another Gary doppelganger. This one was wearing a black cloak identical to my own and looked to be in his mid-sixties. He had a black military uniform underneath the Cloak with a rank badge covered in blue and red squares. On his hands were eight golden rings that had glowing gemstones. A hookah was to one side of his arm as he didn't quite fit the throne and an Xbox controller was inside his lap.

"Oh, it's you," Old Gary said.

"What?" I said.

"I've been waiting for you since, well, I was you," Old Gary said.

"Who are you? Where am I?" I asked, a lot more bewildered than I usually was in this sort of situation.

"I am you. I am also Emperor Gary Karkofsky the First and Only. I am the ruler of the Grand Terran Empire and its dozens of colonies. Most of which, admittedly, are hollowed out spinning asteroids because that turns out to be a lot easier than terraforming planets."

I blinked. "Are you Merciful? Somehow resurrected? I mean, I was hoping you were kind—"

"No, Gary," Old Gary said, feeling his face. "I am you. Future you. This is the scene in *Back to the Future part II* where Jennifer met her older self then fainted before no longer being included in the film. Which, honestly, was a huge waste of Claudia Wells."

I blinked. "Okay, let's just say I believe you."

"Wow, this conversation is getting boring. I wonder how older me tolerated it the first time around," Old Gary said.

"What year is it?" I asked, looking behind me and expecting a bunch of stormtroopers to come and arrest me.

"It's 2250," Old Gary said, offering his hookah pipe. "Want a hit?"

"I'm high on life, nerd culture, and sex with beautiful superhumans," I said.

"Fair enough," Old Gary said, taking a deep puff. "I'm high on those and drugs!"

"Just say no, man!" I said, shaking my hands. "Remember what the Director of the FBI said in all the arcade games! Winners don't use drugs!"

Old Gary blew some of the smoke in my face. "Clearly, he was wrong."

I took a moment to process this all. "So, by touching the Primal Orbs—"

"Hehe, you said orbs," Old Gary said, giggling.

"Oh grow up," I said, fully aware of the irony.

"I've been transplanted to a possible future where I've successfully taken over the world," I said.

"Two Earths, the moon, a Mars base, and lots of asteroid colonies," Old Gary said. "We're members of the Galactic Congregation that is a lot less religious than it sounds but not wholly secular either."

"Great," I said, muttering. "Well, if you'll excuse me I have to get back—"

"Of course, it might not be a possible future but the future," Old Gary said.

"Excuse me?"

"Because I remember the Eternity Tournament and how it successfully screwed up the entire universe," Old Gary said. "I also remember this meeting as I've alluded to several times in this conversation, which means this may end up as a self-fulfilling prophecy instead of a new timeline. More *Terminator* instead of *Back to the Future*."

"Wait, original *Terminator* or *Terminator II*? The others don't count, even the series that was awesome toward the end," I asked. "Because in *Terminator*, John Connor was only born because of sending Kyle Reese back but—"

"Let's stop and never mention the specifics of time travel again," Old Gary interrupted.

"Probably a good idea," I admitted. "Listen, I know this is a big accomplishment and all but I'm not actually interested in taking over the world. I mean, seriously, who wants that kind of responsibility? I really just talk a good game. I'm going to become a hero instead of remaining a supervillain. So, this future? This future is not going to happen."

Old Gary snorted in disdain. "I remember this part too."

"You're really starting to tick me off, Old Man." I narrowed my eyes. "I am not going to take over the world."

"You do," Old Gary said, putting down his hookah. "Not because you want to or because someone convinced you to but because you had to."

"No one has to become a conquering despot," I said, disdainfully.

Old Gary leaned back into his chair. "This is the part of the story where I relay to you the fact it is possible to force someone to become the very thing they disdain. If you live long enough as the villain, you start to want to be a hero."

"That's stupid and even if you reversed the statement, it still wouldn't make any sense."

"Shut up and listen, jackass."

"Only if I get a chair and some popcorn," I said. "I feel like that's going to be a common feature of this tournament."

"Always happy to use an old favorite among my spells." Old Gary snapped his fingers and a lawn chair appeared with a big movie tub of popcorn.

I plopped myself in the former and picked up the second to start eating it. It was exactly the way I preferred it. "Okay, you've bought yourself five minutes."

"I won't need that long," Old Gary said, leaning back in his chair like the Emperor. "In one of the few realities where you successfully win and the multiverse is saved—"

"Okay, that already doesn't make any sense."

"It's like the Wheel of Time, as long as one reality resists the Dark One, they're all saved."

"Okay, one, spoilers, two what is with Robert Jordan appearing everywhere lately?"

"The thing is, all of those heroes and villains teaming up together up against Entropicus and the chaos that followed didn't have the effect people wanted."

"People?" I asked, eating a handful of popcorn.

"Well, me," Old Gary said, frowning.

"I was hoping it would cause everyone to take a look at what was beneath all the costumes and secret identities. I was hoping we could realize that hero and villain were just two sides of the same coin. The heroes could work with the less insane of the villain world. Pay out pardons and money so we could all become rich as well as famous do-gooders."

"That's a stupid idea," I said.

Old Gary shrugged. "What happened, instead, was the War."

"The War?" I repeated.

"Yes, accent on the," Old Gary said. "The final conflict between the heroes and villains."

"Did our side win?" I asked.

"No," Old Gary said, reaching over and stealing some of my popcorn. "Our side most certainly did not. We sat out the war like Achilles, content on believing the two sides would come to their senses before things escalated too far."

"Were we stupid?" I asked, my mouth dry. "Need a soda."

An enormous paper cup, like the kind sold as the largest size in movie theaters, appeared in my lap. I took a sip from its milkshake-sized straw. It was like Coca Cola except even more syrupy and sugary, which I mentally named Merciless Cola.

"Thanks," I said.

"Welcome," Old Gary said, looking down at his feet. "Yeah, you could say we were stupid, but we were really just trying to protect our friends. Being the devoted champions of Chaos and Neutrality we were, we didn't want to end up killing Gabrielle or Mandy or anyone else who was leading the charge against the other side."

"Wait, Mandy and Gabrielle were on opposite sides?" I asked.

"Instead, we just did what rational folk did and hid our families away. Our kids."

"I have another child than Leia?" I asked, intrigued.

"Spoilers," Old Gary said, putting his pointer finger in front of his lips.

"And this isn't?" I asked, annoyed.

Old Gary gave a dismissive wave. "Cities were destroyed, continents were ravaged, and maps were redrawn. The public, showing its usual compassion as well as decency, revived President Omega's genocide plans. They targeted every single superhuman in the world, innocent or guilty, along with their families."

My blood ran cold. "Which would include Leia."

"Yes," Old Gary said, narrowing his eyes. "They went after my family."

"I hope you killed every one of them," I said, putting down my refreshments then balling my fists.

Old Gary's eyes were haunted and empty. "Yes, I killed them all."

I immediately lost some of my enthusiasm. "How many?"

"The number sort of loses its significance after a certain number of zeroes but that wasn't enough for me," Old Gary said, sighing. "It wasn't enough that I kill them. I wasn't going to let the baby-killing pieces of crap be martyred and academics talk about how they went so bad years later. I wasn't going to let the David Irvings or Alt-Rights of the future talk about how the Pure Human Movement was misunderstood or engage in ironic genetic supremacy. So I took the Prime Orbs and I used them to make sure everybody knew exactly what it was like. I made them feel the pain, the fear, and the horror of their victims by inaction."

I let that sink in. "How'd that work out?"

Old Gary looked out the window. "It broke humanity. I didn't leave myself out of the equation but I always knew what I was. What was left turned to me for leadership and generation after generation left me in charge. There hasn't been a war since and violence is pretty tame. The shadow of what we were hangs over us still."

"Sounds almost too good to be true," I said, sensing just how much agony my future self was in.

"Is it?" Old Gary asked, sighing. "The fire has gone out of humanity because we lost our ability to self-delude ourselves about heroes and villains. We're a grey race now, neither good nor evil, and simply existing. I always had an ironic name because I never wanted to be merciless but in the end, I was the most merciless one of all."

I made a really tiny violin noise.

"Really, Gary?" Old Gary asked. "That's what you take from all this?"

"World peace and all the murderous bigots in the world are dead," I said, frowning. "Oh you poor bastard, however will you survive being the absolute ruler of everything you survey?"

"God, I was an immature dipshit," Old Gary muttered.

"Very true," I said, picking up my Merciless Cola with both hands and drinking from it. "Besides, I don't believe in fate. You may be a sad sack of spent misplaced idealism and guilt for being a mass murderer but that doesn't mean I'm going to be. Besides, if you really didn't think this universe was the best possible one then you could just use your powers to go back in time to fix it."

"Maybe I didn't believe I could make things better," Old Gary said. "Maybe I thought I could take responsibility for my actions."

"Ha!" I said, throwing my half-drunk cola to one side then pointing at him. "My theory is proven true: you're not actually my future self! You're a projection of the Primal Orbs trying to do some mind-whammy on me! I *never* take responsibility for my actions!"

"Mind-whammy, really?" Old Gary asked, raising an eyebrow. "Where the hell did you get such a ridiculous notion?"

"I dunno, television maybe? There's a lot of stories about magical artifacts trying to influence their users with visions," I said, not quite buying my theory anymore.

Old Gary put his arms on my shoulders. "Gary, I'm going

take your advice, as ill-formed and badly conceived as it is. You need to do things differently in the past. You need to change what occurred before and do things differently. You need to let Entropicus win."

"What?" I asked, staring at him then brushing off his hands. "That's moronic!"

"There's a reason!" Old Gary said, conjuring a pair of fireballs around his hands. Apparently, my future self was immune to flame.

"No!" I said, falling back on the carpet behind me.

Everything went white again.

I blinked several times as I found myself surrounded by a bunch of zombie Nazis who'd been shot up, stabbed, and torn apart. I did a double take at my surroundings before noticing Mandy, Gabrielle, and Cassius were beside me. So was Jane Doe who was covered in Nazi blood and carrying a glowing staff.

"Okay, what the hell did I miss?" I asked, my head pounding.

"Shooting, stabbing, and strangling Nazis!" Jane said in her best rural Midwesterner voice.

"Dammit, that's my favorite thing!" I said, pausing. "After sex and snark. Well, depends on the day really."

"Jane and Agent G won their second rounds," Mandy said, pausing. "Unfortunately, their last battle was with Nazi Necromancer and General Furher so the battle spilled over here. I think it was an attempt to eliminate you."

I took a deep breath and looked around. "Yeah, maybe, or maybe he was trying to clean up loose ends. Is everyone alright? I don't see G here."

"I got stabbed and he freaked out so he went to the bar," Jane said. "Thankfully, I heal."

"Which way to the bar?" I asked, looking around.

"That way," Jane said, pointing down the hall.

"Thanks," I said, looking over at Mandy. "If you don't mind, I'm going to go get rip roaring drunk. Can you coordinate the salvation of the world in the meantime?"

"Sure," Mandy said, picking up a broken fang up off the ground. "It's not like I'm going to be winning the tournament directly."

"Gary—" Gabrielle said.

"We played into Entropicus' hands," I said, shaking my head. "I need a drink to think of a way I can get stupid enough to be unpredictable."

CHAPTER ELEVEN

DROWNING MY SORROWS
(AND OTHER PEOPLE'S)

It didn't take much effort to track down the bar on Hell Island. It was the kind of dark, smoky, alien and fictional character-filled room that you expected to find in sci-fi movies. Really, I regretted not packing a blaster because incinerating people with my mind just wouldn't have the same effect.

It didn't take long to find G because he was sitting next to a four-armed looking reptile man wearing a red pair of speedos. I recognized the guy and wondered how he felt about Entropicus ripping off his universe so badly. The bar was tended by an enormous spider that I assumed wasn't Shelob because she wasn't killing and eating people. Still, it meant only two people were sitting at the bar and there was ample space to get your drinks.

I sat down beside G and tapped the counter. "Blue Milk and keep it coming."

"Blue Milk?" G asked, nursing his own drink.

"I figured this bar contains everything in all of fiction so I wanted to drink something from the Star Wars galaxy," I said, smiling.

G looked at me with a raised eyebrow. "I suppose that would be a minor fantasy you could fulfill. Have you considered looking for Rey or Young Leia?"

I glared at him. "First of all, I'm married, and second of all they both have people who can love them back on their home universes. Leia is set up to be with Han and Rey will end up with the star of my fanfics Jet McAwesome."

G grinned. "So you don't think there's any value to pursuing a relationship while we're here?"

The bartender served a big glass of blue liquid with a distinct smell of alcohol added. Huh, who knew Luke and the Lars family were such lushes? Still, he added a milkshake sized straw and I tried it. Not bad. It made me wonder what they grew on Tatooine to make grain alcohol milkshakes. "Relationships are different from hooking up, G-man. Which are you talking about?"

G paused and stared forward. He had the expression of a man who was fighting off a broken heart—that was weird since we were only here a day. Then again, he was drinking a kind of weird glowing scotch and that couldn't be good for your mood. "Jane."

"The teenage weredeer?" I asked, surprised.

"She's twenty-three," G said, frowning. "The first few books happened a long time ago in her past. It's like meeting Hermione as an adult and being like 'hey, you look like Emma Watson' but people getting upset because they think of Hermione as a child."

I stared at him.

"What?" G asked.

"Sorry, it's just I feel like we should be best friends," I said.

G chuckled and shook his head. "That's part of the reason why I'm irritated. Jane is smart, funny, and doesn't mind the fact I'm a robot assassin."

"Those are qualities you need to cross universes to find. Either that or go to the local comic con," I said, slurping my drink.

Wow, was I hallucinating banthas or was that a vision from the Force? Nope, it was just the kick of the Blue Milk.

G leaned in. "It's not the fact we're in love or anything. We barely know each other but it's the fact I won't be able to that bothered me. My world doesn't have dimensional travel. Hell, my world doesn't have magic. Quite a few people don't believe in anything like gods or a purpose to the universe."

"Eh, same in my world," I said, shrugging. "Familiarity breeds contempt. It's hard to believe in an all-powerful god when you have actually all-powerful people trying to help where the real deity seems so hands off."

G gave a bitter chuckle. "Believe me, I'd still take your world over mine any day."

"What is your planet's deal, anyway? I get Jane comes from the *Cabin in the Woods* meets *Underworld*."

"Careful on the pop culture references," G said, pausing. "Too many and you dilute their effect."

"I'll try and avoid saying anything that requires a doctorate in nerd," I said, raising my glass to him. "But yes, what's your thing?"

"Cyberpunk," G said, chuckling. "Cyborgs, conspiracies, megacorporations, and so on. It started as being all behind the scenes but eventually morphed into a full-on Gibsonian dystopia. Life is cheap and freedom is expensive."

Cindy had actually clued me into a lot of details about his and Jane's life. Apparently, both of their lives completely went to crap in the third books of their series.

"Ouch," I said, pausing. "Mind you, I've always felt like my world was a cyberpunk dystopia. It's just instead of being edgy rebels against the Man, it was just the Man versus a bunch of dissatisfied office drones. More *Office Space* than *Blade Runner*."

"Well, speaking as the artificial human enslaved by the system, Blade Runner isn't all it's cracked up to be," G said. "It's a world with no love, friendship, or trust."

"Really? You've got no one to call Mrs. G? You have to cross universes for a candidate? I would have thought a good looking assassin like you would be fighting off the ladies with a stick. You look more like the James Bond sort of secret agent than middle-aged pudgy CIA bureaucrat."

"Sex isn't the issue," G said, finishing off his drink. "Anyone can get laid if they're sufficiently determined. It's only when you self-identify as an obnoxious unlikable misogynist little troll like some of the jackasses on the internet you have trouble with it. Intimacy is the problem. When everyone is a liar and trying to manipulate you then you can't even have friends let alone lovers. I envy you, Gary, you and your wife clearly have an open and loving relationship."

"It sounds like you need a better class of people to hang out with," I said, thinking about his claim Mandy and I had a good relationship.

"Perhaps," G said. "Still, it's going to be disappointing when this tournament ends and we're all going to go our separate ways. It's like catching a flash of something greater and more wondrous in the universe, only to have it stripped away from it."

"We could also all be horribly killed," I said, being honest with him. "You could also get the wish and save the multiverse. Wish yourself a 7th level *Plane Shift* spell."

"I'm strictly *Cyberpunk 2020* not *Dungeons and Dragons*," G said.

I laughed. "Totally besties. But my advice to you, G, is not to sweat the details. If you like Jane and want to be with her then you should cherish the time you have with her. Maybe it'll be only a couple of days or maybe something miraculous will happen like you immigrating to comic book verse."

"Is that an option?" G asked.

"Would your universe even exist if you weren't there to star in it?" I asked.

"That's a sociopathic way of looking at things," G said.

"Supervillain!" I pointed out.

G nodded. "I suppose you're right. I'll go talk to Jane and ask if she's up for a summer romance except replace summer with video game crossover tournament."

"Just don't sing the 'Summer Loving' song from *Grease*," I said.

"Why would I do that?" G asked, a confused expression on his face.

"I dunno, not every one of my references can be a winner," I said, finishing my Blue Milk. "Also, I don't know what's in this but I think I can levitate."

"You could already levitate," G said, looking at me strangely.

"It's working retroactively!?" I asked, stunned. "I've got to have another!"

I turned around and picked up a second glass the giant spider had laid down for me.

That was when I'd noticed the six-armed man beside me had left and been replaced by Guinevere. She was still wearing her armor and drinking from a large stein overflowing with a frothy brown liquid—like she was straight out of a Medieval B-movie.

"Hey Xena," I said, lifting my Blue Milk to take a sip. "How's it hanging?"

"I see you're still in the tournament," Guinevere muttered, sounding more than a little drunk. "Disappointing. You must be happy, though."

"Yeah," I said, frowning. "I'm just totally overwhelmed with joy at the fact my best friend died trying to save the world and I had to beat the crap out of my ex-fiancé."

Guinevere looked over at me. "Diabloman is dead?"

"Yes," I said, taking another drink from my glass. Wow, that stuff hit hard. I was never going to call Luke Skywalker a wimp again. Yes, I'm a Darth Vader fan. We all knew it.

"Couldn't have happened to a nicer person," Guinevere said.

I put down my drink. "Do you want to throw down? Because we can throw down now, I can eliminate you, and the entire multiverse might end up fried because we're ostensibly supposed to be on the same team. I can also insult you in funny ways like pointing out Guinevere is supposed to be pronounced Jennifer. Your superhero name is literally the same as Jenny from the Block's."

"Who?" Guinevere asked.

"Oh, the horror of aging," I said, already half-drunk. "Every reference I make shall become dated within a year."

Guinevere sighed and put down her stein. "You have no idea how irritating it is to know you're one of the Chosen Champions of the Universe."

"Chosen Champion of Death," I corrected her, sighing. "It's just Death wants the multiverse to survive."

"Yes," Guinevere said. "If we succeed, you'll be the biggest hero who ever lived."

"Well, I wouldn't say biggest..." I said, pausing. "Wait, shouldn't you be happy about this?"

"Happy?" Guinevere said, looking at me like I was crazy. "Why in the world should I be happy?"

Guinevere proceeded to chug her stein.

I looked at her like she was crazy. "I dunno, maybe because it's a *good* thing when people decide to do good things with their life? I've spent my entire life being a selfish bastard of varying degrees. You'd think the biggest remaining superhero of all time would appreciate the effort!"

Guinevere stared down at her drink. "That's not how it works, Gary."

There was an immense amount of bitterness in her voice. So much so that it surprised me.

"What's wrong?" I asked, surprised at how much empathy I was feeling for a woman who literally beat the crap out of me. Also, I'm not using the word literally improperly. I'm very glad I had magic to clean myself up after heavy beatings like that. Most supervillains don't.

Guinevere felt the bridge of her nose with two fingers as if she was trying to stave off a migraine. "Do you really want to know why I loathe you?"

"I have a pretty good idea the answer is 'you're a supervillain' but I admit I don't quite get why you're particularly hostile with me. The Guinevere I grew up reading the comics of was all peace, love, justice, and feminism."

Guinevere looked appalled. "You read my comics growing up?"

"Oh hell yes," I said, putting my hand over my heart. "You have no idea how much I got laid in college due to the lessons I learned. Just make sexy times fun for everyone involved and you get a positive reception—like planning video game night. Don't hit on everyone constantly but keep it confined to appropriate sexy time request zones like parties or bars. Don't make ratings systems—"

Guinevere actually banged her head against the bar counter three times.

"Sorry," I said. "I learned other stuff too!"

"Gary, I fought in World War 2," Guinevere said. "I saw horrors you would not believe."

I dropped my joking demeanor. "I actually would believe them, yes. There was a reason my mother made sure I understood we should just ignore grandma Karkofsky waking up screaming when she lived with us. My family didn't come from Poland by choice."

Guinevere closed her eyes, adopting a soberer look. "There is no such thing as a Diet Coke of evil. There are good and there are bad people in this world. People often talk about the moral ambiguities of life but the fact is the line isn't really that hard. Don't rape, murder, torture, or steal. Good people don't do bad things and bad people don't do good. Do you understand?"

"I understand that's an incredibly reductive and simplistic way of looking at things," I said, offended. "I mean, I've murdered Hitler more than any other man in the Multiverse, including Hitler, and I know there were plenty of decent Germans fighting for their country. It just so happened their actions enabled the monster that killed my grandfather. Partially why I don't sweat slaughtering all the people I need to in order to get at Hitler. By the way, Eva Braun is dangerous. Cindy still has three stab wound scars from her."

Guinevere looked at me. "Gary, you want to know why I dislike you? I dislike you because you deliberately blur the lines. You went out into society and became a supervillain. Not because you needed the money, not because you were a political extremist, and not because you were a monster who liked killing people. No, you did it because you thought it would be cool. Worse, you made it work."

"It was a bit more complicated than that," I said, thinking about my brother. "By the way, you're not allowed to put your magic net around me to check."

"I tried to tell you earlier but people now are starting to become supervillains in imitation of you. They think they can break the law, kill other supervillains, and behave like none of it is going to touch them. You've made being a hero look stupid and that's what really chaps my ass."

"Versus the leather skirt?" I asked.

Guinevere glared again.

"I'm just saying I couldn't pull that off," I replied.

The spider poured us another beer and Blue Milk. I really shouldn't have taken mine but I was already not thinking clearly. So, instead, I just chugged it down before responding.

"So, just so we're clear, the reason you've been treating me like garbage and driving away Ultragoddess. The reason you've gone to elaborate lengths to go after me—even though I saved the world from turning into a superhero run tyranny because Merciful played you like a fiddle is the fact I make you look uncool?" I asked, stunned at the pettiness of it. "I'm sorry, I was really hoping for something better."

Guinevere downed her beer. "It's a lot more complicated than that."

"Is it?" I asked, wondering if we were both underestimating each other.

"I've known many heroes who gave their lives to do the right thing. Not just superheroes but the everyday heroes. Soldiers on the battlefield, firemen, police officers, and EMTs. Regular civilians crushed under rubble during brawls while they were trying to help other people to safety. These people deserve to be respected and you dishonor their sacrifices by saying it's better to be the villain rather than the hero."

"You know I totally agree with you on that. You know who also recently died trying to do the right thing and got no respect for it? A guy who was raised by an evil cult, warped from birth into being a killer, and who did a lot of terrible things before he turned his life around. A guy who didn't fit into your little Manichean world of good vs. evil."

"Gary—"

"He knew no one would ever forgive him because of what he did but he tried to make amends anyway."

"Then he should have let himself be punished in prison or be executed for his crimes," Guinevere snapped.

"Yes, because that would have helped anyone," I said, sighing. "But fine, I understand. I'll never be accepted into your elite club of do-gooders because once a crook, always a crook. That doesn't mean I'm going to keep being a supervillain, though. I've seen how bad things can get under heroes and I've always been a crappy bad guy. I'm going to do what I feel is right, regardless of how any of you feel about it. I'd call myself a Nietzschean Overman for that but given I personally know God that would be rather weird."

Guinevere sighed. "You know, I'm starting to see why Lancel and Moses liked you."

"I'm infectious that way."

"So, did Ultragoddess tell you she's pregnant yet?" Guinevere asked.

I spewed Blue Milk all over her.

CHAPTER TWELVE

ANOTHER SHOCK I DID NOT NEED

Guinevere picked up a napkin off the table and wiped the Blue Milk off her face. "You did that deliberately."

"I admit, I did," I said, staring at her. "What do you mean, pregnant?"

"What do people normally mean with that?" Guinevere said. "It's not like it's a metaphor for something else."

"Pregnant with happiness?" I suggested, trying to figure out any possible other meaning than that.

"No, with a child," Guinevere asked, her voice accusatory. "Is it yours?"

"Excuse me?" I asked, confused and blinking rapidly.

"She has a boyfriend," Guinevere said, looking at me. "Several in fact. I also know you've been sexually active with her."

I thought about when I'd ended up at the Observatory, Ultragod's Fortress of Awesomeness, and found her just binge watching her show on the CW while eating Ben and Jerry's. The torment she'd suffered at the hands of Merciful had left her in a dark place and I'd come to visit her.

I remembered her wearing an Atlas City Titans' sports jersey as she sat in front of the world's largest flat screen television. Universo the Ultradog was snuggled up next to her, looking like a cross between a French Bulldog and a shark. He reminded me of my bull terriers Arwen and Galadriel, both of which passed away under the care of Merciful while I'd been locked up with Mandy.

"Hey Gary," Gabrielle said, not bothering to look at me. "You know I would have moved the giant key to let you in if you'd asked."

I shrugged walking up to her. "Eh, everyone knows the Ultra-Family is weak to magic. I just turned insubstantial and walked through the walls. Strangely, the Ultra-Robots didn't try to evict me once I came in."

"You're on the approved guest list," Gabrielle said, gesturing to a hovering Ultranian servant bot. "My father never bothered removing you when he thought we were going to get married."

I frowned, thinking of Moses Anders and how he'd always tried to support me even when I was being hauled off to jail for my actions. "He must have been very disappointed in who I became."

"I doubt that," Gabrielle said, conjuring a giant glowing pair of tweezers that she used to lift me up and put me down on the couch beside her. "My father believed the best in everyone and you did save his life."

"Yeah, before my double took it," I said, looking at her. "I'd thought you'd never want to see me again after that."

Gabrielle looked down. "There was a time when I blamed you, Gary. When I never wanted to see you again and I regretted ever meeting you."

"I'm sorry," I said.

"That lasted about six seconds," Gabrielle said, looking over at me. "You did everything in your power to resurrect my father from the dead, just like you did your wife, and you also were the only person who didn't give up on me."

I stared at her. "Maybe you're being a little harsh on the Society."

"Am I?" Gabrielle asked. "I'm surprised you don't want to tear down the entire organization after what happened. They kept you and Mandy prisoner as well as let that thing walk around with your identity."

I shrugged. "The fly doesn't expect sympathy from he who owns the swatter."

Gabrielle looked at me with her golden eyes, her glowing irises contrasting with their usual brown. "Yeah, well, when you're a superhero, you expect the others to have your back. You don't expect them to throw you under the bus when it's convenient."

I didn't have an answer to that. I had been deeply disappointed with the S.O.S myself. "Everyone has their breaking point. Honestly, I can't imagine fighting daily against evil for decades like some of the heroes have been doing. Merciful offered them a way out and they took it. He Palpatined them all."

Gabrielle gave a half smile before it turned bitter. "Maybe it's also the fact I was only useful to them as long as I was Ultragod's daughter. When he was gone, I was just another liability."

"Then they're fools," I said, frowning. "You've saved the world on your own like five or six times."

"You've done that too, Gary, and they treat you like shit," Gabrielle said, offering me her pint of ice cream.

"No thanks, I'm allergic to white chocolate," I said, raising my hand. "Besides, I can conjure my own now. After a year of intense magical study, I can do parlor tricks like add milk and sugar to my ice powers."

Gabrielle laughed. "So, is your wife, Mandy, comfortable with you coming here?"

I paused. "Yeah, I don't think she actually cares too much where I go."

Actually, Mandy suggested I come over here and screw Gabrielle's brains out with all the casualness of giving her a gift of flowers. It wasn't the sex that bothered her, as I'd later find out, but the intimacy. Mandy didn't mind if her lovers had dozens of their own but they couldn't care for them—it was bizarre. Still, I chalked it up to having had to deal with an immense amount of stress from trying to be a superhero, spy, and spouse all in one. It was enough to break anyone. But it was tiring coming home to find exhausted half-drained worshipers in my home and the remains of a Goth metal party I hadn't been invited to.

"Trouble in paradise?" Gabrielle asked.

"For better and worse," I said, not really wanting to talk about it. "She knows you're one of the most important people in my life."

I'd never been comfortable with the way my marriage had

changed after Mandy's transformation to a vampire, as much as I denied it. She'd become harder and colder, all of the mercy driven out of her soul by both her undead status and fighting President Omega. I still loved her but there was so much darkness in her soul that I often found myself struggling to love her the way I wanted to. I would do anything for her, kill or die, but I also felt like anything less than those extremes was hard now.

"I see," Gabrielle said, clearly not understanding. "Well, I'm glad you're here. How's Cindy?"

"Cindy is Cindy," I said. "She's not so much living with us as perpetually sponging. Still, she invites herself along on every heist and is never useless."

Truth be told, I was under the impression Cindy was having a midlife crisis of some sort. After having lost her license to practice due to the Merciful-controlled medical board, she'd been somewhat aimless and without purpose. Medicine had always been her dream with supervillainy just a way to achieve it. Mandy's return had also put a crimp in her plans of being a superheroine herself and I suspected Cindy's refusal by the superhero establishment was fueling her desire to keep me out of it. I wished I could help her but mostly, she just wanted to drink vampire blood and bash heads in. I wasn't sure there was a psychologist who dealt with post-superhero depression.

"The perfect henchwench," Gabrielle said.

"Hench*woman*," I said, correcting her. "Henchlady if we're being polite."

"How is your family?" Gabrielle asked "Kerri, Lisa, and your daughter?"

"Decent," I said, not lying. "Lisa just joined the New Guardians. I'm appalled she's decided to go the superhero route but it's easier to get royalties from your work than otherwise. Kerri and Mr. Inventor are settled into their new life together. I don't think they're dating, necessarily, but they live together. I'm still hoping Mr. Inventor will take up the mantle of the Nightwalker. As for Leia? Well, she's a genius and telepath so I'm pretty sure she's destined to take over the world or be the leader of a counterculture band of misfit heroes."

Gabrielle looked at me. "I'd do just about anything to be a part of a family like that."

Apparently, Gabrielle had been ignoring everything else I'd said.

"Are you feeling alright?" I looked at her. "Besides, aren't you still part of the Ultra Family? I mean, yeah, Moses and Polly are gone but—"

"Bark!" Ultradog said.

I scratched behind his ears and conjured some ice cream for him to eat. Ultradogs weren't lactose intolerant so he lapped it up eagerly.

"Ultragodling got in a fight with me over the fact he wants to use my father's name," Gabrielle said. "I'm not comfortable with that even if dad treated his bio-construct like a son. I've considered visiting the Bottled Universe to talk to the Ultranians there but I'm not sure I'd want to come back if I did. I stopped by the 40th century a few times to hang with the Army of Space Heroes but apparently even they have limits for dealing with sulking heroines."

"How about the Shadow Seven?" I asked, referring to her squad of ex-villains and antiheroes.

"More like Shadow Seventeen now," Gabrielle said, shrugging. "A lot of younger heroes don't want anything to do with the Society now but I'm not in the right headspace to lead them. The Human Tank is doing a great job leading them."

"Not the Black Witch?" I asked, having always had a love-hate-hate relationship with Selena Darkchylde.

"She's going through a divorce because she cheated on her wife with a vampire."

I looked over my shoulder. "Yeah, I can't imagine who that was."

"What about you? You own Pizza Hutt now?"

"Sort of their off-brand competition," I said, shrugging. "I could retire now but then what would I do with myself?"

"Be rich and happy?" Gabrielle suggested.

"Pfft," I said, making a dismissive wave. "I'd go crazy if I wasn't raising hell and taking names."

"Still planning on taking over the world?" Gabrielle asked, half joking.

"Honestly, Mandy seems more into it than I do," I said, looking at the screen. "Man, I can't believe they got Rosario Dawson to play you on this version."

"Zoe Saldana was a good choice but I had creative control. I'm just glad they didn't try to cast a teenager."

"You know, they cast Wentworth Miller as me in the *Merciless* movie."

"Who did you have to pay off to get that done?" Gabrielle asked, sounding genuinely interested.

"A lot of people," I said, simply. "Thankfully, it turns out this is still America and people don't look at the bloodstains on your money. I mean, non-lethally obtained money that I obtained legally."

Gabrielle rolled her eyes and reached over to take my hand. "Thank you for coming here."

"Always."

Gabrielle leaned over to kiss me. I didn't resist. Yeah, things had gotten intimate after that. I'd also realized in that moment I was still in love with Gabrielle, every bit as much as I was with my wife. It was part of the reason why we hadn't spoken to one another after the event since I didn't want to betray my wife's trust and it clear being in love with someone else made her furious.

Cindy's reaction to the discovery Gabrielle and I slept together? Not a care in the world other than asking if that meant we'd have to buy a steel reinforced bed. At some point my life had become a soap opera and harem anime without any of the romance or easy conclusions. I didn't want to be the bad guy in all of this but I sure as hell didn't wasn't the good guy no matter what I chose to do. It reminded me of the time Ultragod had lost his memory for a year and regained it only to find out he was married to a mermaid named Penelope Poseidon. God our world was weird.

I took a second to slowly return to the present and shook away my memories. My life was a never ending source of complications.

"Yeah, you could say we were," I said, looking up at Guinevere in the present.

"Your wife and your mistress not enough?" Guinevere asked.

I stared at her. "I don't see how that's any of your business."

"Gabrielle is like a daughter to me," Guinevere said, her voice low and threatening. "I would do anything to protect her."

"Does she know that?" I asked, honestly wondering what had happened to their relationship. "Because every time I see you two together, you're at each other's throats. Usually about me."

"So, once?" Guinevere said, finishing cleaning herself off.

"Once is enough," I said. "Which isn't a pregnancy joke."

Except, apparently it had been.

"Funny," Guinevere said. "Except, I don't find the subject funny in the slightest."

"Do you have any family? I mean, aside from the girl you and the Society of Superheroes raised before abandoning her?"

"How dare you," Guinevere growled with all the fury of an ancient Celtic warrior goddess.

"I'm serious. Humor me and I'll tell you a secret."

I think whatever Guinevere was drinking must have affected her because she paused before outright refusing. "Yes, I had a family."

"Had?"

Guinevere closed her eyes. "I was raised by the Tuatha De Daanan in another universe after my father, King Arthur, killed my brother Mordred. I've fought against the latter after his resurrection a hundred times since as well as our mother Morgana Le Fae. Time functions differently in the Otherworld."

"So I've heard," I said, wondering why Morgana Le Fey named her daughter after Arthur's wife. It sounded like the Pendragons had even more problems than I did, especially if you bought into the story Gawain was the adulterer rather than the potentially fictitious Lancelot. "You've got the whole Lannister thing going, except you're Tommen."

Guinevere snorted. "The gods of the Tuatha De Daanan should have been my family but they're a mean, arrogant, and corrupt bunch. So, I came back to the Earth in the hour of the British Isles' greatest need to fight against the Nazis alongside my father. Arthur during the battle and I fell in love with a Welsh infantrymen."

"What happened to him?"

"He died," Guinevere said, opening her eyes. "Of old age, while I stayed young and beautiful forever. It's not as romantic as you might think it is."

"I never thought it would be," I said, thinking about Mandy and me. The Reaper's Cloak provided longevity but it didn't provide immortality even if Old Gary proved I might be able to live centuries.

Assuming it wasn't just a trick by the Primal Orbs or Entropicus.

"Did you have any kids?" I asked.

"Yes," Guinevere said. "Igraine, Percival, and others. They became heroes in their own right, grew old or died as the whims of fate dictated. That was the curse Moses, Stephen, and I all bore. We got to watch our families go on but forever struggle with the pain of our being immortal."

"Until they died," I said, frowning.

Guinevere stole a nearby bar maid's stein of beer before chugging it down. "Yes, Gary, no sooner did I find a group that I could live among forever than I realized it still came with a horrific cost. I forgot you only had to lose a single battle to die forever and while a few of us have come back from the edge of death, only some of us have returned completely. That seems to be the province of villains."

"Don't I know it," I said, frowning. "So, that's why you're so upset with me. Because Merciful killed Ultragod and you see him in me."

"I told you why you upset me."

"People don't hate as personally as you do me because of ideology," I said, looking at her. "Believe me, I grew up the poor Jewish kid with a supervillain brother in a neighborhood full of skinheads. No, there's something else going on here."

"It's not that," Guinevere said, staring down. "But you're right, there's one more reason I can't stand you."

"Which is?"

"Do you know why I didn't look for Gabrielle?" Guinevere asked.

"I think that's the twenty-million-dollar question," I said, looking at her. "I mean, other than the question of how long it's going to take for NetherRealm Studios to sue us."

"Who?"

"The makers of *Mortal Kom*....err, never mind. Never explain the joke. Honestly, we need to rip off some other fighting games to be less obvious. If only someone made a fighting game about superheroes and alternate realities merging together. We could rip off that instead."

Guinevere felt the bridge of her nose and looked like she'd skipped straight to the hangover portion of her drinking binge. "You, Gary."

"Me, what? Is this about my attempt to kill the Four White Dudes?"

"Wait, what?"

"The boy band!" I snapped, slamming my hands on the table. "They had to be stopped."

"We didn't look for Gabrielle because of you," Guinevere said.

I stopped dead. "What?"

"Merciful claimed Guinevere had gone into another dimension because she was pregnant with your child and was going to raise them in safety. Having children and grandchildren to my enemies, I was willing to believe she was making the responsible choice."

"And you believed him?" I asked, hissing.

Guinevere stared at me. "The only thing all of us believed about you, whether you were good or evil, was that you would never hurt someone you loved. That trust is the reason why Gabrielle was imprisoned."

Wow, there wasn't much to say to that was there?

I stared into my empty glass of Blue Milk. "How far along is Gabrielle?"

"Two months," Guinevere said.

"I see," I said, thinking. "You don't think I...hurt her when

I fought her, did I? I mean, she shouldn't really be in this tournament in her condition."

"She has the Girdle of Nimue," Guinevere said, staring at her. "It will prevent any damage to her child barring death."

I nodded, reassured. "If you'll excuse me, I have to go talk to her."

Guinevere didn't respond as I left.

CHAPTER THIRTEEN

WHERE I DON'T FIND GABRIELLE

Well, about an hour later, I hadn't had any luck finding Gabrielle on Hell Island. Admittedly, half an hour had been spent throwing up on the toilet (thank God this island fortress had indoor plumbing) but I'd done a pretty thorough sweep of the place. I did find out G and Jane went on a date before sleeping together (also they did not like to get interrupted), that Mandy had a big pow-wow with all the other vampires on the island, and had an argument with a Chinese girl who kicked the crap out of me.

In the end, I went to my room for the purposes of getting a good night's rest before I tackled the next round of this tournament. The room service being as ridiculous as it was, I fully intended to order a few copies of vintage comics as well as a season of *Mystery Science Theater 3000* that hadn't come out yet. I was trying to figure out how to get the door open when I noticed Cindy was coming up behind me with a panda following her. She was carrying a bottle of tequila in one hand and carrying a bag of Mercitos in the other. The only corn chip guaranteed to be 70% as tasty as Doritos at the same price. Sort of like Pepsi and Coke.

"Hey, Gary," Cindy said. "You're missing the barbecue on the beach. This big flaming headed guy is smoking a bunch of dinosaurs for the feast. Apparently, this island has dinosaurs... and they're delicious!"

The panda made some noises that sounded strangely like Chinese.

"Quiet, Ling-Ling," Cindy said. "I know pandas are herbivores. You could try some new things."

"The panda talks?" I asked.

"Oh quiet, like that's the weirdest thing we've encountered," Cindy said, nonchalant. "I think he's either from a Disney movie or was trained by a corporate executive to fight his son he dropped into a canyon."

The panda made another noise.

"Oh, sorry, she," Cindy said. "I didn't bother to check. My bad. I guess I need to choose her another name."

I continued to look for a keycard or keyhole in the door while playing with the door knob. "Okay, I'm completely stumped. How am I supposed to get into this?"

"You still haven't had the orientation?" Cindy asked. "It's on YouTube and there's an app for your phone."

"No, I was getting drunk!" I said, staring at the wall. "You know, with our dead friend and all."

"Oh, that's understandable," Cindy said, handing me the tequila bottle. "But I wouldn't get too worked up about it."

"Worked up!?" I asked, appalled.

"Yeah, we're going to resurrect him, aren't we?" Cindy said, shrugging her shoulders. "I mean, we went to elaborate lengths to get Mandy's soul back and we tried to resurrect Ultragod too. You ended up resurrecting an entire world. That's in addition to all the zombies and haunted teddy bears that brought back our old villains."

I stared at her. "The horrifying thing is everything you just said actually happened."

"Even the teddy bear part!" Cindy said.

"Rowr," the panda said.

"Resurrection is not something I can do on command," I said, raising my hands.

Cindy got right in my face. "You will resurrect me from the dead when I die. I will accept being a vampiress but want full on human if it's possible. Immortality is the least thing I should be getting out of working for the frigging Grim Reaper's bitch."

"Wait am I the Grim Reaper or the bitch in this?"

"Obviously the latter," Cindy said. "But you're totally

bringing back Diabloman. You don't have to use your wish to bring him back because I've read *The Monkey's Paw*. You should wish for godlike powers, or no, to BE a god and one of resurrection. We're Jewish, we've got a heritage of that."

"I think that misunderstands what we believe," I said.

"Just do it!"

I sighed. "Yeah, I'll get Diabloman back. I'm not going to leave him in Hell."

"And Cloak too."

"He's ascended to a higher plane of existence. That may be difficult."

"Cloning! Alternate Universe double! Kidnap his past self and create a time paradox!"

"Or reboot the universe," I said, thinking about the possibilities.

"What was that?" Cindy asked.

Yeah, that was a good idea. Well, actually, it was a terrible idea, although it was a *good* terrible idea. "There's also something else I feel like you should know."

"Which is?" Cindy said, pulling out her cellphone and starting to type into it. "Wow, the reception here is really good. Either Entropicus has really outfitted this place well or I made the right decision upgrading to a better data plan."

"Gabrielle is pregnant."

Cindy stopped in mid text then started hitting me with the cellphone in the shoulder. "Goddammit, Gary, you frigging man-slut! I knew you couldn't keep it in your pants!"

"Ow!" I said, defending myself with my arms as shields.

"This is why I don't take you on my sex tourism time travel trips!" Cindy shouted. "I can just imagine you banging Louisa May Alcott!"

I stopped trying to defend myself and let her bang it against my chest. "Louisa May Alcott? Really? *That's* who you're afraid I'll have sex with?"

"Yeah, she has a thing for incredibly handsome yet strangely nerdy guys. I swear it's all I can do not to duct tape your mouth shut so you can stand there and look pretty. So many guys would be perfect if they were like that."

I frowned at her, feeling I was getting objectified. "How do you even know I'm responsible for her pregnancy?"

Cindy hit me with the cellphone again. "Now you're calling my bestie a slut! Besides, you have a history of this thing!"

"A history of what exactly?" I'd asked. I'd only slept around on Mandy when she was dead and in a really dark place plus when Gabrielle had been traumatized but that had been with her permission! Okay, wait, that didn't sound like a very good defense.

"A history of infecting women with parasites! You gave me one."

"You mean *our daughter*?" I asked.

A man in a top hat and Victorian attire with aquiline features walked by us and stared at us.

"Keep walking, Sherlock! This ain't none of your goddamn business!" I said, growling at him.

He threw up his hands and walked by. Which was a smart move in my opinion since I was in no mood to deal with bystanders.

Cindy took a drink of her tequila. "I mean, yeah, it worked out and it became whatshername—"

"Leia?" I asked, really hoping this was a joke.

"Yeah, her," Cindy said. "But still, you should take responsibility for it."

I rubbed my temples. "The times don't match up. They're off by a couple of months."

"Oh," Cindy said, deflating. "That does change things a bit."

"But time has been screwy," I said, thinking about the recent compression.

The panda responded in a rather lengthy set of Chinese.

"What did she say?"

"I dunno," Cindy said, shrugging. "I don't speak Chinese."

"I'm a *Japanese* panda," the panda said in English. "I was suggesting the reason time has been so screwy is because of a bunch of time-travelers have been weakening the fabric of the universe. Apparently, some jackasses have been using it to kill Hitler as well as take vacations."

Cindy and I looked to the side.

"Yeah, I don't buy it," I said. "There's lots of indiscriminate time travelers in this town."

"Yeah, let's blame this all on President Omega," Cindy said, looking over at me.

"I'm cool with that."

Cindy looked back. "So, you could be the father but you don't know because you're a cheating bastard."

"Mandy said to sleep with her!"

"You're *blaming your wife* now?" Cindy fumed.

"It's not a blame situation!" I snapped, dusting myself off.

"Either way, I'm worried about her."

"Well, of course you are," Cindy said, giving me one last bash on the pants. "You're full of attachment and can't let go of your ex-girlfriend—"

"Fiancé," I corrected.

"From a decade ago," Cindy paused. "Wait, is it a decade ago? How old are we now?"

"I have no idea," I said, looking at the panda. "Due to the damage done to the time stream by President Omega of which we are in no way contributors to."

The panda, I kid you not, rolled its eyes.

"Yeah, I care for Gabrielle a great deal," I said, staring at her. "Just like I care for my childhood friend who became the mother of my child."

"That's me, right?" Cindy asks.

"Yes, it's you!" I snapped. "In any case, it's equally awkward because she said she loved me in the caverns."

"Awww," Cindy said, smiling. "That's sweet."

"And that she didn't want to share me with anyone else."

"That witch!" Cindy said. "To think she can't into a proper modern relationship."

"I'm pretty sure there's nothing remotely modern about polyamory. If Abraham and Isaac practiced it, you're very much on the side of traditionalism."

"No, it's modern if the women are also playing around," Cindy said. "Like my affair with King Arthur."

"I would not tell Guinevere about that," I said.

Cindy snorted. "Dude was a lot more liberal minded than

you think. He and Gawain were closer than you'd think. Also, Lancelot was French propaganda trying to usurp Gawain's role. Evil, evil French and their Frenchness. Giving us the Statue of Liberty and being such good kissers. It's a plot I tell you."

The panda walked over to the door beside me, put its paw on the door then gently forced it open before walking into my bedroom and flopping down on the floor.

"Okay, how the hell did it do that?" I asked, looking at the creature and desperate to change the subject.

"Stay on topic!" Cindy said, growling. "How could Gabrielle even suggest such a thing!"

"I dunno, most people aren't into multiple partners?" I said. "Marrying multiple ones is illegal in forty-eight states I remind you."

"Eh, so is everything fun. Monogamy, like polygamy, was an invention of the patriarchy. I very much would be willing to be John F. Kennedy's second wife over Bozo the Clown's first."

"Please tell me I'm John F. Kennedy in this version."

"Well, we're not married, and you're rich so half and half?" Cindy said, looking like she was trying to figure it out in her head.

"Thank you so very much," I muttered.

"I hope you told her to take a hike back to the Ultraverse."

"Not in so many words," I said, grimacing.

"Ugh," Cindy said, feeling her head. "I'm going to have to have a talk with Gabrielle. She's my friend too and friends don't stab each other in the back like that. I mean, you pay for like 90% of my impulse buys as well as serve as free babysitting."

"You know, it's sometimes hard to tell whether or not you're just pretending to be a complete jerk to me or whether you just kind of are."

"As Isis the Incredible once told me, the important thing to find in a long-term partner is an emotional stress ball."

"First of all, no she didn't. Second, you made that up right now."

"True," Cindy said. "In any case, Gary, we need to have a sit down. I swear, it's like you have poor impulse control regarding sleeping with beautiful Amazon women. I mean, if you weren't getting your needs met, you could have just borrowed some of the Goth girls in Mandy's harem."

Cindy and Mandy had an odd relationship. They weren't romantically involved with each other, in part due to the fact Cindy was deeply uncomfortable with the blood-letting aspect of vampire sex. Also, well, the fact Mandy was very much dead and that was a major turn off for the doctor turned supervillain. Cindy, however, admired Mandy and wanted to stand by her no matter what since my wife had died protecting her. Recently, their relationship had been strained, though. Mandy had gotten a lot more extreme in her desire to stamp out crime and Cindy was a lot closer to the supervillain underground than I was. That included friends among several groups and teams which my wife had marked for death. Frankly, Gabrielle being as close as she was to Cindy was a lot more believable these days. Cindy had tagged along on a lot of my dates with Ultragoddess in college and awakened to certain aspects of herself because of Gabrielle. Yeah, they don't put these sorts of things on superhero trading cards.

I shook away those sordid thoughts. "Speaking of which, do you know where Mandy is?"

"Why? You want to try out my suggestion now?"

I stared at her. "No, I want to tell her about this."

"Oh," Cindy said. "Wow, you actually tell your wife about your illegitimate love sprogs? You are totally failing supervillainy."

"I told you!"

"I'm the mistress, I don't count. But in any case, Mandy already knows."

"Why's that?" I asked, panicking.

"She's behind you," Cindy said, pointing behind me.

I looked over my shoulder and saw Mandy was, indeed, standing behind me in a female version of the Nightwalker outfit with a bottled water container full of blood she was sipping from. "Hey, Gary."

"What's with the outfit?" I asked, trying again to deflect the subject.

"Alternate costume skin DLC," Mandy said, as if that made

sense. "Also, my previous outfit was trashed by our fight. It turns out you can commission any sort of replacement costume you want from the machinery here."

"Be careful," Cindy said. "I heard from one of the participants that a superhero did that during one of his tournaments and got possessed by a giant ink monster. He went on to babble about some guy named Toby Garfield and how he was much better than the current one."

"She's a weird one," I said, acknowledging things. "Mandy, there's something I need to tell you."

"I'm sorry for ruining your chances to win the wish and fix everything?" Mandy said, clearly more concerned about other topics than I was.

"I'll be in here," Cindy said, stepping through the open to my bedroom and shutting it behind me. The door immediately locked again.

"Dammit, I just got that open," I said, looking at her.

"Can't you just walk through the walls?" Mandy asked.

I paused, thinking about that. "Dammit. I'm an idiot."

"We knew that. In any case, my plan to steal the orbs was ill-conceived but I have a few other plans to get the ultimate power at the end of this," Mandy said, frowning. "I think I may have to substitute for one of the fighters or possess them, but I know some mages for that."

I blinked repeatedly. "Uh, yeah, that isn't what I was going to talk about."

"Oh yes, you mean the fact you may be the father of Gabrielle's baby."

"Maybe," I said, frowning at my mixed feelings on the subject. "It's more likely probably."

"We should hope so," Mandy said.

"Excuse me?"

"A child of the Ultragod line and the Nephilim lineage that Death cultivated in your ancestors could have the power of the Ultra-Force and Nega-Force. While it won't be possible to harness that power for two decades, it would potentially create a weapon that could destroy any possible opposition to a peaceful world."

I stared at her. "Mandy, are you feeling alright?"

Mandy felt her head. "Sorry, it's just this island is full of negative energy. Entropicus created the vampire race so being around him is making me feeling more vampire-like than usual. They're predatory creatures always playing angles."

"You're not going to turn evil on me, are you?" That was the last thing I needed right now.

Mandy laughed. "No, Gary, not as long as I have a soul full of light and love. This tournament is our chance to finally make a difference in the world."

"I think we've made quite a big difference in the world."

"A lasting one."

I gave her a hug. "I promise we'll make a huge difference."

"Whatever it takes." Mandy patted me on the back before she grabbed me and pulled me close, whispering, "Just remember, Gary, *you're mine.*"

Meep.

CHAPTER THIRTEEN

WHY WE FIGHT FOR MIGHT

The next morning, I woke up to the sound of ringing monastery bells. I slid out of bed, tripped over Cindy's panda, and eventually got myself dressed with Cindy following behind me. Mandy was already gone. Heading out, I found out the tournament's participants were all assembled on the beach. Along the edge of the shore were a vast number of fighters with the sun rising behind them. It was the perfect image for a movie poster if you could get the rights to all the legendary and fictional heroes present.

I walked alongside Cindy toward the gathering of the fighters, getting the impression from her silence my actions with Gabrielle had hurt our relationship far more than I'd let on. Then again, I'd never been able to entirely pierce the barrier between the Cindy she showed the world and the person she was underneath. Cindy had grown up with an abusive mother, an absent father, a life in Southtown Falconcrest City that was as close to being an urban hellscape as you could get without Kurt Russell coming in to clean up the place, and had done a lot of things to survive—things that I had no right to judge but bothered me because she was my friend.

Mandy, by contrast, had grown up with a demanding but loving father who had brought her up in various postage-stamp nations across the planet. Places that sounded fictional until you visited them like New Albion, Ruritania, Skullkovia, and Turkey. He'd wanted to train her as a spy and she'd been put through a regime many Olympians would have balked at.

The end result had been her choosing to rebel and committing crimes that forever blocked her from that path. I'd been a poor consolation prize and after becoming a vampire, she'd ended up being hardened by a war that had never happened—yet still haunted her nightmares.

"Whatcha thinking?" Cindy asked.

"Just about how I've not been a great...whatever the hell we are," I said.

"Pfft!" Cindy said.

"Excuse me?" I asked.

"The problem with you Gary is you think there's a way to balance being a great anything with being a bad guy," Cindy said, shaking her head. "Embrace your inner *Grand Theft Auto* protagonist and realize the purpose of life is to be as spectacularly bad as possible."

"Uh-huh," I said, deadpanning. "Why didn't I think of that?"

"Because I'm smarter than you," Cindy said, putting a hand over her chest. "Also, prettier."

"Fair enough," I said, admitting the point. "But the entire point of being a supervillain is I do what I want and sometimes I want to do good."

"Ugh," Cindy said, covering her face. "No, you fool! That's not how it works."

"Who is the henchwoman here?" I asked.

"I am a co-villainess now!" Cindy said. "We should form a team."

"We aren't already a team?" I asked.

"Not until we get an awesome supervillain lair."

The tension lessened between us for a bit as we started to mingle with the hundred or so people gathered on the beach. Mandy was easy to find and was not that far away from Jane, Guinevere, the Prismatic Commando, and G. There was no sign of Cassius or Gabrielle.

"Gary?" Cindy asked.

"Yeah?" I replied.

"What are our chances of making it out alive on this?" Cindy asked.

"No idea," I said, sighing. "The problem is that the participants are of such a wildly and incredibly diverse range of power levels. The Ultragods are fighting alongside the Robin Hoods with all of the Splotches in-between. Yeah, there's been some upsets, but I don't even know why us Muggles were invited."

"You've already eliminated Ultragoddess and killed two evil gods," Cindy pointed out.

"I know! That kind of fluke is not good!" I said, raising my hands. "Gabrielle should be the one who is the big hero in all this. She punches asteroids and space gods. I mostly fight clowns and—"

"The occasional kaiju, evil presidents, yourself—" Mandy asked. "Honestly, I think we've all pulled some upsets in our career."

"Thanks," I said, glad for her support. "Still, we're remarkably outclassed in all this. You know what that means?"

"We take a dive for the greater good?" Cindy asked.

"Hell no!" I snapped. "We find some people who have magical or technological doohickeys then take them! That way we can be better prepared to win the tournament and use the wish to rewrite the universe as I see fit."

"Don't you mean as we see fit?" Cindy asked.

I shrugged my shoulders. "No, I'm pretty sure I mean as I see fit. The problem is I got to visit the universe as I ruled it and it is kind of shit."

"Really?" Mandy asked, sounding way too interested for casual conversation. "You managed to conquer the world in an alternate future?"

I nodded, taking a deep breath. I was more disturbed by the vision than I wanted to let on. "It wasn't the fact I was a bad person that bothered me. I've crossed that line enough time. It was the idea eventually the heroes and the villains would eventually turn on each other with such savagery they'd need to both be put down. Which resulted in the public destroying itself as well. It was like some kind of nightmare scenario."

"Funny, it sounds like real life to me," Mandy said, giving a half-smile.

"What?" I asked.

"Gary, President Omega tried to kill every superhuman in the world and almost succeeded. Merciful took over Falconcrest City on a law and order campaign that gave people everything they could ever want except freedom. Which they took gladly. The superheroes and villains have also been doubling down killing each other."

"So, what you're saying is that said future might actually happen," I said, unsettled.

"What I'm saying is, Gary, you're the only one in the world who thinks supervillains versus superheroes is harmless fun. That's what scares everyone else because the only reason you aren't taking over the world is because you don't think you're supposed to."

I stared at her. "Really? That sounds...crazy."

Mandy shook her head. "People don't want or care about doing the right thing. That's the big thing you need to know in the struggle between good and evil. Julius Caesar was one of the first absolute dictators but he was actually pro-pleb and giving them land versus the super-wealthy having it all with endless numbers of slaves. Napoleon was considered the guardian of the French Revolution and if he'd won, he would have spared Europe an endless number of wars."

"He also reinstituted slavery after the French Revolution outlawed it so screw that guy," I said.

Mandy sighed as if my point was irrelevant. "What I'm saying is it's not megalomania if you actually are capable of taking over the planet. You'd also do a lot better job than most people. It's why I spend all of my time on these secret black ops missions for the Foundation for World Harmony. The Society of Superheroes is the only thing keeping a lot of nations from collapsing and they could do more if they took over completely—which they won't. The problem isn't the people in charge of the world being assaulted by those who want to take over. It's the fact the people in charge of the world don't want any of the responsibility."

"Wow, that's a love letter to fascism."

"How many times have you had to kill Hitler because people

wanted him in charge? On how many worlds? If people cared, then the answer would be none."

"I'm not going to become Merciful."

"No one wanted you to. I'd want you to be King Merciless."

"Why not Queen Mandy?" I suggested.

Mandy laughed then frowned. "Don't tempt me. Really don't."

"What? Afraid in the place of a Dark Lord that I would set up a queen?" I asked.

"Yes," Mandy said, looking to the ground. "Yes, I am."

Cindy's theme music app started playing "This ain't no place for no hero" by The Heavy.

"I'll bear that in mind. No tempting my bi wife," I said.

"Mandy's bi, I'm heteroflexible," Cindy said.

"Uh huh," I said, blinking. "I have no idea what that means."

"Look it up on the internet," Cindy said. "There's a spectrum about these things and I'm on the end that mostly loves dic—"

"Yo!" Jane called to us from inside the crowd. She was standing next to G and Mandy. There was also an unexpected guest in the Prismatic Commando. There was no sign of Cassius, Guinevere, or Gabrielle, though. Thankfully, there was no sign of Entropicus, either, though his brown robed minions were setting up an arena in the middle of the beach with wooden posts and rope around a bunch of marble tiles being set around in the center.

I'd always wondered who were the guys who set up these things. I guess I'd always assumed there were little intelligent hyperactive yellow square people serving every other major villain but me.

"Hey guys," I waved, walking over. "What's happening?"

"I'm just talking with Captain Paladin here," Jane said.

"That's a silly name for a superhero," I said, snorting.

"Yes," the Prismatic Commando said. "During World War 2, I was known as the Red, White, and Blue Commando."

"Why did you become prismatic?" Jane said. "Not that I don't love rainbow colors. It just seems a bit of a lateral career move."

"I felt it was necessary to represent all the peoples of the world to champion the cause of liberty and justice for all," the Prismatic Commando said, putting a gauntlet covered hand over his heart.

"Uh-huh," I said, trying not to choke on the glurge.

The fact was the Prismatic Commando was one of the few superheroes I actually respected at this point. He'd resigned from the Society of Superheroes and fought against Merciful's domination of the United States when others had been willing to take him at his word for being a good guy. He was one of the moral centers of the team without as much blinding anger as Guinevere. Then again, it was possible every hero secretly had feet of clay just as every villain had a story that showed them to have some humanity. Oh, wait, quite a few villains were actually just pure evil so what was I talking about?

Cindy elbowed Jane a bit. "So, have a fun night. Eh, eh?"

"Uh, yes," Jane said. "Yes, I did."

Cindy beamed. "Good."

"Am I missing something?" I asked.

"I encouraged Jane to make a pass at the Ryan Gosling Terminator," Cindy said. "Which is you, G."

"Yeah, I got that," G said, smirking. "Gary—"

I shook my head.

G nodded, getting my message. "So, what do you think is going to happen next?"

"Something awful," I replied. "Because Entropicus is an awful wizard-god. He does awful things and acts in a generally awful manner. Not a cool awful manner like me but a dirtbag uncool manner."

Everyone looked at me.

"What?" I asked.

"Don't ever change, Gary," Mandy said, her voice a bit sad. "No matter what happens in the future, stay exactly the same."

"Oh, that would require me to mature and that's completely impossible," I said, giving a dismissive snort. "So where are Gabrielle and Guinevere?"

"Gabrielle is still sulking about what happened?" Mandy said.

"Ouch, really?" I asked, grimacing. I couldn't imagine how

she felt about my complete non answer to her loving me. The fact was I'd made a commitment, though, and I wasn't about to break that.

"Specifically, you eliminating her from the tournament and making sure our chances of saving the multiverse are significantly worse," Mandy corrected.

"Oh, that."

"What else would it be?" the Prismatic Commando asked.

"So, where is Guinevere?" I asked, turning to him.

"Yeah, where is the most powerful superhero left in this contest that suspiciously looks like a Bollywood actress despite being an English heroine?" Jane asked.

"Some things we don't question in life," I said.

"She's looking for her magic sword," the Prismatic Commando said. "Caliburn apparently got dumped in a pool of acid and she's having trouble calling it back."

I grimaced. "Yes, an awful terrible villain did that."

"You're a villain," the Prismatic Commando said.

"Like I said, Stephen, an awful terrible villain," I said, grimacing. "I can call you Stephen, right?"

"I'd prefer you not to," Stephen said before shrugging. "Mostly because I have a secret identity. How do you even know that?"

"It's on your Superpedia page," I said, pausing. "Err, you know you can get that removed, right?"

"Oh dammit," Stephen said, removing his helmet and feeling his face.

I looked at him. "Listen, Stephen, I want you to know that despite the fact I'm a supervillain, I support you in wanting to save the multiverse. I—"

"I don't think you're a supervillain," Stephen said.

"Excuse me?" I asked.

"What?" Cindy added.

"That was unexpected," Mandy added at the last second.

Stephen sighed. "Mister Karkofsky, I think you're an annoyance at worst. You're a kind of prankster who is, yes, guilty of thievery and assault but has also saved many lives over the course of his career. I can't find any record of people you've killed who weren't trying to kill you or innocents. Have you used excessive force? Yes, certainly. You've also saved the United States from a time-travelling Nazi, the world from an ancient evil demon, and the Society of Superheroes from an alliance of villains. Not all of us forgot that."

"Thanks," I said, pausing. I wondered how friendly he'd be if he knew I'd killed Shoot-Em-Up when I was fourteen and a bunch of other worse-than-normal villains just because I could. The only reason I wasn't guilty of murdering the Extreme was because they wouldn't stay dead. They were heroes too, at least technically.

"Which makes me wonder why you don't live up to your potential by becoming a superhero," Stephen said.

"Because he doesn't want to be lame!" Cindy said, growling. Stephen looked at her strangely.

"What's lame about being the good guy?" Stephen asked, with a sincerity I didn't think was possible.

Cindy didn't respond before looking sideways. "I don't know."

I looked up at the sun. "I don't know whether I can pull off being a good guy. I've tried very hard to be a villain and it turned out I didn't have the stomach for the worst elements. I loved too deeply and hated the people who made the world objectively worse. I can't pretend to be a role model, though, or someone who can be looked up to. I'm going to make mistakes and I'm going to be tempted by anger as well as greed. I don't know if I'm going to rise above those feelings, Stephen."

"Being a superhero isn't about ignoring those kind of feelings, Gary," Stephen said, putting his hand on my shoulder. "It's about trying to rise above those feelings. To believe there's a light in the darkness no matter how awful things get. To try to do the right thing when you don't see a reward coming or think it'll end up okay. To burn brightest in the darkest by simply not giving into what's easiest. Even when you feel. Good and evil aren't places, they're roads and the direction we walk depends solely on us."

"Wow, that was actually a moving speech," I said.

"I wish we had more guys like you on my world," Jane said.

"Or mine," G said.

Mandy looked down. "I wish I agreed."

"You don't?" I asked.

"When I was a little girl, I was a huge fan of the Texas Guardians," Mandy said, frowning. "I used to watch them on the news no matter where I was, whatever godforsaken country my father had dragged us too, and collected their history comics with my allowance. I was especially in love with Spellbinder the half-Great Beast sorceress."

"Diabloman's sister?" I asked.

"Don't call her that," Mandy said, frowning. There was something personal in her tone, intensely so. "Her name was Maria Gonzales and she was more than a supervillain's sister. Spellbinder struggled against the demonic side of her powers and was dark as well as brooding. A loner who didn't like the spotlight and was an outsider. The perfect role model for a queer teenager looking for an outlet. I remember how she was treated when SKULL outed her. I remember how she was raked over the coals when the Guitarist died at the hands of her brother. I also remember what happened when she died sacrificing her life to kill one of the Great Beasts."

"Which was?" I asked. I hadn't been a big Texas Guardians fan and kind of regretted that fact now.

"Nothing," Mandy said, frowning at me. "She died saving the world and everyone forgot her a week later. It taught me a valuable lesson."

"What lesson?" Stephen asked.

"Being good sucks," Mandy replied. "Be good for yourself and not for the public."

"I'm not sure you can do that," I said, feeling a lot more emotion in Mandy's voice than I expected in that story. I knew the story of Spellbinder but there was something about the way she said the tale that made me wonder if there was something else going on there. I'd also never heard her express any real love for the half-demon sorceress until now. Before, I'd always heard Mandy talk about the Nightwalker as her favorite hero.

That was when Entropicus appeared in the middle of the beach arena with a puff of smoke like the Wicked Witch of the

West. "It is time for the next round to begin!"

"Oh joy," I said, turning around. "Today's festivities have begun."

"Our first match will be the *Prismatic Commando*—"

I patted Stephen on the back, making a boing noise. "Good luck, Captain."

"Colonel, actually," Stephen said.

"Versus *Stingray: The Underwater Assassin.*"

What?

CHAPTER FOURTEEN

ENTROPICUS BECOMES EVEN MORE DESPICABLE

Stingray. Keith Karkofsky. My brother. My *dead* brother. Keith Karkofsky was the reason I was a supervillain. He'd been a semi-famous supervillain on the West Coast during my childhood. Despite the fact he'd been a guy with a wetsuit and a harpoon, he'd managed to bedevil Aquarius and the Silver Medalist for years along with his fellow Nefarious Nine. Being a supervillain hadn't been a successful career for my brother despite, or perhaps because of, his notoriety. He'd spent the first decade and a half of my life in and out of jail, which was impressive since he'd been about fourteen years older than me.

In the end, he'd finally gotten his life turned around following a parole from the government for some off-book work against bad guys who didn't need costumes. He'd forsworn the criminal life for good and broken all contact with his fellow crooks. I'd been too blind to see it, though, because I'd chosen to believe my brother's career was cooler than being a hero. Even when he was having his brain matter splattered all over my face by Shoot-Em-Up in an ill-advised spree killing of "bad guys."

"Wow," Jane said, looking down at her cellphone. "According to this Tournament app, I'm actually the alternate double of Lara Croft! I don't believe it."

G looked over her shoulder. "I don't either given you're American, biracial, and not an archaeologist."

Jane glared at G. "I'm short and have brown hair. That's enough."

"Your hair is actually black," G pointed out.

"Angelina Jolie version?" Jane asked. "I mean, I have the body for it now."

"Guys," I said, looking over at them with barely concealed rage. "Now is *really* not the time!"

"Sorry," Jane said.

Mandy reached over and placed her hand on my shoulder. "It's probably a trick, Gary."

"No," I whispered. "It's probably not."

Moments later, I saw the figure of my brother step out of the crowd, wearing a hooded robe over a modified version of his Stingray costume. It looked less like a wetsuit with a diving helmet and more like a suit of power armor. His harpoon was replaced with a kind of weird energy lance that I assumed would be lethal for anyone underwater but someone immune to electricity like, say, someone in insulated armor.

Or a zombie.

Stingray proceeded to remove his helmet, as if to make sure I recognized him. It was Keith alright, but not the Keith I knew. He was younger than me now, about the age he died, but with marble white skin and long black hair in place of his previous dirty blond. His face was gaunt and his cheeks sallow while his eyes were a pale shade of yellow.

Being the expert on the undead I was, as much due to obsessive D&D playing as actual magical studies, I recognized him as having made the transition to becoming a *Jiang Shi*. Chinese vampires or a kind of physical ghost, they were a favorite weapon of necromancers across the globe. *Jiang Shi* had all the intelligence and power of their living selves but they were fueled only a negative image of their living selves. It was as if someone figured out how to pour out all of the good in a person and leave only their asshole traits. Normally, the only thing that could do that was the internet, politics, or the crappy money-based religions. Having my brother's corpse animated by his dark side would have been bad enough, believe me it was, but there was another fact to *Jiang Shi* that made it even worse. *Jiang Shi* were prisons for the soul. The person who they were was dragged from whatever afterlife they had earned for themselves and forced to be fuel for the black magic that caused them to kill for their masters. Saint or sinner, you would eat a baby if your master commanded it and the entire time you would be aware of it.

"Son of a bitch must pay," I muttered, starting to walk toward Entropicus and the unholy perversion of my brother's memory.

Mandy grabbed me by the shoulder. "No, Gary."

"Please don't let this be an undead solidarity thing," I muttered.

Mandy narrowed her eyes. "Entropicus is messing with your head."

"*No shit* he's messing with my head," I snapped at her. "I would have thought that was obvious by the fact he's *resurrected my brother and murdered my best friend.*"

"That means he's afraid of you," Mandy said, staring at me. There was no sign she was moved by my words but she'd survived a zombie apocalypse and imprisonment by Merciful so I wasn't sure that anything could phase her anymore. "Entropicus is trying to bait you into doing something rash."

"It's working!" I snapped at her.

I had no idea why Entropicus would be cautious around me since, like Gabrielle, he was fully capable of squishing me like a bug. I'd punched above my weight class more than a few times and managed to come out on top but like Little Mac in *Punch Out!*, eventually I got myself knocked out. Entropicus was a top tier villain that had fought and defeated the entire Society of Superheroes before.

Honestly, it was entirely possible he could fight the majority of the participants of the tournament here by himself all at once. If he was stopping to screw with the mid-tier magician antivillain who was best thought of as a B-List Supervillain with some lucky breaks, I put it squarely in the context of a kid frying ants with a magnifying glass.

"It's my job to fight him," Stephen said, looking at me. "I'm sorry about your brother."

"It's not my brother," I said, my voice low. "It's the corpse a demon is wearing. Do whatever you want to it. You can't harm him."

"Wow, cold," Cindy said. "I'd be thinking all manner of ways of bringing him back from the dead. Seriously, we could bring your brother back the same way we did Mandy and could build our own personal version of *The Munsters*."

"Cindy—" I started to speak.

"You can be Herman!" Cindy said.

I closed my mouth. "Yeah, okay, I have no one to blame but myself for the disrespectful way everyone talks about the dead."

"Yeah, you really don't and I've known you like a day," Jane said.

"Wish me luck," Stephen said, giving me a salute.

"Just promise me you're not three days from retirement and have a sweetheart back home," I said, looking at him.

"But I do have a sweetheart," Stephen said.

"Shh!" I said, holding a finger to my mouth. "Do you want to become a person I have to avenge?"

"You'd avenge me?" Stephen said, patting me on the shoulder. He reminded me a bit of my dad in that respect. All he needed to do was scream at the TV during football games and complain about how easy kids these days had it and the effect would have been perfect. "I knew you weren't all bad."

I felt my face. "You Golden Age heroes are way too good to be true."

"Thank you." Stephen put his helmet back on and raised a fist in the air. "Entropicus, I challenge your vile monster and choose to liberate its soul! I do so in the name of humanity and all freedom loving people of the universe!"

The Prismatic Commando charged into the arena like a professional wrestler. Entropicus took a position between them and conjured a throne to sit down upon. The battle was joined and the two proceeded to fight it out.

"He's going to die, isn't he?" Cindy asked.

"Yep," I said, sighing. "This was a trap for a hero."

"Come on!" Jane said. "He's a flag superhero! There's no way he'll lose! That would be Un-American."

"Oh, now you've jinxed it," G said.

That was when Guinevere arrived moments later. She was

covered in blood, smelled of acid, and was carrying Caliburn. "Entropicus is trying to eliminate the most powerful of heroes one by one. This includes bringing back the dead as monsters with vast powers."

I looked over at her. "Uh, sorry about that sword getting dumped into the sewer of toxic waste."

"I'm judging everything about our brief encounter to be the result of temporary insanity," Guinevere said.

"You see, Gary, this is what you get with heroes," Cindy said, shaking her head. "Like the time I time travelled back in time to the forties and ended up sleeping with the Nightwalker. Do I get any appreciation? No, it's just 'give up being a thief' and 'we can't be together because you're bad.' I also wasn't the only bad girl either! Makes a girl feel awful."

I did a double take. "You slept with Lancel?"

"Only like twice. It turns out the 1940s were not actually that much fun to visit for a Jewish girl," Cindy said. "On the other hand, I killed Himmler with an exploding dreidel."

I applauded Cindy for having the ability to distract me from my undead brother about to fight in a death match against the Prismatic Commando. Also, her gross hypocrisy.

"Begin!" Entropicus' voice echoed across the beach.

The Prismatic Commando glowed with a golden rainbow aura before flying up six feet in the air then starting to blast at Zombie Keith. The Underwater Assassin responded by simply knocking away the blasts with glowing fists, aiming the equally glowing harpoon at him, throwing it and then impaling the aging hero. The harpoon was attached to a metal chain forged from the fires of hell before Zombie Keith began to swing around the hero like a ball and chain.

"Stingray?" Guinevere asked, looking at the sight. "Why in the world would Entropicus bring back that loser, power grade or not?"

I shot her a withering glare.

"You know, I used to admire you," Mandy muttered, adjusting her sunglasses. "You were the best of the heroines. You are a real tool in person, though."

"I'm only angry when around evil," Guinevere said.

"And yet somehow the Society of Superheroes works with politicians," I said.

"That is a cheap joke," Guinevere said, pausing. "Cheap but true."

Stephen managed to regain control of the fight and delivered numerous devastating punches to Zombie Keith before blasting his upper torso off. "I'm sorry, but you're undead so it's okay to kill you."

"That's racist!" Mandy called out from the crowd.

"Well, that was an unexpected outcome," Cindy muttered. "I had fifty bucks on Zombie Keith."

"Not cool," I said, knowing it couldn't be that simple.

"Hey, he's family!" Cindy said. "Sort of! I'm really serious about resurrecting him. We can bring back all of the people we like and screw everybody else! You just have to promise me my dear departed mother will stay dead and burning in hell."

"Rotting in hell," I corrected. "She's in the section where people decompose but don't die."

"Good," Cindy muttered, crossing her arms.

My fears proved justified as the missing upper torso of Zombie Keith became a blue pyre that transformed into a new fleshy growth, like he was a Resident Evil monster. The monster then stretched out its arms and wrapped around the Prismatic Commando. Stephen let out a scream as the blue flames burned him and reduced his armor to useless junk.

Stephen was a warrior, though, so he didn't give up. The WW2 hero shrugged off his injury and charged at Zombie Keith with his bare fists. Zombie Keith drew back his arms and let forth and unholy growl before turning his arms into a pair of bone knives like some arcade fighter game character. They ended up stabbing the hero again, though the stomach.

"Dammit," I muttered. "Just because I don't like the guy doesn't mean I want him dead."

"You don't like the Prismatic Commando?" Mandy asked. "He's like patriotism without all of the unearned pride and xenophobia."

I didn't want to respond. "Listen, Guinevere, I—"

"No," Guinevere said, looking down. "Not again, I'm not

going to let another friend die."

Oh hell.

Guinevere lifted up Caliburn and summoned forth the Shield Perilous as a glowing disc around her arm before charging at Zombie Keith. A rousing battle score started playing and for a second I thought it was Cindy's cellphone app working again. Instead, I realized it was merely my mind providing music for one of the greatest heroes the human race had ever produced. As prickly as I found Guinevere, she was a woman who wasn't going to abandon her friend and that thought shamed me.

Unfortunately, it occurred to me what was really going on wasn't a heroic rescue but a trap. I kept thinking of Entropicus as the generic Evil Overlord/Sauron figure that history comics had taught me he was. However, he was the Chosen of Death or at least had been. That meant if he was anything like me then he was a guy who knew the kind of stupidly noble drives that inspired heroes to displays of self-sacrificing idiocy.

The trap then became clear. This wasn't an attempt to destroy me by using my brother against me. No, it was a feint. A sleight of hand that had a far bigger and more impressive target in mind. It was a trap set for Guinevere.

"No!" I shouted, levitating upward and launching myself at Guinevere like I was a video game boss.

Guinevere moved too quickly, though, and drove Caliburn into the heart of Zombie Keith. The undead abomination exploded into a collection of burning bones, saving Stephen's life, but breaking the rules for the tournament. I hadn't had a chance to study the rules but even I knew that was going to have awful consequences when the guy arbitrating the tournament was very close to Asmodeus himself.

"Interference," Entropicus said, shaking his head. "The battle is forfeited to my champion. The punishment for those who broke the rules? Elimination!"

"Do your worst, fiend!" Guinevere said, lifting her sword and shield. "I should never have agreed to participate in this foul bloodsport to begin with. I shall smite you and bring an end to the threats you have brought to creation!"

Entropicus smashed down the bottom of his staff against

the ground right before black and red lightning descended downward upon both her as well as Stephen. I was beside Entropicus by the time it happened, ready to attack him, only for a terrible glow blinded me. Moments later, I turned to see both Stephen and Guinevere had been transformed to stone like Diabloman.

"You do not fight my power," Entropicus said, laughing. "You fight the power of the tournament and my authority within it is absolute."

I stared at the sight of two more fallen champions and realized the Age of Heroes was over. The Nightwalker, Ultragod, Guinevere, and Prismatic Commando were all fallen. Worse, I'd done almost nothing to make the world a better place as it had happened. I'd killed a few people worse than them but without these pillars to build a new tomorrow then there wasn't anything worth saving about the current age. What was the point of being a villain if there were no heroes to fight? There was just darkness and worse darkness.

"You bastard," I gritted my teeth.

"I merely followed the rules," Entropicus said, chuckling to himself. "She was the one who chose to break them."

I turned around. "Well, there's no rule so absolute as to not have a loophole. I challenge you, Entropicus! Right here, right now!"

Entropicus gave a rictus grin, the little bit of flesh on his face allowing him the parody of a smile. "You have to win two more battles before you are able to reach the tournaments finale, Merciless. You will not because I will—"

I turned around. "I challenge Agent G and Jane Doe."

"I surrender," Agent G said.

"Me too," Jane said. "Though I could totally take Entropicus. I just don't wanna."

"I don't want to die so I'm surrendering too," Cindy said. "I totally am getting bribed for this, though. Like, a small planet and at least three Hawaiian Islands. The good ones, not the leper ones, as Homer Simpson would say."

"You got it," I said.

A glowing light descended upon both me and Entropicus.

It was a sign the Primals had accepted my thinking. Almost immediately, the other contestants on the beach disappeared and left only my friends where once had been a vast crowd. A few others were left over, seemingly without rhyme or reason, but it was an effective signal the tournament was over. Almost over. Now all I had to do was battle the God of Evil and win.

Okay, this plan seemed to be a bad one in retrospect.

CHAPTER FIFTEEN

WHERE THE ENORMITY OF MY STUPIDITY IS MADE CLEAR

Entropicus' look was one that could have obliterated me and I meant that literally. Entropicus had used his Hate Beams to eradicate every hero he'd fought but Ultragod and Guinevere. However, he didn't fire said beams but just looked at me for a long time.

"Very well," Entropicus said. "I accept your challenge."

I lifted my hands before balling them into fists. "Prepare to be punked like Ashton Kutcher used to do to people before celebrities started suing him for horrific mental trauma!"

"That's a terrible threat, Gary," Mandy said.

"Back me up here," I muttered, not at all confident of my chances here.

"I will decide the rules of the contest, though," Entropicus said, his voice like the wrath of God.

"Oh come on!" I snapped.

"The nature of arbitration," Entropicus said, glaring. "It will be a contest either to the death or three falls."

"You want to go two out of three with me?" I asked, confused.

"Yes," Entropicus said.

"O-kay," I said, blinking. "Not exactly what I was expecting."

"It will also be done at the height of the sun," Entropicus said, gesturing to the sun above. "In the Castle of Ultimate Sorrow."

"Castle of Ultimate Sorrow?" I asked, confused. "Who names these things?"

"I do," Entropicus said.

"Oh, well that explains it," I deadpanned. "Where's the Castle of Ultimate Sorrow?"

"There." Entropicus gestured to the Chinese castle on the hill. We had been staying under it the entire time with the tournament monks keeping us away from the castle proper.

"Oh," I said, looking at the castle. "That's a lot closer than I expected."

"One more condition," Entropicus said, chuckling like the Devil.

"Which is?" I asked, now annoyed with the Supreme Master of Evil as well as wanting him dead.

"*Say please*," Entropicus said.

I stared at him. "You raised my brother from the dead as a soulless monster. Your children killed my best friend and damned him. You murdered legends."

"That's not what I want to hear."

I took several deep breaths, quaking with fury. "Please."

Entropicus chortled. "You will lose, Gary Karkofsky, because you have no ability to commit to anything in your life. The path of villainy, the path of heroism, your lovers, and even your own ambition. You invited a monster into your ranks and treated them as family when they were your enemy all along."

I assumed he meant Diabloman. "Balance in all things. What exactly do you have to show for conquering the universe and making it hell? The desire to end everything? To make no God, universe, or even memory of humanity? Do you get off on it? What?"

"When you live past your family, you will learn to treasure the present. When you live past a century, you learn to dream of building empires. When you learn to live past civilizations, you learn to hate everything and everyone. When you live past the lifespan of worlds and the epochs of time, you understand what a cruel joke existence is so that the only mercy that exists is for nothing to ever undergo the horrors of life. When you die, at a time of that I decree, you will not under the illusion of your petty joys justify your awful existence. No, instead, you will reach up, your eyes full of despair, and say—"

"Eh, what's up, Doc?" I interrupted him.

Entropicus didn't say anything else. Instead, he turned around and walked away.

"I just made the worst mistake of my probably soon to be very short life, didn't I?" I asked, to no one in particular.

"Pretty much, yeah," Jane said, pausing. "I mean, you know, if he wins then he's going to wish the universe unmade and the Powers that Be are going to let him because the universe sucks."

"Hey, this is on you too now! You trusted me to forfeit your position in the tournament!" I said, faking horror at myself—which wasn't really all that fake. "Why in the world would you do something so dumb?"

"I don't know!" Jane snapped. "It looked really heroic and only sounded stupid in retrospect!"

"Well, I hope you've learned your lesson!" I said.

Jane crossed her heart. "I solemnly swear to never think you know what you're doing ever again."

"Jane, you are like my second sister," I said. "Expect me to horribly prank you and scare your boyfriends."

"I already have a brother so I'll pass." Jane checked her cellphone. "Actually, according to this app, we're alternate doubles of each other."

"Wait, I'm Lara Croft?" I asked. "That horrifies my fourteen year old self."

"Does Gary have any chance of actually beating this guy?" G asked, walking up to the battle arena.

"Let me paint a picture," Cindy said, walking up. "Imagine Godzilla fighting Harry Potter and you have a rough estimation of how any fight between Gary and Entropicus would go. Except, Godzilla in this metaphor is also a wizard."

"Am I Godzilla in this metaphor?" I asked.

"No," Cindy said, staring at me. "No you are not. Which you know."

"Don't be surprised at my infinite capacity for self-delusion," I said, making finger guns at her. "I'm fully capable of believing that if I want it enough, I can have it."

"That's like the very definition of stupidity," Cindy said.

"I know!" I said, stretching out my hands. "Yet look at my life! It seems to work for me."

"Millionaire, superpowers, vampire secret agent as a wife, hot redhead as his mistress, hot superheroine is in love with him, and he has a hulking badass as a henchman," G said, looking over at me. "Yeah, you have a point there. I've read fanfic characters with less wish fulfillment."

"I've suffered for it," I said, thinking of all the people I'd lost over the years. The suffering, imprisonment, beatings, and shocks to the system.

G smiled. "You should visit my world. I think you'd like what the media has to say about you. Mind you, on my planet you're considered a cheap knock-off of Doctor Impossible."

"I resemble that remark. In any case, I'll try and get all the comics about me from your world and Jane's when this is all done," I said before pausing. "Wait, you read fanfic?"

"Only for *Game of Thrones*," G said. "It's the only way Sansa will ever catch a break."

Mandy walked over to the stone figurines of Guinevere and Stephen before kneeling before them.

"Mandy?" I asked.

"One hundred and fifteen," Mandy said, lowering her head.

"Excuse me?"

"That's the number of times Guinevere and the Prismatic Commando saved the world or were part of a group that did," Mandy said, looking at them. "I remember only about three. The Atlantean invasion, the defeat of Tyrant Sun, and the time the vampire plague spread throughout the world with everyone infected."

"Yeah, I recall sleeping through the last one," I said, not even aware of the majority of horrific events that happened during my life the Society of Superheroes or their affiliates had stopped. I lived in a world where there was a weekly attempt by people like me to rule the world, kill the population, or turn everyone into zombies.

In retrospect, it made sense why Guinevere had such a horrible attitude as the planet's constant peril would wear down even the strongest souls. Worse, those who had once seemed invincible were broken one by one. The fact I'd eliminated quite a few of the bigger named horrors didn't mean there were less problems, though.

Just different ones.

"They deserve to be treated with more reverence than serving as statues in Entropicus' trophy room," Mandy said, looking to the beach. "We should find a place to bury them and give them the proper respects they deserve."

"Much as the Klingons, the real Klingons rather than the knock-offs they're trying to pass off as the real thing on *Star Trek: Discovery*, I believe the body to be just a shell," I said, looking at the stone statues. "Besides, I'm not going to let them stay dead."

"What?" Mandy said, doing a double take.

I frowned. "I want to be a hero but I'll screw the natural order a couple of times before I die."

"I wish I had someone like you when I died," Mandy said.

"Excuse me?" I asked.

"Nothing," Mandy said, looking back. "Do you really think you can bring them back?"

"I don't intend to wish anyone back," I said, pausing. "I intend to give reality a reboot!"

"Really? Are sales of your comic dipping?" Jane asked.

"Funny," I said.

"Not kidding," Jane asked. "That's usually the only reason anyone does them and they always make things worse."

"Think about it," I said, ignoring her. "This reality has gotten far too dark and edgy. Superheroes are a shadow of their former selves and supervillains are, well, not cool anymore."

"They were never cool, Gary," Mandy said, showing the barest hint of fang. "You basically assumed they were because your brother was one, but they've always been a gang of murderers, rapists, and thieves."

"This is true," Cindy said, giving a nod of agreement. "I mean, heroes still suck but screw the rest of our kind. The only thing worse than the good guys is another villain."

I pretended to be shocked. "Really? I hadn't noticed that. You know, what with my decision to become a superhero and all. Something I'm doing now. You know, by saving the world."

"Which *you haven't done yet*," G pointed out. "Also, is highly unlikely to happen for myriad reasons."

"I'm the plucky underdog," I said, ignoring his advice. "I'm bound to win against Entropicus. Look at *Rocky.*"

"Rocky lost three fights in the movies, four if you count Apollo Creed beating him in the gym rematch," Jane said, surprising me with her knowledge of movie trivia as much as made-up superheroes. "Furthermore, you lampshaded the fact you're an underdog so the laws of dramatic irony mean you have to lose."

I stared at her. "I'm starting to think we have too many hot snarky people on this team."

Jane shrugged. "You can find a new job."

I tried to smile before turning to the others. "Basically, my plan is to wish for a newer and better reality. All of the old heroes will be there: Ultragod, Nightwalker, Guinevere, and the Prismatic Commando but they'll be younger! Hipper! We'll introduce superhuman powers and alien invasions as a new thing except when origins are tied to a specific event. No more of this time compression thing, we'll just have a new date for our Age of Heroism! Bad guys will have not murdered millions over the past century but be introduced gradually! Clear out some of the crazy too! No more Psychoslinger or Mercifuls!"

"Will Diabloman be back?" Cindy asked.

"Yes," I said. "Maybe not as a universe murderer either."

"But my mother will be dead," Cindy said.

I looked at her. "You're really insistent on that."

"Remember when you first met me?"

"As a teen prostitute?" I asked, trying hard to ever bring that up around her. Cindy didn't seem to mind talking about her brief 'career' before meeting me but spoke about her home life with the kind of fear and disgust you'd expect from where she'd worked. I didn't have to be a criminal genius to put together what it had probably involved or why she'd latched onto my family the way she had.

"Yeah," Cindy said. "Ask how I got there and why it was a step up from where I was."

I pointed at her. "This is the kind of thing I'm talking about and should have no place in our new world."

Mandy walked up to me and took my hands. "Gary, I want you to look into my eyes."

"Because you're going to mesmerize me into making sure vampire bites don't hurt and I shouldn't think about how arterial spray is actually a gusher rather than a sucking thing?" I asked. "Because that wasn't cool the first few times you did it."

"No," Mandy said. "Please accommodate me, though."

"You got it," I said, looking into her eyes.

"Besides, if I could mesmerize you then you wouldn't be nearly as annoying," Mandy muttered.

"Mind tricks don't work on Gary, only money," Jane said.

I stared at her in horror. "Did you quote the Prequels at me?"

"Better than *The Last Jedi*," Jane said.

"Point taken."

Mandy moved my chin back to parallel with hers. "Gary, look into my eyes."

"I'm looking. They're very beautiful and predatory," I said. They were also different from my wife's living eyes. They'd changed in a way that I was only now trying to figure out the implications of.

Mandy smiled at the compliment she'd thought I'd given her. She then frowned. "Gary, that is a *terrible* idea."

"Oh."

Mandy closed her eyes. "This is, quite possibly, your worst idea ever."

"I wouldn't go as far to say worst."

"No," Mandy shook her head. "Don't do this. The world needs to move forward. We can't just keep recycling the same stories, the same heroes, the same villains, and the same plots over again. Sometimes, stories have to end."

"I don't want them to end. I want them to keep going forever like Toni Basil's 'Hey Mickey' once it gets in your head."

I started humming it.

Mandy glared at me.

"It's there now, isn't it?" I asked.

"Dammit," Cindy muttered. "I hate that song."

Mandy took a deep breath. "Gary, I want you to win this

battle against Entropicus. We just need to wish carefully."

"But imagine the kind of wonderful hijinks that might ensue if I misuse it." I paused. "I suppose I could give it to you."

Mandy's stare had no mercy in it.

"Seriously, you'd do better than I would," I said, shrugging. "I just don't want to become Old Gary and dominate the solar system if it makes me as miserable as he looks. Imagine yourself with the power to control everything."

Mandy didn't respond as there was a hunger inside her eyes. "This is just because you want me to forget you and Gabrielle are having a baby."

"Obviously," I said. "Assuming we are."

"You knocked up Ultragoddess?" A pasty-faced Keith Karkofsky said, walking up beside me, his upper costume completely destroyed while his hair had turned bleach white. "Wow, did I misjudge what women like. Apparently, it was geeks all along."

I did a double take at him.

"Hey bro," Keith said, giving a thumbs up.

I screamed like a victim in a slasher movie.

CHAPTER SIXTEEN

WHERE I MEET ZOMBIE KEITH

"Yo!" Zombie Keith said, pulling out a white chocolate candy bar marked Braiiiinnnnns and taking a bite out of it. "Wassuuuuup!"

I screamed again. I sounded like a yodeling schoolgirl being thrown off a cliff.

Jane walked up behind me and gave me a dope slap. "Calm down."

"Stop that," Mandy snapped, staring down at Jane. "He's my husband. Only I get to slap him."

"Spousal abuse is never funny," Cindy said, a lot more serious than normal.

"It's consensual," Mandy said. "Like the chains, handcuffs, lingerie, and leather."

Cindy blinked. "Does Gary wear the leather or lingerie?"

"Seriously," Zombie Keith said. "Dude has got some serious Austin Powers mojo going on here. I don't get it."

"Regular awesome sex. It's how I get my boyfriends back home to cooperate," Jane said. "You just need to express the value of sharing."

"I don't like sharing," G muttered under his breath.

Zombie Keith raised his hand. "So, Gary, high five!"

"What the hell are you doing?" I said, finally regaining control over my senses. "Also, my brother did not act like this."

"Well, I'm just your brother's dark side," Zombie Keith said, talking with his mouth full before swallowing. "I'm back to the time he was a surfer dude catching the New Angeles waves.

The waves around this island are pretty radical but I'm dead so I can't really enjoy them. Bum—"

"Don't say bummer or I will have to kill you," I said, staring at him.

"Wouldn't be so bad," Zombie Keith said, looking over at the arena. "I just, like, killed two superheroes. That's a drag. Hey, are you actually a wizard?"

"Yes," I said, trying to fake being cheerful as I stared at an empty shell imitating my dead brother. I still wanted to hug him.

"Could you like conjure me up some Doritos?" Zombie Keith said.

I waved my hand and a bag of Mercitos appeared in his hand.

"Awww, it's the crappy generic kind," Zombie Keith said before tearing open the bag and shoveling them down his throat.

"Okay, that's nasty," Jane said, wrinkling her nose. "It's like he's combined corpse and frat boy."

"No, no surfer dude and corpse," I said, looking over at her. "They're both still pigs when eating but surf zombies loves the environment."

Zombie Keith wiped away some of the toasted chips from his face before speaking. "I wanted to tell you some information about Entropicus."

"Really, the guy who brought you back from the dead," I said, trying not to scream and set him on fire.

"This isn't life, dude," Keith said, frowning. There was a genuine look of bewilderment on his face. "I don't feel anything. I don't feel love, hope, joy, or friendship. All I feel is hate. I hate Entropicus most of all. As soon as he finds out I regenerated from Caliburn then he's going to send me after you. Maybe he'll send me after my, Keith's daughter, Fireworks or his ex-wife. Actually, probably not since Keith hated her too. She was screwing the milkman."

"They still have milkmen in New Angeles?" Jane asked.

"Time in my world is weird," I replied.

"Hey, how is the Human Tank?" Keith said.

"She's fine," I replied, nodding my head. "Misses you, Keith, the person you once were."

Keith seemed to ponder that. "I'd like to tell you what I know about Entropicus' plans as well as weaknesses in exchange for a favor."

"You want to give us information, even though you're a being of pure evil enslaved to another being of pure evil," I said, processing that. "Who in all likelihood is lying because using my dead brother against me is exactly what a diabolical mastermind like Entropicus would do."

"Yes," Zombie Keith said, staring at me. "If I tell you what I know then I want you to kill me. Permanently."

I stared at him. "How would I do that?"

"You're the Chosen of Death," Zombie Keith said. "You can kill anything. That's literally one of your powers. Just like it's—"

"One of Entropicus'," I said, frowning.

Entropicus hadn't managed to destroy the Age of Heroes until today but he'd certainly devastated it. There were hundreds of worlds other than Earth where their local heroes had been crushed, broken, and corrupted. There were places in the Multiverse where he was the god that humans prayed to. I wasn't sure if there would be much will to resist him if he invaded again, not without the four greatest heroes of Earth to inspire humanity. No, Entropicus had to die during this tournament or he'd just return and defeat humanity. If that meant making a deal with my brother's haunted corpse, so be it.

"Yes," Zombie Keith replied. "Do we have a deal?"

"Yes," I said. "I'd like to know what you know. Tell me why Entropicus keeps dialing back on killing me."

"He can't," Zombie Keith said. "If he kills you then he loses everything."

I blinked. "Excuse me?"

"What?" Mandy added.

"The Primals have a bunch of rules that apply to their Chosen Ones," Zombie Keith said, shrugging. "They can kill each other but they can't hurt the Chosen of the same Primal. Their powers won't work against one another and if they kill one another then they lose all of their powers."

"Bullshit!" I said, staring at him. "That is completely made up and unmentioned until now!"

"So, we're not just riffing on *Mortal Kombat* now but outright plagiarizing it?" Jane asked.

Everyone looked at her.

"It was a rule in the second movie!" Jane said, throwing her hands up.

"The second movie does not count!" I snapped, appalled she would even mention that. "That's like counting *The Last Jedi!*"

"Even worse than the Prequels, huh?" Jane asked.

"Obviously," I said, still angry about that movie. "Because blankety blank happens and that ruined *Star Wars* forever!"

"Blankety blank?" Jane asked.

"Well, spoilers are still sacrosanct," I said, looking over at Zombie Keith. "So, is that it?"

"I think that's pretty important," Jane said. "I mean, you're basically immune to Entropicus' powers and that's pretty awesome as the only believable reason he hasn't killed you."

"Well it's still unbelievable because he could send an army to kill me at any time," I said. "I mean, basic Doctor Evil logic is he could shoot me on the commode, but I suppose it's slightly less ridiculous I haven't been squashed like an insect the first time I stood up to the guy. Especially if he loses his powers if he kills me indirectly."

"Wait," Jane said, looking at me. "So, if you do win against Entropicus you're going to lose your powers?"

"Yeah, probably," I said, having not really given it much thought. "Eh, it happens."

"Really?" Jane asked.

I shrugged. "It's a small sacrifice to see the end of the biggest bad guy in the multiverse taken down. I'm entirely capable of getting myself some new powers when this is done."

"What if it kills you?" Jane asked.

I blinked. "That would suck."

"I could make you a vampire," Mandy said, reaching over to hold my hand.

I didn't take it. "You recall how that ended, right? There was a year of you murdering about a hundred people, all of them bad, and soul-crushing despair from your loved ones as we tried to get your soul back?"

"It was three weeks now," Cindy said.

"What?" I stared at her. "That doesn't even make any sense! I am totally fixing that in the reboot."

"There will be no reboot!" Mandy said, raising her voice and pulling her hand away. "Also, Gary, are you actually saying you think I wouldn't do the same for you? That I wouldn't scour the Earth and heavens to get you your soul back?"

"I'm saying you already spent years trying to save me when we were caught in Merciful's time loop," I said, referring to one of the incidents during President Omega's reign. "I wouldn't want you to do that again. Don't turn me into a vampire. Even to save my life. Please."

I wasn't happy about the prospect of dying but I'd gone into this business with my eyes wide open. I didn't want to live forever, though I was happy living for a long time, and was comfortable with the idea of eventually clocking it for a greater cause. In that respect, I did have something in common with Anakin Skywalker. As the Kurgan said, it was better to burn out than to fade away.

Mandy, however, didn't see it that way. "So, what you're saying is, you'd rather be dead than be like me."

"Mandy—"

"You'd rather leave me alone to face eternity?" Mandy stared.

Jane grimaced. "Yikes, they haven't had the T-Talk."

"T-Talk?" G asked.

"Turning talk. It's a common storytelling trope on my world's fiction because, well, vampires are real and public," Jane said. "Every human and vampire couple has to eventually discuss whether or not one is going to be turned or not. It's the ruination of a lot of relationships because vampires are inherently selfish parasites."

Mandy glared.

"On my world!" Jane corrected herself before turning into an adorable doe, which made it impossible to hate her.

"Yeah, well I understand that," G said, looking at Gary.

"Cyborgs don't live very long on my world. I'm already past my sell date."

Jane turned her head, still in animal form, and looked like he was an oncoming truck. Apparently, the two had managed to form a stronger bond over the past day than I would have thought possible.

"I didn't know that I'm sorry," Jane said.

"The only thing I don't want to face more than the possibility of dying soon is dying on a world where there's no hope," G said.

Cindy put her hand over her heart. "Well, I for one am entirely happy living forever but only if I remain young and beautiful as well as live in absolute pampered luxury. That means we need to go find some gods, kill them, and take their stuff."

There was a crack of thunder in the distance.

Mandy looked down at the ground. "Maybe you should be with Gabrielle, Gary, if you're so fond of growing old and dying."

"Actually, she's going to live forever unless killed like her father but that's not—" I started to say.

"Do I still need to be here?" Zombie Keith said. "Do your conversations normally drift off like this during events of multiversal importance?"

"Yes," I said.

"Cool," Zombie Keith said, nodding. "Epic. So, if you're going to do that, could you maybe conjure a board and let me do one last surf?"

I looked at him and remembered the earliest part of my life, before Keith became Stingray and when he was just a teenager enjoying surfing. Before his future wife had gotten knocked up and he'd turned to crime to find a way to make ends meet. He hadn't been this bad but there was enough of my brother to remind the toddler portion of my brains of my brother. I wanted to resurrect him but that was for me rather than Keith. When I'd spoken to my brother's ghost, he'd been happy in heaven. Zombie Keith just drew his soul from where it belonged.

"Do you know anything else?" I asked him. "Useful, I mean."

Zombie Keith paused as if thinking hard. "Is our dad dead?" I blinked. "What?"

"That occurred to me and I'm wondering if it's true. I know things I shouldn't despite being a corpse of a guy who died decades ago," Zombie Keith said.

I closed my eyes. "Yes, Keith, he's dead. Heart attack."

"Who is taking care of Lisa then?" Keith asked.

I stared at him. "She's a grown woman now, Keith. That means she mostly spends her time asking me for money to finance her pop career. Well, country-music pop career. I bought her a studio so she should be fine."

Keith was like no *Jiang Shi* I'd ever encountered. "I want to feel something about that but I can't. I don't know anything else. Just, do me one more favor other than kill me."

"Which is?" I asked.

"Tell Kerri I love her," Keith said. "I miss her too."

"I'm sorry you didn't ever get to meet Leia," I said, looking at him. "I tell her stories about you all the time."

"I hope you lie," Keith said, grabbing his head before his eyes turned black. "Because you're a gutless loser who could have resurrected me but didn't. Instead, you just wanted me as an excuse to do whatever the hell you wanted. You never cared about me or anyone but yourself and I'm going to rip off your face."

"Ah," I said, nodding. "There's the *Jiang Shi* I know."

I snapped my fingers and concentrated all of my power into burning the undead creature into a thing that could no longer be resurrected. In the fires, I saw Keith's consciousness, his soul, disappear into the alternate dimensions that existed between physical as well as mental space. He was free, hopefully, forever. But only if Entropicus was destroyed.

"I'm sorry, Gary," Mandy said, standing behind me. "I know this had to be hard for you."

I looked back. "It wasn't hard for me. I carry my brother with me wherever I go just like you carry me."

I walked over to the stone statue of Guinevere before looking at Caliburn, resting in her arms alongside the Shield Perilous. I managed to pry them both out of her hands before walking over to hand them to Mandy. "She'd want you to have these."

"Guinevere considered me a blood sucking abomination and tried to kill me twice," Mandy said.

Guinevere, to my knowledge, had never tried to kill Mandy and while it was possible she'd done that during one of my wife's many covert missions—something about this didn't feel right. Still, we had bigger problems right now. "Then take them because you're the only person here who knows how to use melee weapons."

Mandy nodded and did so.

"So, everyone here ready to be my ring crew for my upcoming Badass Battle of Badassitude?"

Everyone was.

CHAPTER SEVENTEEN

IF WISHES WERE FISHES, WE'D ALL STINK

"Wow, this is a far more badass castle than I was expecting," I said, walking through the open gate to reveal a massive interior with Tron lines going up and down bare stone. There were free-floating blocks moving in regular patterns as well as random beams of light firing from pits into the sky above.

"Really? Badass?" Cindy said, looking at the interior. "I swear I've played this level in *Assassins Creed*."

"There're free floating blocks!" I said, gesturing upward. "I mean, what if I made a jump and smashed my head against them! They might pop out mushrooms or stars! If I can get thirty seconds of invincibility then I can take Entropicus out, easy!"

"Can we have a ban on making video game references when we're trying to save the entire multiverse?" Mandy asked, looking around the place with a look of sheer disbelief.

"You're a sexy vampire entering a castle with a magic sword and shield," Jane said, looking at Jane. "How the hell are we not going to make any *Castlevania* references?"

"By *not making them*," Mandy said, looking more than a little pissed off. She was still mad over the fact I didn't want to become a vampire even in a life-saving emergency. I mean, don't get me wrong, I didn't want to grow old and plop over like Lancel Warren did but I wasn't a fan of vampires outside of my wife. Anne Rice aside, who I would never be able to read the same way again, vampires were people living under a dreadful curse. You had to be a vicious sociopath to not see the downsides versus the benefits and I seemed to be the exception as one who couldn't.

"Whatever you say, Alucardette. Honestly, I feel like I'm among my people," Jane said, glancing to her. "It's like being in a Joss Whedon film. Something I suppose is appropriate since he used to make superhero films you've probably got not equivalent to in your world."

"What do you mean? Joss Whedon made the *Society of Superheroes* movie," I said, blinking. "Love that film, even if it is ahistorical."

Jane blinked. "I'm still wrapping my head around the fact you still have superhero comics in a world where they're real."

"Do you have vampire and werewolf movies on your world?" I asked.

"Yes," Jane said. "They're a bit different since the reveal of the supernatural in 2008 but we've got everything from *Dracula* to *Underworld*."

"There you go," I said, looking around for guards or some sign of Entropicus' people. The weird monks who inhabited the island weren't anywhere to be found and I hadn't seen Gabrielle since I'd accidentally eliminated her from the tournament.

"I've often thought of getting myself infected with lycanthropy," Cindy said. "I have gotten numerous power ups with my toys over the years but the simple fact is, I'm kind of running low on super-abilities. Being a werewolf who dresses as a sexy Red Riding Hood strikes me as something that could work me."

Jane's face wrinkled into a nasty expression. "Yeah, that's not how shifters work on my world. We're all born to it. We're not an STD."

Cindy snorted. "Oh, I wouldn't want to be a were-DEER anyway, seriously. I'd want to be something cool."

"Grr," Jane growled, sounding wholly unlike a deer.

"Wait, would it be transmittable via sex?" Cindy asked, completely ignoring Jane's point. "I mean, that sounds like a much-much easier way to get transformed than the surviving a mauling thing. Would it have to happen when they're in wolf-person form? Would I have to swallow—"

"Time out!" I said, making a t-gesture with my hands. "We're not going there. This is a PG-13 universe."

"Except for all the swearing, murder, and adultery," G said.

"Do you want to move to a world where magic is real or not, Tinman?" I asked, looking back at him.

G raised his hands in surrender. "Just don't try and pass off a watch as my heart and we're good."

"If I was Dorothy, I'd have brought Aunt Em and Uncle Henry to Oz. Screw Kansas. This is why the books are better," Cindy said.

"There are books?" G asked.

I was about to explain when a pair of glowing force fields appeared behind me and behind my friends, trapping them.

"Well, that's a sudden but inevitable betrayal," I said, looking back at them. "Mind you, it's a bit subtle for Entropicus and involves less disintegrating us with his Hellazons."

"Hellazons?" Jane asked.

"His all-girl army of Goth demigods," I said, looking at her. "That shows he can't be all bad."

"I'm afraid to disappoint you, Gary," Cassius spoke from the other side of the room before walking out.

Cassius walked out wearing a bizarre skin-tight bodysuit with a flowing cape and helmet that left his face exposed. It glowed with little dots as there was a metal box on the side of his shoulder. His sword and belt had been upgraded with technology from Entropicus' world and he looked very much like he'd stepped out of a seventies sci-fi epic.

"Oh hey, it's you," I said, looking at him. "Why are you dressed like…"

I paused.

"You know, I actually have no pop culture reference to compare you to." I looked back to the others. "Help me out here."

"Buck Rogers?" Jane suggested.

"Flash Gordon?" G suggested.

"Captain Pornstar of the Eighth Dimension?" Cindy said.

Everyone looked at her.

"I should know I won awards for my supporting role in that," Cindy said. "The industry has become a lot less sleazy since the dawn of the 21st century."

Everyone looked at her still.

"I did it for the art," Cindy said, crossing her arms. "It's also been on HBO Late Night so it's a real movie!"

"Well, there went our PG-13 rating," I muttered.

"It was a mercy killing," Mandy said, solemnly.

Now everyone was looking at her.

"I can be funny!" Mandy said. "It's just people don't notice because I'm in the clown car that is this group."

"That's a fair cop," I said.

"Silence!" Cassius shouted, raising his electricity glowing sword. "I'm sorry, Gary, but I can't let you battle Entropicus!"

"Where did you find this guy?" I asked, looking over at Mandy.

Mandy shrugged. "I got dumped into his universe for a couple of months while in the future that never was."

"I thought she was crazy," Cassius said, shaking his head. "Who believes in vampires, after all?"

"*Everyone,*" Jane muttered. "Anyway, I think I got that issue on Free Comic Book Day."

I kept my vision on Cassius. "Okay, you do realize we're trying to stop the end of everything, right? May I ask why you're getting in the way?"

"I need to be the one who gets the wish," Cassius replied, approaching with his sword. "You may have lawyered your way to getting to challenge Entropicus but I haven't been eliminated from the tournament and still want to win."

I stared at him. "Listen, I like Malcolm Reynolds and Han Solo as much as the next guy but I'm not betting on them in a battle with Wizard-Satan."

"I managed to acquire a Century Box," Cassius replied, tapping the little device on his shoulder. "It's provided me with a battle suit that significantly upgrades my combat capacity. I also intend to blast Entropicus from orbit with my starship. That's in addition to the fact I have a patron who knows how to weaken exploit the tournament's rules."

I tried to think through the implications of what he was saying. "Well, it's not a *terrible* plan but it's still like those fighting video games where everyone is evenly distributed power wise despite the fact some characters should be objectively impossible for others to beat. People can come up with excuses for how the underdog can achieve an upset but it's stupid rather than cool."

Cindy leaned up against the force field holding her in place. "Psst, Gary, isn't that what we're doing?"

"Shut up!" I snapped back. "This is completely different!"

Jane covered her face. "Oh God, the fate of the universe is in the hands of the world's biggest dork."

"Not world's biggest," I said, pausing. "Maybe third or fourth but I'll never be the world's biggest as long as Basement Dweller Man and Nerdy Jewish Guy exist."

That was when Cassius fired a blast of energy from his sword, which I barely turned insubstantial fast enough to avoid. "Hey! You could hurt someone doing that!"

"That's the idea," Cassius said, sighing. "It's set on stun but I am fully capable of killing you if it comes to that. Regardless of the consequences."

"The consequences being we kill your ass immediately afterward," Mandy growled, narrowing her eyes. "I like you, Cassius, but you're not going to be able to hurt my husband even if he's an incredibly flawed individual who'd rather be married to one of the good guys!"

"That is not true!" I snapped.

Mandy lowered her eyes. "I can hear the truth in your voice. You hate the undead and mourn the Mandy I never was."

"Get your hearing adjusted!" I snapped, perhaps not taking the ideal path to dealing with her.

Cassius looked at the shield. "The Century Box has taken control over the Castle of Ultimate Sorrow's interior workings. You'll be kept harmless in this location while my crew keeps Entropicus' cheating bastards busy. Every one of them is willing to make sacrifices to achieve our goal."

I stared at him. "You want the wish, no matter the cost."

"Correction," Cassius said. "I want the orbs."

"It's always about men and their balls," Cindy said.

Jane and Mandy nodded.

G rolled his eyes.

"What do you want to wish for?" I asked, having decided against my reboot plan. Unfortunately, that meant I had no idea what I wanted.

"My planet back," Cassius said, simply.

I blinked. "You got Alderaaned?"

Cassius frowned as if offended by my comparison. "Yes. Yes, I was. My wife, my people, and my comrades in arms were all killed in a war across the cosmos. With my wish, I'm going to return them to life. No, I'm going to wish the war that killed them never happened."

"Good wish," I said, not joking. "I'm not sure how to phrase my wishing since wishing for more wishes seems like it'd fail and if I wished for unlimited power, I'll probably end up trapped in a genie bottle."

"You're referencing something I don't get," Cassius said.

"So, no *Aladdin* in the future but *Star Wars* is alive and well?" I asked. "I can live with that."

"Don't make me destroy you," Cassius said, lifting his sword and approaching in a very Darth Vader-esque fashion.

"You're not going to destroy me," I said, completely confident in my conclusions.

I hadn't had a chance to talk to Cassius but I actually remembered him now. There had been a story Gabrielle once related about how the Texas Guardians had fallen into a space age world where magic and psychic abilities didn't exist. The story had helped inspire the crappy SyFy channel movies I'd seen as the historical comic book publishers were shills who'd do tales about anything that smacked of superhero "truth." One quality that had been demonstrated by the Cassius of those stories was the fact he was a man of his word. The one man who actually had a code of honor in a universe that considered those things ridiculous and stupid. Because, well, codes of honor were ridiculous and stupid. I'd rather be good than honorable. I'd also rather *win* than be honorable.

"Surrender and stay alive," Cassius said, his sword held in a perfectly formed fighting stance.

"If you wanted me to surrender and were really committed then you would have already won," I said, rolling my eyes. "But you're too nice a guy."

"Excuse me?" Cassius said, pausing a few steps away.

"Listen, if you really wanted to get me to surrender then you'd just use the force fields imprisoning my friends against me," I said, pointing to them. "I'd surrender to avoid you crushing them into paste."

"Gary, what are you doing?" Cindy asked, looking at me.

"Stop helping!" Jane said.

Mandy, however, just smiled.

Cassius stared. "This is a very peculiar strategy."

"It's like the easiest way to get superheroes to back down and the one thing that I won't do," I said, throwing my hands out. "You're a soldier and strike me as a fairly honorable sort, despite the fact you tried to nick the orbs without winning the tournament. So, you can't threaten my loved ones and you have only a small chance of actually beating me."

"Wow," Jane said, staring. "This is the worst plan I have ever heard and we started with your boyfriend defeating the Dark Lord."

"Husband," Mandy said. "For now."

"Eh, you're only married to him until death," Cindy said. "Afterward, I suggest asking out Aquarius. He's pretty awesome despite his 'talk to fish' power."

"Etu, Cindy?" I asked.

Cindy put her hands over her heart. "I love you Gary, truly, but there's a reason I keep your will updated to include me as well as Leia. It's only a matter of time."

"I like my chances," Cassius said, advancing. "Say a prayer to what god you worship."

"Or," I said, taking note my plan wasn't quite working as well as I'd hoped. "You can join Team Merciless and then when I win the tournament, we proceed to bring your world back on the ten page document I'm going to have my lawyers go over before making a wish on. All I need to do is make it a run-on sentence so I can wish for everything I could possibly want or just wish for everything on my list."

Cassius stopped. "Do you think that would work?"

"Yes," I lied, offering my hand. "What do you say?"

"I don't want to hurt anyone else in my life," Cassius said, looking down. "I've killed far too many over the years."

"Thanks," I said, walking forward then blasting him with my fire powers. "Sudden but inevitable betrayal!"

"What the hell, Gary!?" Mandy asked.

"Villain!" I said, chuckling.

That was when Cassius got up, unharmed, and charged. I turned insubstantial but a glowing field encircled his proton sword and caused it to pass through my flesh anyway. I was impaled through the back and started to bleed out onto his arms.

"Ah, dammit," I muttered.

CHAPTER EIGHTEEN

WHERE I DON'T DIE
BECAUSE THIS IS MY STORY

Well, I wasn't dead. That was a good sign. Mind you, I had earlier boasted about not being afraid of death. It wasn't true. I think everyone who says they're not afraid of death is lying, even if they had proof positive it wasn't something to be afraid of like I did.

For example, I could have just been hallucinating Death during our frequent encounters or it might have been a sufficiently advanced alien taking advantage of my desire to see a Grim Reaper who could usher the souls of the dead to distant shores where they might be cared for. Sort of like some near-death experiences were actual visions of the other side and others were dreams you had while high on anesthesia.

The truth was, though, I didn't want to die. I had lived a life that was full of amazing moments but they'd mostly happened in the last few years. Dying here, at Cassius' hand, seemed to be something of an anti-climax to it all but I supposed that was to be expected. Death was rarely someone who actually took you when you wanted her to.

The Nightwalker had died of a heart attack fighting three muggers after defeating everything from Great Beasts to the Laughing Wizard. Ultragod had died at the hands of Merciful, a man who only managed to shoot him with an ultranium bullet because of our dubious friendship. Guinevere, Stephen, and Diabloman didn't deserve to be killed as signs Entropicus wasn't to be screwed around with.

In fact, I had an uncle I'd never met named Jerry Karkofsky. He had been my father's older brother. Jerry had been the golden boy of my father's family and a United States Marine. Both my father and he had signed up to fight in the Second Vietnam War not out of a desire to be heroes but just because they'd thought it was their patriotic duty. There had been pictures of Jerry on our mantelpiece, in my father's study, and I'd grown up hearing plenty of stories about the guy. He'd been a great football player, a straight A student, a ladies man, and apparently knew how to play guitar.

However, none of these stories had ever involved the war where my father had distinguished himself. I'd found out, one night, when dad had been loaded after a failed parole hearing for my brother Keith (he'd broken out of prison with the help of the Nefarious Nine). Jerry had died during one of his first patrols, killed by friendly fire, because the guy fighting beside him had panicked and opened fire on one of their fellow Marine groups approaching. All of Jerry's potential had vanished in a moment and my father had learned the lesson "heroes" rarely got to be rewarded for their bravery because it was the survivors who wrote the tales of them. At the end of every battle were ignominious endings to what had once been living stories of people who someone, somewhere loved.

As I lay there, a huge hole in my chest from where Cassius stabbed me, I found myself realizing this kind of reminiscing was probably going to get me killed. Why did I always get philosophical whenever I was close to death? Dammit, I needed to be actively trying not to die during those times!

Summoning my remaining breath, I shouted, "Listen, jackass, I haven't accepted your challenge and the tournament is over so killing me doesn't help!"

I had no idea if that was true but I imagined if I died here then Entropicus wouldn't mind. As arbitrator of the tournament, he probably would judge me a forfeit and declare himself the winner by default. That was the benefit of being the guy who made the rules, you could usually break them with impunity and Entropicus had repeatedly proven himself to be a cheating bastard.

"I'm actually trying to heal you," Cassius said, lifting his Century Box. "I don't want you dead, Gary, I just want to save billions."

He then, reluctantly, pulled out the sword and used the Century Box to seal up the wound. Century Boxes were things that had shown up repeatedly in the conflict between Entropicus, Abaddon, and the Earth. They were apparently tools from the realm of the Ultranians, people who worshiped the Ultraforce, and could do just about anything related to matter as well as energy manipulation. Within reason. The Century Boxes had many limitations but what they were was a mystery to me. They were sort of like *Star Trek* technology in that they could reverse your D.N.A from being an iguana but apparently not cure blindness.

In seconds, I was alright again. "Thank you, man, I appreciate that."

"You're wel—" Cassius started to say before I punched him in the face. It was like punching a brick wall. Apparently, humans in the future made extensive use of either bio-engineering or cybernetics and that was cheating.

Cassius was about to rebuke me when I grabbed his sword and started swinging it around at him. I managed to climb to my feet and continued to take swings at him while he moved back and forth.

"Oh for God's sakes," Cassius muttered as I ineffectually tried to assault him with a weapon I'd never used before. "Wait, is this a challenge?"

"No, it's an attempted murder!" I said, swinging again.

Cassius sidestepped one of the attacks and grabbed the sword before sheathing it. "No, because if you were doing that, you'd use your powers against me."

"That and I like swinging around lightsaber-esque weapons," I said, frowning. "Listen, who put you up to this insane scheme since it is clear your heart is not in it. You only stabbed me because I attacked you."

"Why did you do that again?" Cassius asked. "I thought we had a deal."

"Villain!"

Cassius' expression told me he didn't find my statement to be the least bit funny. "I grew up on a world ruled by a fascist dictatorship and genetically-engineered nobility. The whole idea of playing a pantomime villain for laughs isn't really amusing to me."

"This is the world you want to bring back?"

Cassius shrugged. "Not the dictators but the people under them."

I could understand that. "The offer is still on the table but only if you tell me who gave you the Century Box."

My question was answered by the wall to the castle being smashed down before Guinevere, alive and unstoned, was smashed through it by Gabrielle. The two of them were having an old fashioned, knockdown, drag out fight between superheroes that used to be common. That was back when superheroes were actually friends, ironically, and yet still always seemed to end up having throwdowns. Now, ironically, they mostly just scowled at each other since it seemed no heroes really liked each other anymore.

"Her," Cassius said, pointing to the dueling women.

"Guinevere!" I shouted, pointing at her. "I know you don't like me but this is just low! How could you frigging set up an attempt to take my place in the tournament."

"You witch!" Mandy shouted.

"Actually, no, I meant Ultragoddess," Cassius said, pointing at her.

"Wait, what?" I said, doing a double take.

"Run away, Gary! She's gone *Fatal Attraction!*" Cindy shouted. "If she can't have you, no one can!"

Guinevere looked over at Cindy in sheer confusion before Gabrielle knocked her across the room into the wall, effectively ending the fight. "It's not like that Gary. I gave Cassius the Century Box with explicit instructions to goad you into a fight so you could be defeated and your place usurped."

"That's what we just said!" I said.

"But that you weren't to be harmed!" Gabrielle said, wrapping Cassius up in glowing fist and squeezing him. "I was explicitly clear about that."

"Why the hell would you do that?" I asked, genuinely stunned she'd betray me like that.

"Because she doesn't want the father of her child to be killed," Cassius said, pausing. "Because Entropicus cannot be defeated by you."

"And you think you have the ability? That is some brass balls there, Star Lord," Jane said, shaking her head.

"Star Count," Cassius corrected. "That's the name they've started referring to me as."

"Say one lightsaber, ah-ah, two lightsabers, ah-ah," Cindy said in an exaggerated Transylvanian voice.

"No," Cassius said, struggling against the glowing fingers of his prison.

"I have a plan," Gabrielle said, looking at me. "But yes, Cassius is expendable, while you're not."

I looked over at Cassius. "Are you okay with that?"

"There is a word for a soldier who doesn't prepare himself for death in the line of duty," Cassius said, looking over at me with a stone cold empty expression. "Fool."

"And what about her?" I asked, pointing at Guinevere. "You stayed dead for like fifteen minutes!"

Guinevere took a deep breath and picked herself up off the ground. "Knowing the entire world was at stake, I fought my way out of Arawn the Celtic God of Death's realm in order to rejoin this group. I then decided I needed to make sure Gabrielle didn't make a terrible mistake by threatening the multiverse's best hope for victory."

"Thank you," I said, touched.

"I meant herself," Guinevere said. "Since Entropicus is going to win the tournament, that means we need to have a backup plan involving the entire Society moving against him before he can make his wish."

I sighed. "Man, no one believes in me, do they?"

"I believe in you, Gary," Jane said, looking at me with sincere faith in her eyes. "Like, all of these people are from your universe so that means this has to be your comic. If it was my comic, it'd be littered with my supporting cast."

"Thanks, I think," I said, looking at her. "I'm totally buying you a salt lick after this."

"That's racist," Jane said. "Also, accepted."

"Well, I have a decent chance against him," I said, crossing my arms.

"You just got stabbed by Cassius," Gabrielle said. "That is not a good sign since the whole point of my replacing him with you is that he'd be underestimated."

I walked over to Cassius and stole his Century Box, causing his futuristic gear to vanish before attaching it to my shoulder, causing the Reaper's Cloak to gain a bunch of blue Tron lines as I felt the Ultraworld technology alter my body to be the best version of itself. I could feel years of fast food, general neglect, and drinking vanish along with the micro-polyps from living in Falconcrest City's hellhole. Honestly, it was amazing I looked as good as I did despite all that. The Century Box also increased my magical output by several manifolds, providing me genuine invulnerability and flight to go along with my fire as well as ice powers. I could even turn insubstantial enough to avoid magical attacks like the kind that normally could stab me. I was powerful now.

An A-lister.

"Okay, good," I said, crackling some electricity between my fingers to test my abilities out. So far, so good. I still needed a few more edges, though. "New plan. Mandy, I need you to give me over Caliburn."

"Like hell," Guinevere said.

"I'm going to also need to loot your picnic basket of holding, Cindy."

"Double hell!" Cindy said. "You can't just take my gadgets! We've got a whole theme you'd be interrupting!"

"Trinkets aren't going to be able to defeat Entropicus, Gary," Gabrielle said, looking over at me. "My father lost a number of battles against him and even his victories were never conclusion. He is perhaps the ultimate threat to the universe."

"The multiverse, actually, but Entropicus can't use his powers against me," I said, looking between them. "Death obviously had a plan to defeat him so she made it so the two of us are going to evenly matched when we confront one another."

"Except he's a god of evil and can punch through planets," Guinevere said. "Every time the Society has conclusively beaten him, it's turned out just to be one of his avatars. The real thing may have not even have been encountered."

"I have a way around that too," I lied.

"I can sense when people lie to me," Guinevere said.

I shrugged. "Well, the worst thing that could happen to me is I die and that was your plan anyway."

Guinevere paused. "You raise a very good point."

"You know, I totally regret saying you had the best movie of the Society of Superheroes release," Cindy said, looking at Guinevere. "The Shadow Seven movie was much better and not just because I was in it."

"Please, you were the only good thing in that movie," Mandy said.

"Best film where I wore clothes the entire time," Cindy said.

"I object to that statement," I said.

G shook his head. "I'm sorry, I'm too dazzled by the fact I'm seeing all of this happening to offer any advice. I will say that I think you should screw the tournament and try to take out Entropicus before it ends, though. If he wins then it's the end of everything, so almost anything is justified to get it done."

"Ah, but if the tournament is derailed then he's almost certainly going to win by default," I said, pausing. "That is probably why he did it in the first place. No, we must trust in Death's plan."

"You mean the Death who made him a god in the first place?" Cindy pointed out.

Dammit, I hated logic. "I was going to go with the Death who could take him out at any time anyway so yeah. Stupid mysterious ways of gods."

Gabrielle put down Cassius then looked at me. "Gary, I don't want to risk your life on this."

"I think we're a little past that," I said, pausing. "Besides, even if Entropicus does destroy everything and everyone then we'll just have to rebuild afterward."

"That's....moronic," Guinevere said.

"It's hope, that Carrie Fisher gave us," I said, lowering my hood and putting my hand over my heart. "Yo, Century Box, lower the force shields on my family."

"Affirmative," a metallic reverberating voice said.

They did.

Mandy charged at Cassius before stopping just short of ripping his head off, hands outstretched. Her eyes were blood red and her fingernails had extended into claws. Cassius didn't flinch or even try to resist. He was a man who didn't care whether he lived or died.

"Well," I said, walking toward Gabrielle. "I really should be getting going to my match with Entropicus but I need to talk to you first. In private."

Gabrielle lowered her head. "Alright."

"Thank you."

I had no idea what I was going to say during this conversation.

CHAPTER NINETEEN

THE TALK OF TALKS

I followed Gabrielle into one of the alcoves of the castle, finding no sign of any inhabitants or furniture. Really, the place felt more like the inside of a circuit board than it did an actual building. Still, the two of us ended up in a chamber that had its own running river that led out to the rest of the island.

Gabrielle walked over to the edge and leaned over to put her feet in it, causing her boots to dematerialize. "So you want to reboot the universe?"

"You heard about that?"

"Ultra-hearing," Gabrielle said, tapping her left ear.

"Ah," I said, walking over and putting my feet in the water as well. It was freezing cold but surprisingly invigorating.

"You realize that's not far from what Merciful wanted to do, right?" I asked.

I closed my eyes. "I think that's what everyone wants to do on some level. Seeing Keith again, the way he was, and watching heroes die makes me wonder if this world is worth saving."

"It's not about the world today, it's about the world to come," Gabrielle said, glancing at me. "My father always used to say that."

"He would have liked my dad," I said, smiling, "They were both crusty old farts with too much patriotism and belief in a better tomorrow."

There was a significant pause.

Gabrielle took a deep breath. "Gary, are *you* happy?"

I took a deep breath. "Yes."

"I see," Gabrielle said.

I stared forward. "Every day, I'm happier about my daughter being alive and making sure she's safe as well as loved. Even now, having lost Cloak and Diabloman, I'm not afraid because she's there."

"What about Mandy and Cindy?" Gabrielle asked.

I didn't answer for a time. "Mandy isn't happy."

"She's not?" Gabrielle asked.

"No," I said, looking down at the water rushing over my feet. "Not since she got her soul back. It was fine when we had an opponent to fight and direct our anger against. That's not been the case since and I can feel her chomping at the bit. Honestly, she spends a few days at a time at the mansion while she's out being a vampire, spy, or vigilante."

Mandy spent most of her time hunting, going on missions, or training. It was something deeper than her dislike of Diabloman. The few times Mandy opened up to me, it was like she was holding back something terrible and couldn't spit it out. I could tell Mandy was in love with me, that she'd do almost anything for me but it was like she'd had to fall in love with me all over again. Honestly, the happiest the two of us had ever been was when we were forced to live together as a brainwashed 1950s couple in Merciful's prison and she didn't have to be honest with me.

"Love isn't easy," Gabrielle said. "She fought a war in the future for you."

"Maybe. There's a lot about her story that changes with each conversation. I'm not saying she's lying but I wonder if she remembers it accurately. Time has been changed many times in the past and maybe that's in effect now." There was also something else, something I couldn't quite put my finger on, but which had become increasingly clear the more time we spent together outside of Merciful's brainwashed prison.

"You'll do anything for her. I know you will." I could tell Gabrielle was trying to convince herself of that.

"Perhaps." I paused. "Is that why you told me you didn't want to share?"

"That was selfish of me, Gary, and I apologize. I've been

selfish since being freed. When we first kissed back on New Avalon, I was reminded of what it was like to have a normal life and someone who loved me. I grew jealous of the happiness I saw in your home. Then I needed comfort and you were already sleeping with someone else. Two someone elses."

"Yeah." I grimaced, trying to figure out whether I felt guilt for being a supervillain and living by my own laws there. I didn't have anything against nontraditional couples but I'd loved Gabrielle first. She deserved better than to be caught up in this soap opera drama. "Cindy is my best friend with benefits."

Gabrielle grimaced. "Not a mental image I needed. She was my bestie in college too, if you remember."

"Yes I do, small universe syndrome writ large. She misses you too."

"How do you make it work?" Gabrielle asked.

"I don't think we do," I said, simply. "The thing about relationships, though, and this is speaking from a guy who has either been married for ten years or five or a few weeks is that you're not supposed to live for the good times but work through the bad."

"And sometimes that isn't enough," Gabrielle said.

"No," I said, pausing. "Sometimes, it's not enough."

There was silence between us as both of us had done a pretty extensive job of avoiding the main subject to our conversation.

"So, is the baby mine?" I asked. It wasn't a question I wanted to ask but it had to be discussed and discussed openly.

Gabrielle closed her eyes. "I don't know. It's either yours or the Gary of Opposite Earth."

I paused. "You slept with my doppelganger from the world I created? Really?"

Gabrielle shrugged. "He reminded me of someone I knew."

"So, genetically, the kid is my child or my nephew via identical twin?" I asked.

Gabrielle looked at me with her big beautiful brown eyes. "Does that make a difference?"

I didn't want to be honest here because honest was complicated, messy, and would possibly lead down to a road I didn't want to go. "No, because it wouldn't matter if the child was General Asmodeus' or President Omega's."

"Have I been impregnated against my will or am I a whore for supervillains in this scenario?"

"Okay, bad examples."

"You think?"

I paused. "What I mean to say is, Gabrielle, you're my family and always will be. I love you, I always will, but I'm not going to break up my family. I wouldn't be the person you cared for if I would do that but that doesn't mean you can't turn to me, that I won't always be in your life, and that I won't be a loving father to our child if you will let me be. You'll never be alone, Gabrielle, because I'd rather be your hero than the world's villain."

"Thank you, Gary," Gabrielle said, reaching over and squeezing my hand.

Then we had sex.

"Dammit," I muttered, lying naked on the ground with an equally unclad Gabrielle wrapping her arms around me. "That was not what I was going for."

"Yeah, I got the impression it was a 'let's be friends' speech but you overdid it with the sincerity." Gabrielle kissed me on the cheek. "You have the problem of being extremely endearing while also having poor impulse control."

"Yeah."

"I don't want to be anyone's second," Gabrielle said, leaning her head on my chest. "On the other hand, feelings aren't ones we can control. I don't know where this is going, whether this is a mistake, or if I'm endangering either of us but it feels nice right now."

"Really, guys? Now is not the time to Netflix and chill," Jane said, as she walked in on the alcove with her hand over her eyes. "Especially when there's no Netflix."

"I wish I'd known this was going on," G said, walking in. "I would have asked Jane to spend some time with me in the alcove."

Gabrielle created a modesty curtain around us before standing up to start getting dressed again. "Are your friends always this rude?"

"I've literally known them for a day," I said, pausing. "Albeit, one of them may be my opposite universe clone as well as Lara Croft."

"I actually just programmed that in to the tournament app along with a bunch of other nonsense," G admitted. "One of the benefits of having a cybernetic brain that can more or less hack anything because it doesn't obey the normal laws of computing."

"What?" Jane said. "Did you touch the rules?"

"No," G said. "I'm not an idiot. That could endanger you."

I ran around the modesty curtain. "Wait, your app has the rules of the tournament?"

"Gah!" Jane said, turning around. "I saw your family jewels."

I stared at her, annoyed. "You're welcome."

I snapped my fingers and once more was attired in the Reaper's Cloak. "Still, I need your cellphone."

Jane turned around. "Wait, are you always naked underneath there?"

"Sometimes," I said, adjusting the fabric. "It's very flexible attire, magic."

Jane tossed her phone over her shoulder. "The password is 1-2-3-4."

I opened my mouth in shock. "We have the same password?"

"Wow, it's like you're a human shaped Bugs Bunny," G said, sticking his hands in his pockets.

I entered Jane's password and started looking over all of the tournament's rules. There was a lot of legalese and wiggle room designed to give the arbiter disgusting amounts of power. It was also a trap because the arbiter *had* to finish the tournament once it started. He also couldn't do any damage to anyone unless they violated the rules or challenged him. In other words, there was a reason why he'd tolerated my disrespect with barely disguised contempt—because he knew I'd eventually have to face him. Not because I had a special way to defeat him. No, I had to believe I had a trump card and I hadn't just been sent here to die so Death could witness the end of everything. That wasn't her style.

"Okay, I think I see a couple of loopholes," I said, thinking about various plans that would make sure my battle against

Entropicus didn't end with him blasting me with his eyes and winning. Indeed, a part of me wondered if the reason Entropicus had arranged all of this wasn't just because I was the wild card in all this and he could kill me easily but as a deliberate slight against Death. The only way to strike at a being who was literally second only to God was to eradicate Death as a concept by killing everyone everywhere for all tim

e and to slay her new favorite to do it.

"Gary, your wife is here," Jane said, speaking up. "She's with Fetish Girl and Stabman."

"No, I don't think they were invited to the tournament," I said, looking confused.

"Wow, this is a terrible world," Jane muttered. "Superheroes or not."

I looked up to see Mandy, Cassius, and Cindy entering the room. Mandy was looking worse for wear with her eyes bright red as well as her skin less pale than corpse-like with blue veins visible across her skin. Her teeth were elongated completely while her fingernails had decayed into claws.

"Wow, your wife is going full Mileena," Jane asked. "You'd still hit that, though, right?"

"Jane, I really think we may need to limit our team ups," I said, shaking my head. "There's really only so much sass one universe can take."

Honestly, I wasn't sure what to say to Mandy now or do. I wasn't going to deny what happened, futile as that would be, but would accept whatever consequences had happened. If she wanted to leave me then that was understandable. There was something broken in our relationship and we had to confront that. The worst part was I couldn't say I was sorry because I wasn't. I did love Gabrielle and didn't regret we'd made love. Yeah, some superhero I'd turned out to be.

"Entropicus' power is at its zenith," Mandy said, clutching her fists together. "It's hard to resist the darkness that accompanies it."

"Ah," I said, staring at her. "Which probably isn't helped too much by—"

"You passing the salami to Ultragoddess while we're on

a mission? No! No it's not," Cindy said. "You didn't even ask permission, which is a basic requirement of any proper master-slave relationship!"

"Am I the—"

"You're the slave," Cindy said.

"Right," I said.

Mandy gave a gallows' laugh, which didn't sound remotely human. "Gary has always loved too much, too freely. He and Gabrielle are always drawn together like flames and a moth."

"Mandy—" Cindy started to say.

"I don't need your sympathy," Mandy said. "Besides, it was never going to last. The truth was always going to come out."

"What truth?" Cindy asked.

Mandy, however, didn't respond. "Let's just focus on getting this done."

"Alright," I said, knowing that was probably for the best.

"That was a really shitty thing to do to Mandy," Jane said, her voice echoing in my mind.

"Wait, what?" I thought back. *"You're a telepathic deer?"*

"More like a shaman," Jane thought back to me. *"But yeah. I've got most psychic powers as a basic ability and have been reading everyone's surface thoughts. Still, my point stands."*

"Yes, it was," I said back, projecting my thoughts. I was no stranger to telepathic contact.

"So why did you do it? I assume it has to do with the fact she's been cheating on you for months."

"It's not cheating if I don't object."

"That's the broken-down spouse defense," Jane said. *"I am sensing some guilt here, though."*

"I'm the reason why Mandy was killed, I'm the reason she became a vampire, and I'm the reason why she's since become a murder-happy vigilante and assassin."

"That's a lot of responsibility to take on your shoulders versus the fact you banged your ex-girlfriend ten feet from her—which is most definitely your fault. What is the central problem between you two now?"

"*I worry my wife is evil now.*"

Jane blinked. "*That is a big deal. It still doesn't excuse what you did, though.*"

"*No, it doesn't,*" I replied, feeling immense guilt. "*I fear that I've ruined her.*"

"*Women make their own choices, Gary.*"

"*Yeah and the Mandy I knew would never be evil,*" I said, pausing. My eyes then widened.

"Gary?" Jane asked.

I looked at Mandy then back at Jane. "Not a word."

"Gary and I have a special connection," Gabrielle said, stepping out in her costume. "It just got the better of us."

"Yes, the special connection called being outrageously hot but still knocked up," Cindy said, then pointed at Gabrielle. "Shame!"

"Shame for which?" Gabrielle asked.

"Shame!" Cindy said. "Also, since I'm sleeping with Gary as well, I need to know your last six months of partners. If there's any extraterrestrials, we're going to have to have you tested since everyone knows they're all carriers of virulent STDs."

"That's xenophobic," Cassius said, looking bored. "Also, a sensible precaution."

"What are the aliens in your world like?" Jane asked.

"Giant slimes and tentacled things generally," Cassius said. "I, thankfully, don't have any inclinations in that area. I did know a man at the academy, though, who—"

That was when Guinevere ran in, carrying Caliburn. It was soaked in blood. "Entropicus' forces have started invading the Earth. The Hellazons attacked me and informed me of this."

I looked over at her. "Cute. He's trying to distract us while we fight."

"It's working," Gabrielle said, looking at me. "I should go out and help since I've already been eliminated."

I took a deep breath. "No."

"No?" Gabrielle asked, doing a double take.

"I know how to beat Entropicus," I said, looking at every one present. "It's going to require everyone's help, though."

"Our help?" Jane asked.

"Actually, more like all of your powers." I gave one more look at Mandy then focused on taking down Entropicus.

Then I decided my 'wife' and I would need to have a very long talk.

CHAPTER TWENTY

WHERE I EXPLAIN MY PLAN TO EVERYONE

I explained my plan to everyone.

"I was wrong," Mandy said, looking at me as her eyes lost some of their red glow and became merely menacing. "This is your worst idea ever."

"All of our powers combined? That's your plan?" Jane said, covering her face. "I mean, you don't even have a bunch of transforming robots to join together."

"We had those on my planet," Cassius said, snorting in derision. "They're militarily impractical."

"Can you even do that?" Jane asked.

"Yes," I said, sighing. "The benefit of everyone's powers here being magical in nature except Guinevere and the Ultra-Force is basically the Force so it's magical adjacent."

I was ignoring G's powers being cybernetic but that was the benefit of sorcery in that it was flexible. I was more interested in his skills, too, since I wasn't exactly a trained fighter. I'd learned everything I knew about fighting from getting beaten up by heroes.

"If you think gravity or consciousness is magical," Guinevere muttered. "I don't think you actually understand what you're suggesting."

I took a deep breath. "Listen, the big problem that we have is the fact Entropicus is more powerful than me."

"Really?" Guinevere said, looking at me. "You don't say."

I pointed at her. "You don't get to be sarcastic. We're already dividing that role on the team like five or six ways."

"We're a team now?" Guinevere asked.

"Team Merciless!" I said, pointing at her.

"We're not called that," Guinevere said.

"We really are," Jane said. "He called dibs."

"Yes, Gary, we know he's more powerful than you," Gabrielle said.

"Well, he won't be if I have a bunch of superpowers that he doesn't have while he can't use his powers against me," I said.

"Why can't he use his powers against you?" Guinevere asked.

"Because Gary's dead brother, reanimated by the very guy we're trying to kill, told him the secret weakness of said aforementioned guy we're trying to kill despite the fact he's a mindless slave," Jane said, crossing her arms. "Everybody got that?"

"Well, when you put it like that then it sounds stupid," I said, deliberately exaggerating my voice.

Mandy licked her fangs with her tongue. "So, you want to somehow gain our powers but don't want to become a vampire."

I looked at Ultragoddess. "In simple terms, my plan is to transfer the power of the Ultra-Force to me, temporarily, as well as infuse myself with the magic of Guinevere's fae-based magic through Caliburn. That will give me a source for all of my Reaper's Cloak abilities while not actually drawing from Death. I will also be able to draw on the rest of your abilities through Jane's telepathy once I set up a biometric link through the Century Box. I'll go from zero to hero in an instant."

"So, our plan rests on the cop out ending to Season Four of *Buffy the Vampire Slayer.*" Jane said.

There was a pregnant pause as no one responded.

"Oh come on, that is not the most obscure reference anyone here has made in the last *ten minutes* let alone ever!" Jane snapped, putting her hands on her hips.

"I'm sorry, I hated everything after Season 3 with the exception of Tara and the musical," I said.

"Isn't this against the rules?" Cindy asked, raising a finger in protest. "You know, the rules that got Guinevere killed for about an hour? Which, by the way, if you can show me how to come back from, I would totally love to learn."

"No," Guinevere said, not even bothering to turn to face her.

"It's within the rules to prep yourself pretty much how you see fit," I said, looking at her. "The only thing you can't do is do so in such a way as that it makes it impossible for the other subject to win."

"So, while we're cheating, Entropicus is going to be cheating too," Jane said.

"Yes," I said. "Because you know, *he's been cheating this entire time.*"

"I don't know," Gabrielle looked down at the ground. "Humanity's defenses have been severely compromised in the past few years."

"Because almost all of its heroes are dead," Jane said, nodding. "Yeah, we got that."

"Not cool, Jane," I said. "Yeah, we're at a severe disadvantage."

"I'm the heaviest hitter Earth has and is Guinevere is the immediate runner up," Gabrielle continued.

"You just keep telling yourself that, Gabby," Guinevere said, smiling. It was the first smile I'd seen on her face since Ultragod died.

"If Earth is being invaded by Entropicus then there may not be a planet to return to when this is done," Guinevere said. "We can't just do nothing."

"We have to trust that Earth will produce the heroes necessary to repulse an invasion," I said, putting my hand on my chest. "That the good on the Earth will rise up to defeat the bad and that our belief the Earth can't function without its legendary heroes is wrong. Because everyone has the potential to be a hero."

Moments passed.

"Yeah, no," Cindy said. "Got any other ideas?"

"Fair enough, I didn't believe it either." I shrugged and pulled out Jane's cellphone. "I'm going to text the Squadron of Superheroes on Opposite Earth and ask them for help. They have an abundance of goodies on that world."

Opposite Earth had an exact set of duplicates for Ultragod,

the Nightwalker, Guinevere, Gold Medalist, and a bunch of other classic heroes despite the fact it ostensibly was set in our present times. It was one of the reasons why I *hadn't* visited the world since I'd more or less created it with a bunch of stolen magic.

I couldn't go to a world where so many lost and familiar friends were still alive. I'd lost the urge the moment I'd done a phone book check (yes, they still had phonebooks) to note my brother and dad were still alive on that world. Still, I had connections there since I'd sold the internet, solar power, Velcro, and the microwave to the planet.

"Cellphone reception reaches other planets now? Wow, people actually get their monthly payment's worth here," Jane said.

"I'm sending it through the Century Box, which can do anything but what it can't," I said.

"Uh-huh," Jane said. "Well, that's uninformative."

"Say hi to Opposite Gary for me," Gabrielle said.

I looked up from my text.

"Or not," Gabrielle said.

"This settles all of my objections to attacking Entropicus," Guinevere said, shaking a fist in my direction. "If you wish to kill a dragon then you must strike at its head."

"Aren't you supposed to go after the soft underbelly?" Jane asked.

"Real life is not *The Hobbit*," Guinevere said. "Saint George knew better. He was a true Englishman."

"Actually, Saint George killed the dragon by poisoning it with a sheep and then spearing it. He also was a Byzantine knight if he ever existed," I said, correcting her. "Also, screw dragons."

"I like dragons," Jane muttered.

I used to love flying breathing reptiles but now I hated them. It even affected my love for Game of Thrones. I'd fought a dragon a few years (?) back when Falconcrest City had been overrun by a zombie horde. It had been a dragon, or at least a wizard transformed into a dragon, which had killed Mandy and forced me to resurrect her as an undead monster. It was still the worst memory of my life and what popped up whenever the Halloween Man used his Scare Gas on me.

Guinevere snorted. "Maybe *your* Saint George was Byzantine but not mine."

Mandy was about to respond when she barreled over and felt her stomach. "The castle is changing."

"Wait, what?" I asked.

Almost immediately, a swirling portal appeared in the middle of the chamber that opened to reveal a hideous industrial hellscape that belched fire as well as smoke into an empty void. I sensed an immense amount of despair radiate off the buildings, accompanied by the feel of screaming souls that were bonded to the machinery. I knew, in an instant, it was Abaddon the capital of Entropicus' multi-dimensional empire. It was also where the final bout was supposed to take place.

"Oh come on!" I snapped, looking at the portal. "He said it was supposed to be in this castle."

"The Castle of Ultimate Sorrow is located on Abaddon as well as whatever dimension it is bonded with," Guinevere said, as if I was an idiot. "This was all a trick to make you accept a battle on Entropicus' home turf."

"I would have accepted anyway," I said.

"Then you're an idiot," Guinevere said.

"Duh," I said, not denying it. "But I'm also a savant at bullshitting, lying, and *Dance Dance Revolution*."

"He's lying, he sucks at that game," Cindy said.

"The others are definitely true, though," Gabrielle said. "Are you sure you don't want me to substitute for you?"

I looked at her. "You were willing to go to incredible lengths to keep me from fighting, why should I feel the same?"

"Grr," Mandy made noises akin to a wolf.

"I'm feeling some hypocrisy here," Cindy said, frowning. "I'm just saying."

Mandy's stare could have melted steel.

"Maybe she's just feeling a bit peckish," Jane said, elbowing me.

I ignored her. "So, do I have everyone's permission to steal their powers in what any other supervillain would refuse to return because they're evil but I will because I'm Chaotic Neutral?"

"I don't think that alignment exists in 5th Edition," Jane said.

"You've actually upgraded?" I looked at her. "What is wrong with you?"

"Yes," Gabrielle said.

Guinevere grimaced. "I suppose we have no choice."

"Not sure how you're going to gain the power of cybernetics without multiple surgeries but whatever you think," G said.

"You can have my skill of being awesome," Cindy said.

"You need my skills because I don't think you otherwise know how to use a sword," Cassius said.

"The pointy end goes in the other guy," I said. "Which is from the Zorro movie as some of my fans online have indicated I don't give enough citation for the quotes I make."

"You have our support," Mandy said. "All of us. Goddess help us all."

"Thank you," I said, nodding before tapping the Century Box. "Can you do that?"

"AFFIRMATIVE," The Century Box replied.

"Good," I said. "Do it."

"Wait, you didn't check with it first?" Cindy asked.

My cloak turned a brilliant shade of gold and white as everyone else glowed. I felt my mind surge with knowledge of combat, combat styles, tactics, mystical knowledge, and everything relevant to Entropicus the Society of Superheroes knew. There was also the Ultra-Force, Jane's, and Guinevere's magic that merged into a single awesome singularity within me. Golden lightning crackled up and down my body.

"The power fills me. Yes, I feel the universe within me! I am... I am a part of the cosmos! Its energy flows... flows through me. Of what consequence are you now? This planet, these people - They are *nothing* to me - the universe is power, pure, unstoppable *power* ...and I am that force, I am that power!"

G leaned over to whisper to Jane. "Is he reciting Skeletor's lines from the crappy eighties live action *Masters of the Universe* movie?"

"You shut your mouth!" Cindy snapped, pointing at G. "That movie was awesome whenever it wasn't awful. It had Courtney Cox *and* Dolph Lundgren."

"KNEEL BEFORE YOUR MASTER!" I shouted, cackling.

Jane walked up to me and slapped me across the face.

I blinked a few times.

"We good?" Jane asked.

"Yes, I'm fine," I said, taking a deep breath. "Muhahhahahaha!"

Jane lifted her hand again.

I backed down and raised my arms up defensively. "The maniacal laugh is the last bit, I swear! Bwhahahah."

"Yeah, this was a great idea," Mandy muttered. "This is why I hate Chosen One plotlines. The least qualified, least talented, and least stable person is always the person who everything depends on."

"That's a terrible thing to say about your husband," Gabrielle said.

"Husband," Mandy muttered before chuckling. "Yeah, I suppose it is."

"I am a god!" I shouted, my voice echoing through the chamber.

Jane proceeded to kick me through the portal to Abaddon.

"Ahh!" I shouted as I felt all of my atoms forcibly relocated through time and space. I ended up slamming against the cold, hard stone of Abaddon. The air smelled of sulphur and industrial chemicals even as the aura of pure evil radiated out from every direction. Surrounding me was a coliseum as large as any in ancient Rome, full of cheering slaves from a million different species spread out across time.

Abaddon, itself, was the only thing remaining in the last moment before the universe's destruction, sort of like the Restaurant at the End of the Universe. Its people were from the worlds Entropicus had conquered or destroyed across uncounted millennium and every single one of the citizens was as nihilistic as their master. Supposedly, Ultragod had once scored a conclusive victory over Entropicus only to have his followers all band together to resurrect him. They wanted the universe's worst monster to rule them rather than be freed. All so they could be monsters to each other. It was like a planet of Objectivists. BA-ZING! Yeah, I'll be here all night.

I wasn't concerned about Entropicus' massive army of slaves, however. Though, the prospect of taking this world over was appealing—sort of like declaring yourself ruler of Space Mordor—I was more interested in their master. Entropicus was sitting in the center of the coliseum on top of an exaggerated twenty-foot-tall throne constructed out of laser rifles as well as energy cannons. It made me want to call George R.R. Martin and ask if he wanted to sue. Standing alongside the edges of the throne were the Hellazons.

The Hellazons were a dozen women who were once superheroes on their homeworlds. Women he'd defeated and then brainwashed into being his servants. They cast aside their original identities and started dressing in costumes that made them look like Goth MMA fighters. There was Lady Whip, the Blood Queen, Murderess, and others I didn't remember the names of. They had male counterparts but the Hellazons were far more famous for reasons relating to the fact most Superpedia writers were male. A few of them were sporting bloody wounds from Guinevere's sword and it was clear she'd managed to drive them back here.

At the top of the throne's steps was Entropicus, who was sitting with an amused expression on his face. The skeletal faced monster looked far bulkier and heavier on his home world, like if Arnold had the face of Satan. This was his reality, sculpted for the purposes of making himself stronger and I wouldn't have been surprised to discover his essence permeated every atom making up the hellscape.

The others exited out the portal behind me and took in the environment beyond.

Jane looked at the Hellazons. "So, if we lose, we're all going to become body-building Suicide Girls?"

"Only until Entropicus kills everyone and everything," I said. "Also, I didn't need that image in my head when I'm trying to concentrate."

"You don't have enough hot babes to keep your attention?"

"I'm not *collecting* them! They just sort of fall into my lap."

"Oh you poor baby," Jane said. "I'd feel sad for you if you weren't living in a world where literally every superperson is gorgeous."

"Yeah, well, the fact all realities are going to die if Entropicus wins is the price for that."

"I'm still not sure how that works or why Skullboy over there thinks it's desirable."

I really didn't think now was the time to make fun of Entropicus and if I was thinking that then it really wasn't the best time. "As the God of Death, he'll rule the afterlife of everyone as all the gods die from lack of living worship."

"Okay, that makes sense," Jane said.

"No, it really doesn't," I said.

When the last of my friends arrived, the portal closed behind them and I wondered if he was going to threaten my loved ones to make me throw the fight.

Instead, he just smiled. "Welcome, Merciless, to the end of everything!"

Well, he was confident.

CHAPTER TWENTY-ONE

WAR AGAINST THE GODS

"I love what you've done with the place," I said, looking around the coliseum. "Very Space Rome meets New Jersey." Entropicus' eyes bore into my soul. "Clever quips and disrespect will not save you, Gary Karkofsky. I have seen your entire history from birth until death. You act as if you are the hero in a grand adventure. That you will always land on your feet and the world will bend to your needs and victory will always be yours in the end. That is not this story, though."

"I think he's calling you a Gary Stu….err, Gary," Cindy said.

I pointed Caliburn at him, threateningly. "You don't know me, Auntie Puss, which I apologize for being a lame comeback but there's only so many variations on a guy with a skull for a head I can make. Any person who knows me knows I'm measured by my failures far more than I am by my successes. I get smacked around by superheroes, I lose my friends, and every time I save the city or world it's only after things have completely gone to hell. I am, in fact, actually, awful at this superhero and supervillain thing."

Jane leaned over to G. "Why are we trusting him with this again?"

"Search me," G said. "I am way out of my genre here. If we were going after international criminals or terrorists, then I'd be in charge but this is beyond me."

I ignored the two. "The thing, I've always had people I could lean on to carry me through the battles against the various bad guys I've faced over the years. First it was Cloak, then it was

Diabloman, and a half-dozen other super-talented people who I tricked into thinking I actually knew what the hell I was doing."

"Does that include us?" Cindy asked Mandy.

"Yes," Mandy said, looking at the Hellazons with shame and regret in her eyes.

"Super," Cindy said. "The world makes sense again."

"In fact, I don't know what I'm doing," I said, pointing at Entropicus. "It's complete and utter lunacy to have trusted me with the responsibility of defeating the Lord of Evil. The guy the Devil prays to. The Supreme High Dingy Doo of Damnation. The—"

"We get it, Gary," Gabrielle said.

"But tell me, Entropicus," I said, walking forward and pointing at him. "Do you think that makes me less dangerous or more dangerous?"

"Less," Entropicus said.

I paused. "Yeah, you got me there."

"I also know why you ramble, equivocate, and speak nonsense," Entropicus said, leaning his head over onto his hand with a bored expression on the remains of his face. "You think taunts and insults will buy you time as well as confuse your enemies. That it will give you a few extra seconds to attack or come up with solutions that will allow you and your companions to survive. You play the part of the fool and the court jester to hide you are an above-average, but not exceptional, tactician."

"That's...not entirely true."

Entropicus leaned forward. "However, I know the truth. The reason you have won so many times in the past is the fact you have *never* been the underdog. The weakling. The David versus the Goliath. The Reaper's Cloak has always provided you a vast array of flexible powers useful in virtually any situation you have found yourself. Your opponents have included zombies, powerless criminals, and yourself. You have never actually faced someone who wields power greater than yourself. Instead, you pretend to fight opponents stronger than you in order to disguise the fact you are a child plucking the wings off insects with the power of the gods."

"You're not wrong," I admitted. "I'm usually scared

shitless whenever I'm fighting the various people I encounter. This despite the fact I can shoot fire out of my hands and ice among other cool powers. Making *Star Wars* references is sort of my way of trying not to scream like a little girl whenever I'm encountering people like you."

"Hey, some little girls are tough!" Cindy said. "Like our daughter! Who, I point out has rescued you too."

"But if I'm a bully picking on those weaker than themselves, what are you?"

"A god," Entropicus said.

Dammit. That backfired. "Well, you're right. I am a stage magician with lovely assistants like G and Cassius here. Everything I do is sleight of hand. I'm not the Nightwalker or the Trenchcoat Magician who has a rabbit to pull out of his hat or pigeons up my sleeve for every occasion, though. I'm still going to win this fight, though."

"And why is that?"

"Because it'd be a pretty crappy ending otherwise."

Entropicus looked down. "Do you wish to know my story, Merciless, before you die?"

"I'd like to buy myself a few more minutes of not dying so, please."

Jane elbowed me for that line.

"What? It's true," I admitted.

Entropicus sat back in his chair, amused to once more have the floor. About the only weakness I'd been able to find in him so far was pride and I was going to try to exploit that for everything I could. Still, I was genuinely surprised by the next words that came out of his lips. "I am...was... Cain."

I blinked. "Excuse me?"

"The First Murderer. The Third Sinner," Entropicus said, repeating various titles. "The Marked One."

"Huh, I thought you were fictional," I said, genuinely stunned that was true.

"I am," Entropicus said, his voice full of disgust. "There was no Garden of Eden, Adam and Eve, or Paradise Lost. It was all the metaphor of your people. However, the Primals brought me forth as a primeval avatar of evil when they desired to make the universe more interesting. I was created from the story of a homicidal farmer guilty of fratricide to be the scapegoat for humanity's endless capacity for horrors. The nature of violence all came from me and even if it wasn't true, because people believed in it, it became true. I was shunned and hated wherever I dwelled until I decided to make the fear generated into a tool."

"That is a raw deal," I admitted.

"It is more than a raw deal," Entropicus said, his voice like venom. "It is foul nature of my reality that I was created as nothing more than stock villain in the pantomime of humanity's mythology. You cloak yourself in the mantle of the villain but have warped the narrative around you that people consider you the hero. For me, I have been predestined to make wrong what mankind makes right because that is my place."

"You could try being...I dunno, *not evil*?"

"Would that I could," Entropicus said, sounding almost sad. "My vision stretches across a thousand realities and I am left with the knowledge no story is ever allowed to drift too far from its original purpose. Each time I have sought a different path to become a better person or even express my free will from the role predestined, I am brought hurtling back to the awful thing I have become. My family is destroyed, my kingdoms laid waste to, or my kindnesses turned to ash. The Primals do not wish me to be anything other than Death's scourge on the living so a villain I must be until I escape it this day."

"By destroying reality?" I asked, trying to figure out the logic.

"By remaking reality," Entropicus said, his voice a low whisper. "My curse is not only limited to myself, you see, but for heroes as well as monsters. The decent are punished along with the vile because it makes a more amusing tale that way. We are the amusements to the gods and never allowed to stop rolling Sisphysus' boulder up the hill it continually rolls down. King Arthur's kingdom is never allowed to stand but must always succumb to Mordred's treachery. Robin Hood will never triumph because John will always become King when his brother passes. The Earth will only be saved by its messiah at the end of the world."

"Yeah, happy endings never last because everyone eventually dies," I said, unimpressed with his completely batshit view of the world. "What kind of moron has the hubris to think they can just reboot reality?"

Everyone looked at me, but I made a zip it gesture to them.

"The universe is an absurd place and one that does not deserve to exist in its current state," Entropicus said. "The gods hide from humanity and science continually finds itself rebuffed from the secrets of the universe it promised to reveal. But most of all, the reason that it does not deserve to exist is the horrors of the abyss."

"The abyss?"

Entropicus stretched out his hand to Abaddon. "This place, just one of the many like it, where souls are continually tormented for all eternity. Where the guilty are punished by having their own crimes done against them, repeatedly, for all eternity. It is a monstrous thing and worse than oblivion as it makes the righteous infinitely worse than the damned."

I stared up at him. "What have you done with Diabloman's soul?"

"Allow me to show you," Entropicus said, snapping his fingers.

What I saw was a vision of a horrific prison of a million souls held in individual cages over a vast abyss. In the center of it, suspended by four chains pulling his arms in four directions was Diabloman, naked, without his mask, and having blood drip into his eyes. I tried not to look at his face, which he'd never shown me, but I caught a glimpse of the sad middle aged man underneath.

Tortured, forever.

"Each drop of blood is filled with the essence of regret," Entropicus said, whispering his next words. "He'll experience all the worst moments of his life over and over again for eternity. A fitting punishment for the world's worst murderer, wouldn't you say?"

"You were the one behind his destruction of the old universe," I said, staring up at him. "Just like you've been behind most of my troubles, haven't you? You wrote *The Book of Midnight* so you brought the Great Beasts to my world, you created vampires, and you were probably behind Merciful too."

"Your doppelganger was his own man," Entropicus said, chuckling. "But I do know a secret about his actions. A secret that will break you and leave you without the will to fight on. A secret that will end this sad display of defiance by showing you that everything you loved, everything you fought for, was a lie. Do you know what that secret is?"

"I do," I said, looking up at him.

"Oh?" Entropicus said, looking surprised. "What do you believe it is?"

I looked back at Mandy. "It took me a while to figure out?"

"Gary, don't believe anything he tells you," Mandy started to say.

"It's too late," I said, looking at her with a sad expression on my face. "I'm sorry, though, for what it's worth. I don't think you started as a bad person."

"Gary, what are you talking about?" Cindy asked.

I looked at her. "That's the secret Entropicus was holding back as the one-two punch of tonight's proceeding: she's not our Mandy."

For a coliseum full of screaming fans, the next few seconds were surprisingly silent.

"Hahahahaha," Entropicus burst out laughing and it wasn't the smug humor of a Dark Lord but the kind of giddy laughter of someone who had just heard the funniest joke of his life.

Cindy pulled away in disgusted horror. "You monster!"

Mandy didn't deny it, though. "I may not be your Mandy but I am a Mandy. All of her memories and thoughts were given to me when I came here. Everything we had was true."

"Lady, I wouldn't believe you if you presented me a signed affidavit that water was wet," I said, looking back at her. "How?"

"Merciful gave me your wife's body in exchange for spying on you. I chose to stand with the side of the angels, though. I had a lot of experience resisting the darkness in my life." Mandy looked at me with a sad expression on her face. "Besides, I liked you Gary, you were funny and sweet. If you weren't so in love with the memory of your wife and your flying doll, we would have been fine together. I didn't even mind you screwing your psychotic henchwoman."

"Mandy died for me!" Cindy pulled out a sword from her picnic basket. "Wait, a damn minute, I wasn't even mentioned in the list of obstructions?"

"I object to the term flying doll," Gabrielle said. "Even if I have a bunch of dolls made of me and can fly."

"Eh." Mandy shrugged. I decided in that moment to name her Fake Mandy. It felt childish and stupid given the monumental nature of her betrayal.

"So my wife has been dead all along," I said, realizing all of my efforts to bring her back had been for nothing. "You could have told me. If you cared for me in the slightest, you would have."

Fake Mandy looked down. "I tried. Many times, I tried to tell you the truth. That I wasn't who you thought I was. I spent centuries with variations of you in the future. I told you then. We fell in love then. But there was always pain. Beyond pain. Every time I told you, you felt betrayed."

"BECAUSE I WAS BETRAYED!" I shouted. I'd let her drink my blood, have sex, and more. I felt…soiled.

"We even had children," Fake Mandy said. "The children your Mandy never wanted to have."

"Like hell!" I snapped.

"Yeah, he has enough of disgusting things!" Cindy added.

I glared at Cindy. "Stop helping."

"Death would have told you if she wasn't Mandy!" Gabrielle said, looking at me. "Right? I mean, she—"

"Death is not kind," Entropicus said, sounding almost sympathetic. "She takes on the form of the person you most love and the people you trust the most but she is not human. She has never been human or anything approaching such. Instead, the Lady of Endings is a force of nature. I learned the lesson you learned long ago: do not trust the gods."

"Who are you?" Gabrielle asked Fake Mandy, her expression containing several reactions. There was shock, horror, confusion, but also something else. Gabrielle was looking like she was trying to see the face of a friend in Fake Mandy's. I had a sneaking suspicion who Fake Mandy's real identity was but that didn't matter right now.

None of this mattered.

I almost collapsed but I held myself up. "Let's put a pin in the whole identity crisis thing."

"A *pin in it*?" Cindy asked, staring at me. "Are you serious? This imposter has been—"

"I *know what she's been doing,*" I said, staring at her. "Probably everything she's told us has been a lie: from being from the future to caring about us."

"It's hasn't been," Fake Mandy said, her voice almost wistful. "I reminded you, I sided with you against Merciful. I helped you fight against my master and I've done my best to return to the old ways of heroism. You have no idea how exhausting it was pretending to be her every moment of every day. I could never quite achieve a perfect union with her memories but—"

"Lady, just shut the hell up," Jane said, speaking for all of us. "Nobody cares about what you have to say now."

"Thank you, Jane," I said, deciding she was permanently on my Hanukah list. "You never told Diabloman you were alive, Maria."

Fake Mandy looked down. "He killed me, Gary. I can't forgive him for that."

"Then how can we forgive you?" I said, not expecting an answer.

"I'm rethinking coming to this universe if this is the kind of thing you guys have to deal with," G said. "I've had to deal with imposters pretending to be the people I loved before and it's a nightmare no matter where it is."

"Yeah, we can deal with it now," Cindy said, stepping forward with her fire ax. "Decapitation, last time I checked, was a good way of dealing with vampires."

Gabrielle stopped her with her arm. "Let's find out more before we act rashly."

"Gabby, all we do is act rashly!" Cindy snapped. "It's sort of our thing."

"Maybe that has to stop," Guinevere said, looking over at Mandy. "Did you know who she was, Cassius?"

"Yes," Cassius said. "I know who she really is. That is why she approached me. That doesn't mean I approve of what she does. A man who has lost his wife will believe anything if it means he can speak to her, hold her, or be with her again. It is the ultimate lie."

"And I fell for it," I said.

"We all did," Cindy said.

Fake Mandy didn't respond for a moment then said, "This is what Entropicus wants."

"The Devil has got it right," Cindy said. "Mandy, the real Mandy, died for me. A person who mattered gave their life up for me and you took her life and made it something awful! Lady, you are worse than Entropicus!"

"No she's not," I said.

"Gary—" Cindy started to say.

"We have bigger things to worry about," I said, looking at Entropicus. "I've still got a multiverse to save."

"You would continue to serve Death's wishes even knowing how she manipulated you?" Entropicus asked.

I felt empty, bereft of purpose and sucker punched in the soul. This, of course, was exactly what Entropicus had been hoping for. I understood why he wanted me to be the last participant in the tournament now. It hadn't just been because he wanted to spite Death or the rules prevented him from killing me outright. No, he wanted to break my faith in her and make sure she was nothing more than an enemy when I fought Entropicus. The last insult to his former master. Unfortunately, he'd made one small error—he'd given me something to hit.

"I'm not so supremely selfish as to want to endanger everything to get back at someone who wronged me. Are you?"

Entropicus' silence spoke volumes.

"Yeah, that's what I thought," I said, rolling my neck around with some basic yoga. "Let's get this over with."

Entropicus stood up and slowly descended the stairs. "So be it."

Now I just had to kill Abaddon's god.

CHAPTER TWENTY-TWO

ROUND ONE: FIGHT!

E ntropicus stood across me, the throne looming in the background. My associates were off to one side, met by the Hellazons who were prepared to take the fight to them should they try to save me. They were also there for the purposes of slaying us all should we manage to beat Entropicus. I had no doubt he would rather lose the tournament than die as he only had to win once in order to end everything. He wouldn't get another chance.

I just didn't know how I was going to do it.

"You have a small measure of my respect, Merciless," Entropicus said, looking down. "You are willing to die and send the entire universe careening to its doom for the momentary salvation of your pride. That is delicious hubris."

"Eh, I'm the most expendable one," I said, triple checking my battle strategy. I had no idea if it would work but it was all I had. "After all, you have to live long enough to make a wish after all this."

"Which is why I have my people prepared to massacre Guinevere and Ultragoddess when you die but before they regain their powers."

Ouch. That was definitely a downside of my plan. "Why do you even want to destroy the universe? Just between you and me before we fight for the wish."

"It is my nature."

"You realize a Primal named Destruction isn't going to just let you rule over the afterlife, right? Death is a transition but oblivion is an ending. He's going to want the destruction of everything everywhere."

"I think I know the being a bit better than you."

"Who can know the mind of gods? After all, we're only human."

Entropicus' eyes glowed. "I am going to break you."

"Bring it, Ivan Drago."

Cindy's cellphone started playing, "Anarchy in the UK" by the Sex Pistols. It was a song more traditionally associated with the Trenchcoat Magician than me but Mandy, the real Mandy, had done a cover of if called "Anarchy in Falconcrest City." I promised myself I would listen to it once this was done.

"Begin!" Entropocius shouted, his eyes glowing and shooting out a pair of Hate Beams powered by all the despair and anger of Abaddon fused into physical form.

The Shield Perilous, which I'd hidden over my arm with petty illusions reinforced by the Century Box, blocked the Hate Beams as I created a cone of refraction that sent them spiraling back into Entropicus himself. The blast struck him in the chest, sending him back only a couple of feet.

"Clever," Entropicus said, before smashing his fist down into the ground and sending the ground up beneath me in an explosion of rubble.

Entropicus moved with blinding speed, pounding me in the chest and face with a series of brutal punches that would have liquefied me if I wasn't empowered by the Ultra-Force. He then grabbed me by the head and I slipped out from his grasp behind him.

"You cannot use the power of Death against me," Entropicus snarled, turning around faster than I could attack him.

"Not using it on you," I said, vanishing into the dirt beneath him. "Using it on me!"

Entropicus could and would have ripped out the ground then and there but, instead, ended up being attacked by a flying construct of Ultragoddess. I felt my mind merge with hers, which was very awkward to say the least, as the two of us began pounding away at the God of Evil. Gabrielle was faster, stronger, and a better fighter than I could ever be. She was also a better fighter than Ultragod himself, having learned from the best in the Society.

Unfortunately, being a construct limited her to just rely on punches, blocks, kicks, and jumps. I'd brought out our biggest gun at the start, which was possibly a mistake, but I wanted to weaken Entropicus enough that everyone afterward would have a chance.

"You assume there's going to be anyone afterward," Gabrielle said, in my thoughts. *"You should have a little faith in me, Gary."*

"I have more faith in you than anyone else alive," I thought back through Jane's telepathy. *"Especially now."*

"I know who your wife, I mean, your fake wife is," Gabrielle thought back. I could feel her emotions that were a mixture of excitement, happiness, shock, and shame. She knew I'd been deceived into loving a woman who wasn't Mandy. Hell, technically, I'd been married to the Fake Mandy longer than my actual wife—but there was a feeling of affection there that made me mad. Apparently, Gabrielle had difficulty turning her back on her friends, even when they committed awful crimes.

I'd never thought I would be unhappy about that.

"Focus on the fight, please," I said, hoping she could succeed against Entropicus. *"Please."*

Ultragoddess leapt into the air and slammed down Entropicus against the ground, only for him to grab her by the neck then slam her in the chest with a glowing fist. I tried to absorb the pain of the attack but that just caused her construct form to become less and less stable. Entropicus then blasted her in the face with his Hell Beams before tearing the construct apart. I heard Gabrielle scream as I felt it alongside her.

Our psychic connection broken.

"Is she alright?" I asked Jane.

"Yeah, just unconscious," Jane said, through our bond. *"Actually, being unconscious is really bad for you and if you don't—"*

"I know," I thought back.

Entropicus started blasting through the ground with his eye beams before I struggled to concentrate on creating another construct. Guinevere arrived moments later and I pulled upwards long enough to give her Caliburn and the Shield Perilous. I didn't want to share my mind with her and every bit we did was embarrassing as well as uncomfortable but she put a heavy pounding on Entropicus while I hid away from the battle field.

In a way, I was grateful for all the beatdowns I'd received as it allowed me to concentrate despite the immense amount of pain I suffered with every blow. Guinevere's movements were even faster than Ultragoddess but our connection was weaker. Still, she managed to hold up against Entropicus for almost a minute and a half. Then he grabbed her hand, reversed it, then stabbed with Caliburn through the construct's nonexistent heart. What followed was him decapitating the construct with a backhand.

"*Son of a bitch!*" I said, hiding underneath the throne.

The pain was agonizing.

"*Gary, I don't know if I'm going to be able to maintain this,*" Jane muttered.

"*You're feeling it too?*" I asked.

"*Fraid so,*" Jane muttered. "*It's like being attacked by a cougar.*"

"*An attractive older woman?*"

"*Shut up, Gary. I can only do one more,*" Jane grunted.

"Century Box, how much damage have we done to Entropicus?" I asked, hoping it was good news. "Frame it like a health bar."

"23% of the damage necessary to disable him has been done," the Century Box said.

"Well, shit," I said, feeling Entropicus coming over. "This plan was not a good one."

"Affirmative," the Century Box said.

I had to make a decision. Using the Ultra-Force was like making an illusion with magic, a skill I knew a bit about. You created the image in your mind then poured your energy into it. That was the reason why I was able to create the constructs, even though I doubted I would have been able to manage them nearly as well without their hosts working through me. I was pushing the rules to the limit for this tournament but would have to push them even farther.

"Let's hope this works," I said, feeling Entropicus right over me. *"Sorry, Jane."*

I projected my plan to her.

"I'd say I'm surprised it's crazy but I'm not," Jane said. *"When this is over, you're going to have to buy me a forest."*

I was about to be torn apart by Entropicus when the alien god was smashed by a glowing golden deer who transformed into an Ultra-Force Jane before she unleashed a lightning kick. No sooner did Entropicus lift his fist to crush her, he was stabbed in the back by a glowing construct of Cassius. Then dozens of glowing Ultra-Force bullets slammed into his chest as G started attacking him with two pistols.

What followed took every single bit of my concentration and will to keep all three of their constructs in existence. I was generally impressed with how fast and capable the three of them were. Jane summoned her own magic to fight, throwing lightning and white magic, before moving fast enough to dodge Entropicus' counter attacks. Cassius fired glowing blasts of Ultra-Force from his fake pistol and actually managed to deflect another Hate Beams blast into Entropicus' face. G fought like a John Woo character, moving faster than Entropicus' fists or kicks. Skill was serving as the perfect counterpart to Entropicus' skill.

"57% done," the Century Box said.

"Yes!" I said.

Then Entropicus grabbed G by the face and crushed it, destroying his construct. He then fired his Hate Beams, let Cassius dodge it, and then turned the blasts around in mid-air to striking Cassius from behind. Entropicus proceeded to stomp on Star Count's head, destroying his construct. The pain of having my head crushed almost severed my connection with Jane.

"This isn't working!" Jane shouted in my head.

"Have faith!" I shouted, levitating out of the ground.

Jane did a backflip over Entropicus' back and grabbed up Caliburn, charging at him with the blade that had inflicted a genuine wound to his back. "Die you son of a bitch."

Then Jane's construct exploded as Entropicus punched

through her chest and out the other side. I lost all contact with her. I had no idea if any of them were alive, some of them, or all of them. Entropicus had smashed the hell out of my allies and I had no more tricks up my sleeves.

"I am now officially out of patience," Entropicus said, turning around to face me.

I came out of the ground, standing there in my insubstantial form. "Well, that's just too bad. I'll find a way to take you down, even if I have to sacrifice my powers."

I was relying on my insubstantiality exclusively now. There was nothing I could do to him that would even pierce his skin. Still, there was nothing Entropicus could do to me until I turned substantial again.

"You don't have any time left," Entropicus said, turning his hand substantial and grabbing me by the cloak before pulling me forward to his face.

"Ah," I said, realizing how screwed I was. "My insubstantiality works on Ringwraith rules where everything insubstantial is solid to each other."

"I'm afraid so," Entropicus said, his eyes glowing as he turned insubstantial too. "Goodbye, Merciless."

I used the Ultra-Force to fling Caliburn at Entropicus. Entropicus dropped me then grabbed the sword in midair, catching it in his palms.

"Shatter," Entropicus said, his voice full of inhuman power and unnatural energy.

Caliburn, one of the Great Relics and the only weapon in this dimension that could hurt him, shattered.

"Oh hell," I said, looking at that.

"Yes," Entropicus said, grabbing me by the throat then slamming my body into the pavement of the ground. He then grabbed me by the leg and smashed me against the ground back and forth like a doll held by a toddler.

"Fu…" I said, my head banging from the horrific beating I was getting.

"I was honestly expecting more," Entropicus said, looking down. "Even at the end, you tried to rely on the power of others."

"It's called having friends, jackass," I said, through a mouth of broken teeth and blood.

"Yes, I remember having friends," Entropicus said, walking over to me before taking my arm and breaking it in one easy gesture. "You know what friends do, Gary? They die. They betray you. They let you down or they forget you when you're no longer providing them amusement. In the end, you can only rely on yourself."

Entropicus then lifted me up one last time and hurled me in the air before blasting me with his Hate Beams full on.

I caught fire.

Then fell to the ground, landing with a thud.

I was surprised to find myself anywhere after it happened, especially since all the pain was gone from my body and it seemed I was healed. I found myself in a sunny bright field with Douglas firs nearby and a light mist pouring down from the clouds above.

"So, I failed," I said, face down in the mud.

"Not quite," a voice that was surprisingly nasal and obnoxious sounding, spoke above me. "I mean, yes, you're probably going to die horribly but the Level 15 Invulnerability you've inherited from Guinevere and Gabrielle as Ultra-Merciless. You were a limited edition released as the character in Amazing! Cards Universe and a lot of people thought you were overpowered but it's the best use I could get out of your deck."

I blinked, trying to process the sentence that I had just heard. Rolling over on the ground, I found myself across from a chunky white man with a reversed baseball cap, shorts, and a t-shirt that showed the line, "DungeonCon 1999." He was redheaded goatee and was chowing down on a bag of Mercitos.

"Don't take this the wrong way but aren't you the guy who ran the comic book store nearby my house in New Angeles?"

"I am, indeed," the man said, crunching away. "I ran said establishment for the purposes of safe guarding our cultural heritage of toys, video games, and comic books. It was an island of geek heritage in a sea of Philistines who did not appreciate the intricacies of the medium."

"If I'm dead, you're not exactly who I expected to see," I said, staring at him. "You know, since I actually know Death."

"I'm not Death," the man said. "I'm her brother, Destruction."

There was a short pause before I responded. "Yeah, not what I was expecting."

"So, I have been told. However, if it benefits you, I should note that I take the appearance of what your feeble mortal brain can process of my true form."

"But you ran a comic book store in the suburbs of California's largest yes."

"Yes."

I pulled myself up. "Aren't you the person behind Entropicus?"

"*He* perceives me as a nine-dimensional eldritch horror that consumes universes, rends souls, and is made of black holes."

"Yeah, I feel a little cheated here."

"That's to your deterrent not mine," Destruction said. "I've brought you here to have a conversation regarding the stakes of your fight with Entropicus before the second round where you probably will lose. Probably but not necessarily."

"You have a higher opinion of my chances than I do." I shook my head. "Wait a damn minute, aren't you the guy who is trying to obliterate the universe?"

"No, not at all. You misjudged me a great deal, Merciless. I hate my job and want to change the nature of it."

"What?"

"I want to stop destruction. I want to make it so that the stories I like are repeated endlessly and preserved for future generations across countless realities. Ultragod vs. Entropicus, you versus the Typewriter, Guinevere versus Morgana Le Fae, and all your new friend's battles like the little deer girl versus the baby killing dryad."

"Baby killing dryad?" I asked, before shaking my head. "Wait, my fight against the Typewriter is my iconic conflict? That guy?"

"I think you're better as a street-level protagonist than all the cosmic battles you've been fighting lately."

"How is eradicating the multiverse going to help with the fact you apparently love to play games with mortal heroes and villains?"

"Getting rid of the other Primals will allow me to make the universe as it should be."

"I've known you like a minute and a half and I'm pretty sure you're even less qualified to reboot the universe than I am."

"You may change your mind when you explore my realm."

"Don't have time for that." Mind you, encounters with gods generally took as long as they deemed fit.

"Even to meet your actual wife?"

CHAPTER TWENTY-THREE

THE VALUE OF CONTINUITY

I stared at Destruction with a dangerous expression on my face. "You know, Entropicus may have cut me down a few pegs and pointed out I'm not nearly as dangerous as I seem but I am not in the mood to have anyone joke about my wife. God or not, I will kick your ass if you bring up Mandy again."

"The real Mandy," Destruction said, simply. "Is here, in Limbo."

"Limbo," I said, blinking. "Jewish people don't believe in Limbo."

"They also don't believe Samael is a hot Goth chick but you still see my sister as that," Destruction replied. "Limbo is the realm between the land of the gods and the world of mortals. It's the place I store the souls of those who I'm not done with."

"Not *done with*?" I asked, each word bitterer than the last.

Destruction held out his hands. "Death's hold over mortals is something I've struggled with for many years and have almost always won against. You saw how I brought Guinevere back from the dead a few minutes ago. I'll do the same to Stephen, Moses, and Lancel eventually but I want to experiment a bit first. Maybe have a female Prismatic Commando or have four Ultragods that all turn out to be imposters. Two of them could be cyborgs!"

I stared at him. "Lancel Warren is dead, so is Moses Anders. I thought I brought Mandy back from the dead but I didn't."

Destruction threw out his arms. "Yes, silly, I still need the *illusion* of change. Death should appear threatening even if the only people who will stay dead are the uninteresting ones. But come now, haven't you noticed your villains have a distressing habit of returning?"

"I assumed there was no more room in hell," I muttered, wanting to throttle the man with my bare hands.

Destruction gave a rictus grin that managed to be terrifying despite the fact he looked like the guy who manned the register after midnight at my local big box store. "You can't have conflict if you don't have opposing sides. Good guys, bad guys, it's like shirts versus kins. You can't have one without the other."

"I'm pretty sure you can. It just means a really nice place versus a shitty one."

Destruction gave a dismissive wave. "Come now, Gary, you know I'm right."

"If you're right, why the hell did that imposter fill my bed!" I said, snarling and getting up before coming right up to Destruction's face.

"Because it was more interesting that way," Destruction said, not looking remotely intimidated. "There's nothing interesting about a happily married couple raising a family in safety as well as security. It's why I usually kill the lovers off or erase the children. When I bring back Ultragod, I'll probably do what you suggested and make him a younger hipper version. Get rid of the Polly Perkins romance. Not sure about getting rid of Ultragoddess. I tried doing that a few times but I think she's got a few stories worth telling. Mind you, I'm loving what you've done with her. Making the sweet and innocent heir the world's greatest hero into an adulteress and whore. She'll have to miscarry, though, because no one wants a—"

I punched Destruction in the face, growling in rage.

"You son of a bitch, you stay away from my child!" I snapped.

Destruction felt his jaw, making a few strange gestures with his mouth. "Huh, I actually felt that. That was unexpected."

"I'll kill you if—" I was interrupted by my mouth disappearing. My nostrils had also disappeared and I couldn't breathe.

Destruction put his arms to my side and stretched his back before I charged at him despite my inability to catch my breath and he just teleported out of the way. "Honestly, Gary, I don't see what the big deal is. You are the only superperson who I thought could appreciate what I've been doing. There are so many boring universes out there. Places where heroes get killed and stay dead so you never get to see them in action again. Places where they retire or grow old. Places where they don't get to be constantly pushed to the limits of morality or sanity."

"Mmph!" I screamed a string of obscenities at him before starting to black out.

He restored my mouth and nostrils to me. "You're telling me you've been screwing with the laws of reality in my world because otherwise it would be *boring*?"

"Yes," Destruction said, gazing down at me. "Honestly, did you really think the destruction of the old universe was because Diabloman and Entropicus had a real chance? No, it was to reset the game darker and edgier. I'm also the reason time keeps switching back and forth. You being a father to a five year old is a bit aging of you. I may have to make Leia your kid sister or an orphan you adopted off the street. You're lucky she's amusing. You don't want to know what I did to the Amazing! Family."

"Is...was Mandy ever resurrected?" I asked, having a sinking feeling of horror about what Destruction may have done to my timeline.

"Oh yes," Destruction said, chuckling. "You brought her back but that's way too happy an ending. So I switched her souls and made it always that way. It's amazing what you can do when you're omnipotent."

I tried to blast him with fire from my hands but nothing came out. "You're sick, man."

"Am I? Am I really? You're playing the game because you love it just as much as I do," Destruction said. "You wanted your loved ones back too. You also don't really give a shit about saving lives or being a hero. The only reason you're planning on trying to be a superhero is because it's something new and exciting. I personally think it's a good idea even if it'll never stick. That's why I retconned Merciful into being a deranged fascist by breaking him. You'd be surprised at how much suffering it took to drive him mad. He was much cooler that way than when he was a sickening good guy."

I stared at him. "How much have you done to me?"

"Oh, my friend," Destruction walked up close and put his finger on my nose. "That would be telling. Most of the time it's just a whisper or a word. *Gary can't handle being Ultragoddess' lover and will get himself killed. Being a supervillain is morally equivalent to being a superhero and the best way to honor your brother. It'd be better to lie about being his wife than reveal the truth and have no one to return in this life.* That last bit was for Maria, the woman who is walking around in your wife's corpse from the future. Wow, that's a radioactive bit of continuity. Of course, I could be making all of this up too. You'd never know."

I fell to my knees. "My wife—"

"My wife, my wife, my wife," Destruction repeated, rolling his eyes. "I swear, I'm so glad i put you through the wringer on that because you were so insistent on being a good husband. It made me glad when you finally broke and became the cheating scumbag I always knew you could be. Mind you, technically, you were never married to Maria in the first place but I suppose I can retcon it all away anyway if you say please. Personally, I think a supervillain should never have any relationships that aren't shallow and based on sex."

I grabbed him by the shirt. "Where is Mandy?"

Destruction disappeared from my hands and appeared behind me. "You know, I'm starting to sense some hostility here. Still, I'm in a forgiving mood. I'll send you to the spot where you want to go and let you see the people you've left behind. Maybe afterward you'll be in a better mood to appreciate all I've done for you."

He vanished.

I looked around the forest and noticed a signpost with three arrows on it. One pointed to "Heroes", another "Villains", and third "Sexy Cosplay Convention."

"As tempting as the last may be, I'm going with heroes," I said, following the sign's direction in hopes of finding some damn answers. I wasn't sure if I wasn't having some sort of dying dream or last minute hallucination but if I began to question all the insanity of my life then I wouldn't believe in anything at all. I mean, what was more likely, that I was the plaything of omnipotent omniscient monsters who wanted to play with us like action figures or I was insane? Obviously, it was the former.

What awaited me a few acres away down a yellow brick road was one that caused me to almost fall to the ground weeping. I couldn't believe what my eyes told me but in the face of truth, the soul recognized what was real.

There, in another grove, was Mandy wearing a pair of gym shorts and a tank top practicing archery. She was standing on a picnic table cloth, shooting arrows into a round target with an English longbow. She was still pale but no longer a vampire, looking as alive and fresh as the day she...died.

God in Heaven.

Beyond her, I could see other people I recognized. There was Moses Anders, sitting at a picnic table, carving a turkey for a group of people dressed in 40th-century costumes. Stephen was sitting next to a beautiful woman who was dressed like a stereotypical member of the French Resistance during WW2. I also saw Lancel, standing there in full-costume, looking brooding. I also saw other people in civilian attire that I didn't recognize. I wanted to visit with all of them before realizing there was only person I needed to speak with.

"Mandy!" I said, running up to her and embracing her before trying to kiss her.

She stopped me.

"Mandy?" I asked, pausing.

Mandy smiled brightly. "Gary, I know where your mouth has been in the past hour."

I blinked. "Oh shit."

Mandy laughed then kissed me anyway. "You're not dead, right? I saw you take a pretty nasty beating from Entropicus. Time doesn't have much meaning here."

"Not yet," I said, hugging her tight. "Hopefully, not ever."

"Death holds few mysteries," Mandy said, staring at me. "Even though it should."

"Wait, what?" I said, looking around. "I mean, this is great. Destruction was telling the truth. You guys are alive-ish and are coming back! It's enough to get me to almost forgive the fact he threatened my dau...actually, no, fuck that guy. However, I hate him slightly less than before. Wait, you don't even know who Leia is, do you? Crap, this is going to be awkward but—"

"I know about your daughters, Gary."

"Daughters?" I asked, stunned.

Mandy's expression was sad. "I know how history is supposed to go, Gary. You're meant to have a happy and joy-filled life."

"How can I have that without you?" I asked, looking at her.

"I've never left you, Gary," Mandy said, putting her hand over my heart. "However, Destruction has made a mockery of life. Returning superheroes to life only to let thousands of people die at the hands of murderers who can't be incarcerated or killed forever. Time, itself, is slowing down and possibly even stopping."

"Yes, that is totally Destruction's fault," I said, pausing. "Not at all me."

"It's not you, Gary," Mandy said, looking at me with a sad expression on her face. "But you need to bring an end to this."

"Wait, what?" I said, pulling away. "An end to what?"

"The cycle," Mandy said. "That's why Death chose you as her champion? She knows Destruction would be fascinated by you but that you can choose to be different than what he believes. That you can convince him to let time move on."

"Time move on... how?" I asked, very carefully.

Mandy lowered her gaze. "To let the dead, good or bad, stay dead."

"Don't take this the wrong way but....are you crazy?" I asked, stunned the conversation had turned out this way. "I just found you after years of spending time with someone wearing your skin. Your actual skin, I want to clean myself off with a Brillo pad."

"Spellbinder," Mandy said.

"What?"

"Maria Gonzales, sister of Damien Gonzales a.k.a Diabloman," Mandy said.

"You are shitting me," I said, blinking. "That's his name?"

"Yes, Gary," Mandy said, moving her hand up to my face as if she was enjoying just touching it.

"Why the hell would she not reveal who she was?" I asked, blinking. "I mean, to her brother if no one else."

Spellbinder being Fake Mandy was the kind of contrived coincidence I'd become used to since becoming Merciless. Spellbinder had rebelled against the evil cult that had raised her, used her demonically-granted gifts to help others, and had fallen in love with the Guitarist. She was a childhood friend of Gabrielle's and someone who had died saving the world. It was hard to imagine her duplicitous enough to fool me for years. To fool her brother. Then again, I couldn't imagine wanting to live another person's life in place of my own.

"Because her brother killed her," Mandy said, sighing. "Also, because her silence was the price of her resurrection. When she sacrificed her life to destroy one of the Great Beasts, she found herself not reunited with the person she loved but was brought here. A celestial waiting room. She got to watch the Guitarist retconned out of existence and replaced with a murderous asshole who kills people with piano wire."

"Wouldn't a guitar string be more appropriate?"

"Focus, Gary."

"My parents thought I should be on medication for my problems with that. Clearly, they were mistaken."

"You should forgive her," Mandy said.

"Like hell I should," I said, looking at her. "I should have known she wasn't you. I did know she wasn't you. She never acted like you. I just wanted to believe it was true."

"She was a hero," Mandy said, pausing.

"Stakes and holy water," I said, my voice full of venom. "Because of her, I stopped looking to bring you back. Death hid it from me. I'm going to find out why."

"So you'd stop looking. So you'd come to this place. So I'd be here to tell you what you have to do."

"What?" I asked, looking at her. "You seriously want me to stop the people I love coming back from the dead?"

"If you win the battle against Entropicus. You can wish for the multiverse to be free from the loops it's caught in. Not all realities suffer from them but enough of them do. To make a mockery of heroism, sacrifice, and progress."

"Why the hell would I agree to that?" I asked. "Don't mention all the people dying at the hands of immortal supervillains because superheroes are reactive than proactive. Screw those guys. I'd trade the entire world for you instead of them. I'm fine with the Ice Cream Man or Big Ben coming back from the dead perpetually if it means you're beside me. I mean, I just killed the former again last week. At least I think it was him. Dude didn't recognize me but sharpened teeth and acid tuti fruit is kind of unmistakable."

Mandy grabbed my arm. "Gary, he erased my daughter."

I stopped and stared. "Your daughter."

"The one Maria told you about," Mandy said, a horrified expression on her face.

I stared at her. "I thought that was just a story Maria made up. Even when I believed she was you, I couldn't imagine you'd actually kept that a secret from me all those years."

"I wanted to go to New Albion to find her someday but I'm never going to be able to," Mandy replied.

"I'm sorry."

"I can talk with her now but only in the realm of the dead. I might wake up tomorrow as a woman with no memory of who I was, with another past, or as a parody of my former self. We might have never met in my next life."

"I won't let that happen."

"There's only one way, especially if you want to protect your family."

I closed my eyes and cried. "Don't ask me of this. I love you."

"I love you too and I want you to be happy."

"I...can't."

"You have people who love you," Mandy said, kissing me again. "Love them back."

I didn't respond.

Instead, the two of us went over to meet with the other superheroes that were caught in limbo.

Lancel objected to being hugged.

Apparently, you couldn't do that to the Nightwalker.

CHAPTER TWENTY-THREE

OLD FRIENDS LONG GONE

"Stop hugging me, Gary," Lancel said, as he stood there in stoic fashion.

"No," I said, holding my best friend. "You're the Nightwalker, not No Hugs Man."

"I can be both," Lancel said. "I will curse you if you don't."

"Worth it," I said, keeping my arms around him.

Lancel pushed me away by my forehead like a toddler by his father. "Move."

I'd taken a moment to speak with the rest of the people hanging around here in Limbo because I wanted to be absolutely, perfectly, and completely clear about what exactly everyone wanted. Mostly, I was hoping any of the morally perfect heroes present here would have an argument as to why Mandy's idea was insane and we should abandon it.

I didn't get it. "Are you sure your guys are all on board with this?"

Moses Anders nodded. "Life is meant to end, Gary, and I believe in a universe after this. Coming back again and again to fight the same fights over and over again invalidates the purpose of them."

"The world needs Ultragod," I said, looking at him. "You were a beacon of hope and inspiration to people. We're living in a time when Luke Skywalker and Optimus Prime are being corrupted by circumstance. When the paladin and Lawful Good are being derided as unrealistic heroes. When Dirty Harry is bigger than—"

"I believe in humanity, Gary," Moses said, reaching over and putting his hand on my shoulder. "I believe while the power of darkness seems all-consuming, that a single match can hold it back. Good will always create new heroes to fight the darkness and the world is greater than any one man's legacy."

I tried to think of a good argument. "The world is a very crappy place, Moses."

"Then make it better," Moses said, nodding. "The only way that will happen is if consequences happen for good and evil. I promised when I became a hero that I would look after the little guy. How can I say that's true when I'm receiving special treatment? That I come back and more die on the ground."

"Ever see the Third Man?" Stephen Soldiers said.

"In college, yeah," I said, wanting to hear his take on it.

All of the men in the audience looked at me in horror but, well, they were all veterans of World War 2.

"It's a movie about the early Cold War," Stephen said. "One of the most famous scenes is the villain, which too many people took a liking to, said that all of humanity was just a bunch of dots and if someone paid you for every dot you made to disappear then you'd start thinking about how many you'd be willing to sacrifice. The thing is, if we're all a bunch of dots, then that makes protecting each other all the more important."

"That's surprisingly nihilistic for a patriotic hero," I said.

"I prefer anti-nihilistic," Stephen said, blinking. "We're all part of God, the universe, and everything."

"42," I said.

Complete blank expression from everyone but Mandy who rolled her eyes.

"Were you raised by a television set, Gary?" Moses asked.

"No, I had comic books and video games too," I said. "Also, the public library, which is what the pre-electronic internet was called."

That actually brought a smile to some of the heroes' faces.

I looked over at the women. "You okay with this Polly?"

Polly Perkins was an intrepid reporter who had been Ultragod's lover and closest confidant for the majority of the 20th century. It was doubly impressive since she was of Mexican descent and there were plenty of times when their relationship had been illegal under United States law. True love had won out in the end, though, and Gabrielle had been the product of their relationship. I wasn't about to bring up the fact I'd knocked up her daughter if she wasn't but I could tell she knew.

Stupid omniscient ghosts.

"I am," Polly Perkins replied. "I'm glad to be united with my husband but I don't want to return to life if it means being subjected to the whims of an idiot man-child from a higher dimension. Destruction took the form of a leprechaun to torment my husband a few times and often to strike at our love."

"A leprec...you know, screw it, I don't want to know."

"Probably for the best," Ultragod said, shaking his head. "You can't recycle what is good forever but create new stories and legends to inspire each generation of heroes."

"Speaking as a member of the tail end of Generation X, at least for now since time is all screwed up, it falls upon me to make fun of millennials and their entitledness despite the fact it was my generation that ruined everything," I said.

"You really have so little faith in your daughters?" Moses asked.

"Daughters," I said, pausing. "So you know about Gabrielle."

Moses put his hand on my shoulder. "I know you'll do right by her."

"This is a conversation I'd rather not have with my wife's ghost three feet away," I said.

"Same here," Moses said, his eyes flickering with a bit of menace.

"Meep," I said, feeling suddenly very small.

Mandy laughed at that.

"Can I have a moment alone with Gary?" Lancel said.

"Sure," Moses said, stepping away.

"Try not to take too long," Mandy said, pausing. "We're running out of time, even in this place, before Entropicus crushes his head and the universe ends."

"Yeah, speaking of that, anyone got any God-Killing Maguffins around here?" I asked, looking around. "Ark of the

Covenant? Moses' staff? I'll even take the Spear of Destiny and talk with my rabbi about it later. Nobody? Well, that sucks."

Mandy walked away and I watched her depart with every step.

"I'm like ninety percent sure this is all a near-death experience," I said, watching her walk away. "One last gasp of dream hallucination before I die."

"You know ghosts and Death yet you don't believe in near-death experiences?" Lancel asked.

"No, I believe in them," I said, pausing. "I just know the difference between a dying dream and an actual visit to the afterlife."

"Which is?"

"The afterlife sucks," I said, sighing. "At least as far as I can tell. Which is really the argument here, that this place between isn't the real one and it just is a waiting room for the other side that never opens its doors."

Lancel put his hand on my shoulder. "That's why we have to open it. I'll never see my wife, child, and you'll never see your father again if you don't end this."

"You ever wonder if there isn't anything beyond the waiting room?"

"Yes."

I took a deep breath. "I'm not going to persuade you that we should just suck it up and the good you guys do in the world far outweighs the evil by letting the villains back too."

"No."

I thought of Leia. "I can't endanger my daughter either. I'm going to have another daughter?"

"Yes. Mindy Moesha Anders or Karkofsky if you marry Gabrielle."

"Okay, I name her after Cindy AND Mandy? How the hell does that fly?"

"Don't ask me."

"Was Gabrielle just not allowed at the birth certificate? Too high on Ultranian drugs?"

"That's not what I wanted to talk to you about, Gary."

"Oh."

Lancel lowered his gaze. "I'd like you to carry a message to Amanda and Alexander."

He was referring to Nightgirl and Mr. Inventor.

"Yeah?" I asked.

"I'd like them to know they have my blessing to carry on the fight," Lancel said, looking down at the ground. "I became the Nightwalker to try to atone for my mistakes that caused the death of my family and later dishonored their memory. Sunlight, Nightgirl, and Mr. Inventor were unintentional byproducts of that but they made something I considered my cross to be something good as well as pure. I wanted to thank them for that and I'm never going to get the chance."

"You're not convincing me to do this wish, even if I can somehow beat a being who kills gods."

"The trick to understanding how to kill gods, Gary, is to know their power is in their worshipers."

"That's it?" I asked, looking at him. "You can't go with something a little more clear like, 'use the Spell of Aga-ma-hootoo' or he's weak to the color purple? I mean, that's also nonsensical because obviously gods have to gather worshipers so they can't start with them."

Lancel sighed and felt his head. "Entropicus draws his power from Abaddon using his own cloak. Despite serving Destruction, he is still linked to death. That's the only insights I can give you since I don't have any magical powers that can defeat him on me and even if I did—you wouldn't be able to use them."

"Great," I said, sighing. I'll pass it along."

I felt a little disappointed since Lancel had been in my head for years and was one of the few people I could genuinely say I admired. I was a bit of the middle child, though, overlooked compared to those who he had inspired that had followed his path more directly. Mandy, herself, had been inspired by the Nightwalker and it had led to her short but victorious career. Thousands of lives saved during the zombie apocalypse in Falconcrest City only to end saving one.

Lancel placed his hand on my shoulder. "Gary, I want you to also know something."

"Yeah?"

"I'm proud of you."

I blinked. "Really?"

"You were an angry, selfish, impatient, and kind of stupid—"

"Hey!"

"You're right, the stupid part was never true. But you have become a much wiser and more heroic figure."

"Shh, you'll ruin my rep."

Lancel took a deep breath. "I don't approve of everything you've done. I don't have to, though, and I have no room to judge. Instead, I just want you to listen to that little voice inside your head that tells what is right from wrong."

"That voice used to be you."

"Try to be happy, Gary," Lancel said, his voice low and brooding. "I never quite managed it."

"I'll try and figure out a way to do that with my dead wife, family, and friends plus an endless life of fighting."

"Not endless," Lancel said. "Not if you win. Then death is a respite."

"Speak for yourself, I'm never going to die."

Lancel didn't speak for a moment. "Godspeed, Gary."

"Let's hope not. He's a bit slow for my tastes."

I gave Lancel another hug.

"Really, Gary?"

"Quiet, No Hugs Man. Consider this an attack if it feels better."

Lancel reluctantly patted me on my back. "There, there. This is going to make no sense to you, Gary, until you talk to either G or Jane but you're the Jason Todd of my Bat-Family."

"Eh?"

"There's not a lot to do here but watch alternate realities."

"Okay," I said, confused.

"It means, no matter what, you're still family."

I smiled. "Anything else I should know?"

"I do have one question for my friend," the Nightwalker said. "Do you love Gabrielle?"

I closed my eyes. "When I was eighteen and just moved out, I remember meeting Gabrielle for the first time. She wasn't

Ultragoddess, she was just the pizza girl. She was trying desperately to live something of a normal life so she didn't go insane. This despite the fact she was worried she could be saving lives twenty-four seven. The very act of being normal, a part of the lives and suffering of regular people, was important to her so she could not lose perspective on the little guy."

"I remember," Lancel said, sighing. "It was after college she had to give up her normal life completely and live continually as Ultragoddess."

"Back then, though, she was just the overworked, underpaid, and incredibly stressed girl who literally once passed out on my couch every Thursday. That was the girl I fell in love with, not Ultragoddess, and I still see her in Gabrielle. I just worry both of us have changed that we'll never be able to be together."

Truth be told, I'd never loved Ultragoddess versus Gabrielle because I'd always blamed the former for breaking us up, but I couldn't do that anymore. Her sense of duty, desire to help others, and responsibility was as much a part of her as the quirky girl addicted to Kelly Clarkson. Who, by the way, I hate but lied about loving the music of for five years.

I didn't know if we'd be able to reconcile ourselves given the fact the world needed Ultragoddess more than ever and I wasn't about to stop being Merciless—but it was worth a try. Maybe. I didn't know if I was capable of loving anyone romantically after being unable to tell my wife was a girl wearing her skin. What did that say about me?

"I believed the job of protecting others was irreconcilable with love," Lancel said. "Don't."

"Says the man who didn't get his wife killed."

Lancel stared at me.

"Oh right," I said, remembering that was his frigging origin story. "Sorry."

"Mandy died saving the life of another. Don't dishonor that."

I looked over at her. "I never would, but I won't forget she wouldn't have been there in the first place if not for me."

"It was my choice, Gary," Mandy said, apparently able to hear from what I thought was too far away.

"Yeah." I closed my eyes and nodded to the Nightwalker. "Thanks, Lancelot. May you beat up Satan and have a nifty storm cloud to play your harp on."

That was when I felt my rib collapse in or something damn near closer o it. Falling to my knees, I tasted blood.

"I think Entropicus is about to finish me off," I muttered, spitting on the ground.

"Go with God, Gary," Lancel said.

Mandy rushed to my side and gave me one final kiss.

And then they were gone.

Forever.

CHAPTER TWENTY-FOUR

UNDERDOG FOREVER

I woke up to Entropicus hoisting me above his head with one hand. I could barely breathe and I felt like most of the bones in my body were broken.

"Now, you die," Entropicus said.

"Do...you have to...sound...like...an eighties movie... villain?" I managed to grunt out.

Entropicus drew his fist back as he caused it to glow with an unholy purple light.

That was when I used the Ultra-force to jam the shards of Caliburn into his back wound, shoving them in deep before conjuring a glowing alien laser that sealed up the wound.

Entropicus hissed before dropping me. "What have you done?"

"I figured putting some magical holy items in your body would fuck your shit up," I said, trying to figure out Nightwalker's last words.

"I can heal anything," Entropicus said, his skull-like visage contorting in just enough of a manner to let me know he was in agony. "This is my place of power."

"Not the best thing for you to say," I said, slapping my hands down on the ground and drawing from the magical energies below. It was just like when I stole Merciful's entire power source and used it to make Opposite Earth.

In seconds, I felt myself charged above and beyond anything I'd ever felt. It was vile, evil, destruction energy, but it was also the essence of Death. I felt my muscles grow thicker and my eyes glow as Entropicus' power became matched. If not for the fact he was here, he would have been clobbered by Ultragoddess of Guinevere.

"Thief!" Entropicus growled and blasted me with is Hate Beams.

I blasted them back, managing to hold them back until the pawn of his injury caused him to stop. Which was good because he was winning the contest.

Entropicus laughed. "This might actually prove interesting. You are still surrounded by those who would bring about your end. Even if I should fall, you will be torn to pieces by my subjects. Your loved ones will die and their death cries will be the last thing you hear."

I looked over to see Mandy and Cindy fighting against the Hellazons with a depowered Gabrielle who'd managed to steal an energy staff. The others were unconscious on the ground, having expended their power fighting Entropicus.

"Yes, well I suppose that means I have to think outside of the box," I said, turning back to him.

"*Century Box, does this planet have a core? The spinning metal kind or, I dunno, Death Star reactor?*"

"*Affirmative,*" it said, projecting a bunch of information into his brain.

"Gotcha," I said, aloud, before channeling every bit of stolen energy in my hands down through the ground into the heart of Abaddon.

Entropicus blasted me with his Hate Beams and sent me flying through the air, but it was already too late. The entirety of the coliseum shook as towers began to fall and I felt earthquakes start spreading throughout the planet.

"What have you done?" Entropicus shouted, growling.

"I'm pretty sure I'm causing the planet to blow up," I said, pausing. "You know, the one you're drawing all of your power from."

"You don't have the belly," Entropicus growled.

I stared at him, ice cold eyes. "Villain."

Entropicus wasn't the kind of guy who would let his power base die, even if he could rebuild it. He also couldn't take me seriously enough to believe I could possibly pose a threat, stolen energy or not. If I was wrong, well, then I was about to kill however many billions of people on this planet as well as all of my loved ones.

But I wasn't wrong.

"Damn you," Entropicus snarled, blasting the ground with his power to deal with the damage I'd done even as it prevented him from drawing from the planet's power.

That gave me one shot.

So I hit him with every single bit of Ultra-Force in my body. The energy poured forth and struck Entropicus in the chest, burning the remains of his flesh as well as weakening the Nega-Force in his power. They weren't opposites, though, but opposite sides of the same coin. So I drew from the power I'd stolen and converted it into Ultra-Force to continue the attack. I'd stolen as much power as I could from Abaddon and it was enough to shatter planets.

This was much-much more.

In the end, though, I felt the Ultra-Force dissipate from my body. I had exhausted every bit of power in my body as well as all of the magic. It would regenerate in my friends as our connection to it was severed.

Smoke, flame, and ash covered Entropicus in a cloud before it dissipated. There, on fire, stepped out the naked form of the evil god. Looking *tremendously pissed off.*

"Well, that sucks," I said, staring at him.

Entropicus charged at me, his face absent of anything but pure rage. I ducked under his blow and ran out underneath his fists to the other side of the coliseum, the ground cracking beneath us and opening up to burning lava miles below.

"Get over here!" Entropicus called.

I couldn't help myself and burst out laughing, pointing at him, despite being more scared than I ever was in my life.

"What are you laughing about?" Entropicus screamed.

"I'm sorry, it's just that's what Scorpion in *Mortal Kombat* says whenever he throws a dart at his enemies before drawing him back," I said, pointing out. "It's just hilarious. I mean, are you doing this deliberately?"

"Argh!" Entropicus leapt into the air at me, the chasm between us widening tremendously until it was half the length of the coliseum. The heat grew hotter and hotter as the lava raised up into a lake of fire.

He was going to make it, though.

"Century Box, can you make a gun?" I asked. "A really-really big gun?"

"Affirmative," the Century Box said.

"Do it."

An Ultranian gravity gun appeared on my shoulder and I fired it, sending a blast of energy that struck Entropicus in his chest. It increased his gravity a million times and sent him falling into the flaming horror below.

"I cannot be destroyed!" Entropicus shouted, slowly falling like it was an action movie.

"We'll see about that," I said, blasting him a second time and causing him to sink into the lava.

I threw down the gun and then blasted the lava with my ice powers, drawing on the energies of Abaddon for a second time. They sealed Abaddon within as the massive crater became an enormous lump of igneous rock.

I took a deep breath. "Finally, he's dead."

"*Negative*," the Century Box said.

That was when a glowing fist smashed through the top of the rock with Entropicus bashing his way through.

"Oh come on!" I shouted, staring at the sight. "You've got to be kidding me!"

"Round three!" Entropicus hissed.

I floated down into the middle of the crater before shaking my head. "Come on, E, you can't be that mad for destroying the universe! I mean, it's got all manner of cool stuff! Ice cream, sex, and puppy dogs! Objective goods!"

Entropicus started walking toward me but he stumbled with every step, swaying back and forth as if he was drunk. "I am Entropicus, I am the end of all things, and I am the horror that makes humanity fear the dark. I will not be defeated.... by....a wannabe comedian and his shitty plan to stab me with fragments of a holy sword!"

That was when glowing blasts of light shot forth out of holes that appeared across his skin, one after the other. Light started pouring out of his eyes and mouth as he came within ten feet of me before falling to his knees. The monster tried to mouth something before aiming his hand at me then clenching into a fist.

Before exploding.

Burning pieces of dead deity showered over my face and body as I tried to cover myself with the edge of my cloak.

"Holy shit, did that actually work?" I asked, looking at the remains of the Dark Lord.

"*Affirmative*," the Century Box said.

"Wow," I said, looking at the coliseum's fans in the stands. There were only about half left, the others either killed or having fled during the battle. They were silent in pure, stunned disbelief. I could empathize. Raising my hands, I addressed them, "Okay, by the sacred rules of action movies, I am now your king!"

"Kill him!"

"Avenge Lord Entropicus!"

"Ah fuck," I muttered.

That was when a glowing ball of Ultra-Force appeared around me as Gabrielle hovered above with a second one nearby containing the others. Gabrielle had gathered us both up, even the false Mandy.

"The tournament is over!" Gabrielle said, addressing the crowds around us. "This fight is over! The Tyrant God is dead! You are all free!"

"Yeah, because that worked in Iraq," I muttered.

"Technically, there were a wide variety of factors in the failure of Operation: Iraqi Freedom including the dissolution of the Iraq military, the failure of rebuilding, corporate malfeasance, and—" the Century Box started to say.

"Shut up, Box," I said.

"Shutting up, sir," the Century Box said.

Cindy called up to Gabrielle. "Ultragoddess, there's something you need to know. I've always loved you! I mean that sexually!"

Gabrielle looked down, a confused expression on her face.

That was when the skies opened up and the seven Primal Orbs descended. A glowing light covered us all and everything went white. The light faded away and I was surrounded only by blackness.

Leaving me alone with Death. She was standing there, a few feet away, appearing to be Mandy.

"You don't have the right to wear that form," I said, numb.

"I am all dead, everywhere. I am the person who remembers them when they are forgotten and their loved ones are long dust themselves."

"I'm not going to make the wish," I said, taking a deep breath. "I can't lose her."

"You already did, Gary."

I cried in the dark, for I don't know how long.

"Mandy is now reunited with her loved ones. It is a timeless place where you will someday join her. It is a place of no pain, no hatred, or suffering. There is nothing but joy and everything will be alright for her from now on."

"Is that true?"

"Would you want to know if it was not?"

"I guess I'll just have to have faith." I took a deep breath. "So, there's no resurrections from this point on? Death is final. Time and casualty are permanent?"

"Mostly," Death said.

"Mostly?" I asked.

Death gave a sad smile. "The rules are still folding into place. You wouldn't be much of a necromancer if you couldn't speak to the dead and time will always be a river. Even in worlds where magic doesn't exist, life is merely a place in space and time rather than a candle that flickers out then ceases. The future will be open to you as well as the past for future adventures."

"Screw that," I said, looking at her. "I am *done*."

"I'm afraid that bell can never be unrung," Death said, her eyes sad. "Your daughters will both be superhumans and at the center of the conflicts that are coming in the future."

"The racist assholes coming for superhumans," I said.

"And aliens who sense blood in the water now that the

majority of Earth's most famous defenders are dead."

"And the fact there's still many more supervillains than superheroes."

"Power doesn't corrupt absolutely, but it has a very high success rate."

I felt my face in despair. "I don't want any of this."

"You did, once."

"I don't anymore!" I shouted at her. "You lied to me! You said Mandy was back."

"I did," Death said.

"Why?" I asked, betrayed.

"Because you needed to be strong and angry for this final battle. Because you needed to make the wish to set your wife free. Because no one should ever love Death."

"I certainly don't," I said.

Death closed her eyes. "I'll give you one last freebie."

"Excuse me?" I asked, too devastated to care.

"You killed one of my champions, Gary. The rules are clear. I have to take from you your power and never associate with you again."

I thought about that. "Good. What sort of freebie?"

"One last favor."

I thought about it. "Anything I want?"

"You could spend the rest of your life with your wife if you want then both die at ripe old ages."

"Is Diabloman actually damned?" I asked.

"Yes."

"Undamn him."

"That's not really a thing, Gary."

"Make it a thing."

Death nodded. "All of the evil that he has committed, the murders, the torture, and the destruction of worlds is wiped away as if it had never happened. It is the ultimate act of mercy and you may have to choose another name after this."

"I won't tell if you won't."

Death waved goodbye. "Farewell, Gary."

"Is he going to heaven or resurrected?"

"Good luck, my love."

Death vanished and I remained in the darkness of the void. I didn't see anyone else around me but felt my cloak disappear and all of the power I'd stolen vanish. I was a normal, ordinary, all too mortal human.

That was when there was a pulse of light from the ground where Death had once stood. I walked over and reached down, finding a single marble sized orb on the ground. It was the Death orb. I closed my fist around it and channeled the power within.

Sending Mandy's spirit one last 'I love you.'

It was now time to confront her imposter.

CHAPTER TWENTY-FIVE

YAY, WE WON. NOW WHAT?

The Primal Orb of Death rested around my neck as I conjured a black cloak of shadows around me. I didn't want the powers it promised me or the connection to Death, but I wasn't strong enough to resist the temptation. To not have magic at my fingertips whenever someone tried to kill Gabrielle, Cindy, or the other people I knew—who could probably take care of themselves. No, maybe I just did it because I was stupid and selfish.

In the end, I saw the darkness recede and be replaced with the setting sun on Hell Island. I was on the beach and saw everyone else lying on their backs, having been transported from Abaddon. The Castle of Ultimate Sorrow was nothing more than an empty ruin and it would be another ten thousand years before it was the site of the next tournament.

"Yeah, I better not be called back for it," I muttered, walking over to Gabrielle first. "I don't even want to be a DLC or re-skin fighter."

Gabrielle was staring up at the sky. "Well, that was a thing."

I took her hand. "Yes, it was."

"You saved the multiverse," Gabrielle said.

I took a deep breath. "I'm honestly not sure it was ever in any actual danger. The Man Behind the Man™ was Destruction. He wanted to make an amusing story. Bigger stakes and stupider plots."

Gabrielle squeezed my hand, not getting up. "I know Destruction. He's a superpowered fanboy. If things didn't go exactly to his specifications, he would have destroyed everything. Whatever you did, you did the right thing since we're still here."

"Do you remember what I said to you when we first met?"

"Here's twenty bucks and if you want a more personal tip, come on in?"

I grimaced. "I remember our first meeting differently."

"You were kind of an asshole."

"Yeah, I was. Still am," I said, remembering my early college years. I'd paid for it by selling pot and ripping off the local criminals with Cindy. In the end, my parents had kicked me out and I'd bought an older house in Depression Suburbs that was my home until I raised enough money for college. I still thought of it as a more honest and noble means of getting a higher education than taking money from the government.

"What do you recall?"

"I'd been having a party and you looked tired. So, I thought you'd like to come in and enjoy yourself."

"Yeah, a house of petty criminals and local gang bangers. I'd spent the day beating up demons who'd escaped from the Inferno. I should have arrested you all."

"You didn't, though, and fell asleep upstairs."

"Best sleep I had all year," Gabrielle said.

"Are you okay?" I asked.

"I'm intact," Gabrielle said. "Gary, I don't know if you meant what you said—"

"I meant every word."

"You're not in a good place. I didn't know about Mandy not—"

"I'll deal with that," I said, looking at you. "I don't know if I can be everything you want me to be, though, Gabby. Not after what I've lost or what I've done. I'm not sure I'm worth it."

Gabrielle rose up and hugged me. "Gary, all I've asked is you be yourself. I won't make any demands of you. I love you, though, and want you to be part of our child's life."

"I'd like you to be part of my child's life."

"I'd love to," Gabrielle said, holding me and pressing her head against my shoulder.

I moved to kiss her.

That was when Cindy hugged us both.

"Uh, Cindy."

"I was with you guys first," Cindy said. "Also, I feel like we should bond by driving a stake through the heart of the vampire and then having a weenie roast on her burning corpse."

Gabrielle pulled away. "Please, don't kill her. Maria was a good person once."

"So was everybody," I said, getting up and heading toward the Fake Mandy. "We'll talk later."

Cindy wrapped her arms tightly around Gabrielle, and then took a selfie.

"Cindy," Gabrielle said.

"Shh, we could get so many followers from this," Cindy said.

I passed by Guinevere who was kneeling on the ground and praying. I couldn't understand her because she was speaking in Gaelic. I could understand the general gist of it, though. Somehow, she knew she was not going to see her friends again in this life.

I turned to her. "You know, I don't hate you anymore. If, you know, you need to talk."

Guinevere paused. "Thank you, Gary. I'll probably talk with Gabrielle first, though. Still, I suppose we are family of a sort."

"Yes, you're the mother-in-law I utterly hate."

Guinevere smiled. "I can live with that."

I passed by Jane, G, and Cassius who were all lumped together in a pile.

"Great job killing Wizard Satan," Jane said, pausing. "Which I'm assuming is a hallucination because shit has been just too insane to be real."

Cassius stared up the stars. "The universe is full of infinite craziness. Nothing humans have conceived of can be stranger than reality."

G looked up. "I'm moving to Jane's world instead."

"Good call," I said, pointing to all of them. "We're all getting pizza on me before I figure out how to send you back to your realities, though."

G growled.

"Or the reality of your choice," I said, pausing. "Personally, I'm thinking of Rap Video Universe."

Jane laughed. Nobody else did.

"See ya," I said, glad to have them with me. Sadly, there was no sign of Diabloman here. If he was alive somewhere, it wasn't here. I paused before I was out of earshot. "Okay, guys, this is going to sound like a weird question but do any of you know who Jason Todd is?"

Jane and G exchanged a look.

"Uh, yeah," Jane said. "He's the unloved second sidekick of Batman. The fans voted for him to die and he stayed dead for like three decades until they brought him back as a mean anti-hero who kills."

"I think he's cool," G said.

I stared at them then Cassius who shrugged.

"Huh, that was less complimentary than I expected," I said. "Well, stay alive. I like all of you. Well, except you Cassius, since you stabbed me."

"That's fair," Cassius said.

I continued on and found Fake Mandy standing up and cleaning the sand off of her attire. "Hey, Gary."

"Only my friends get to call me that. You are most definitely not my friend."

"No, I suppose that wouldn't be the case."

I gritted my teeth. "Lady, there's a serious double standard going on here. What you did is not an 'oops, I broke a a a plate' sort of deal. There's a serious double standard at work here. If someone possessed a woman's husband and lived with them for years, then you damned well can expect people to want him set on fire."

"Call me, Maria," Maria said, simply. "I also know exactly what you feel."

"How the hell do you figure?" I wanted to attack her, but couldn't because human brains weren't logical and mine was less logical than most.

She looked too much like my deceased wife.

"I probably wasn't always Mandy," Maria said, sighing.

"Destruction could and does retcon things he thinks into better stories, logic be damned. The nastier, the meaner, the better. I wanted to be a hero my entire life and when I returned to the Earth I found my own true love was a horrible parody of his former self. Jim went from being a singing cowboy to a hitman and anti-hero who'd taken up with a succubus."

"Jim Six-Strings, the Guitarist," I said.

"Yes," Maria said. "That was the first time I was brought back from the dead. The next time? The next time I was a vampire. My own personality drowned out in your wife's memories, but left with the despair of losing the people I loved. Your triumph in bringing your wife turned to ashes so it made the pain all the sweeter when it happened."

"I'm sorry, but I'm not going to blame God. You could have told me, you could have told your brother—"

"My repentant brother. The worst murderer in the multiverse."

"Who died trying to make amends."

Maria looked down. "I tried to drive you away, Gary. Tried to make you hate this Mandy, but I wanted a family as well as loved ones. Despite the unholy thirst, the need for pleasure, and the hatred for all life inside me. So I gave you mixed signals."

"Mixed signals." I conjured white fire with my hands, two balls of it, one in each hand. "Lady, you have no idea what qualifies as mixed signals."

"No, that's pretty unambiguous," Maria said. "I'm now the dark and edgy remake of Spellbinder. An adulteress, a rapist, and a liar. A person who has killed hundreds of people as a vampire as well as having switched bodies with an Asian woman. Can you think of something more ridiculous?"

"Quite a few things, actually," I said, looking at her. "I don't want you coming anywhere near my family or loved ones again."

"I'm not sure the universe will let such a simple solution stand."

"Yeah, well, it's a new universe."

Maria stared. "I'm going to change the world, Gary."

"That's your business."

"No, it's our business. We made a promise we would take over the Two Earths and bring an end to the age of chaos that has been afflicting this universe since the Primals became involved in the Age of Superheroism."

"I didn't make a promise with you," I said, dissipating the fire. The time to incinerate her had already passed.

"You've already taken the first step to changing everything. Death will hold villains. You've killed Entropicus forever."

"I'm not sure, to be honest. Assuming the dude works like a lich then Abaddon might be its phylactery. I might have blown it up or I might not have. Either way, I'm mostly hoping to die of old age before he comes back in a few centuries."

Assuming I could now that I was all orbed up. Yeah, I had balls now. The ball was in my court. Okay, now wasn't the time for puns.

"No," Maria said, pointing to me. "This is the dawn of a new age and I'm going to make sure the world knows it."

"Okay, crazy lady, I'll be taking a few steps back now."

"I'm also going to make sure my daughter knows this is for her."

My blood boiled in an instant. "What the hell do you mean, your daughter?"

"I mean the one who I raised."

"The one you barely know who is *Cindy's* biologically?"

"She'll be of my blood once I start feeding her mine," Mandy said, her voice low and cold. "She's the future."

"Like hell, you're going to—"

That was when Maria used the distraction to grab my Century Box. "I'm sorry, Gary, but I really can't have you interfering in all this."

I tried to blast her but a portal was opened up in front of me that sucked me in like a vortex, drawing in others behind me. I was so shocked by Maria's actions I didn't have a chance to react before I slammed against the ground of a wooden ship's bridge.

It was strange looking vessel that appeared to be similar to a Spanish galleon but had helicopter-esque rotors and crystal-powered steam devices attached to it. We were traveling over an iceberg filled ocean and the air was freezing. My eyes looked up toward a ring around the planet as well as two moons.

"Great," I muttered. "I've been transported to another planet. Apparently one that is into *Final Fantasy*."

Then Jane, G, and Cassius landed on me.

"Oomph!" I said.

Then Guinevere, followed by Cindy, and then Gabrielle.

"Oof!" I shouted, now buried under a pile of people.

Turning insubstantial, I passed through them to try and get through the portal before it closed but I missed it by seconds.

"Dammit," I said, looking around.

I'd been snookered. I could be in any part of the galaxy right now. Hell, I could be in any number of galaxies or universes or times. The Century Boxes were some of the most advanced technology in my universe.

Possibly the multiverse.

"Well, this isn't good," I said, levitating myself down and looking at our surroundings. "I don't suppose anyone knows the way back home?"

"I do," a female voice said, sounding very familiar but different.

A second spoke with a light Spanish accent. "Yeah, we've been looking for you for a while, dad."

"Dad?" I asked, turning around.

Greeting me was a twenty-something looking version of Leia who was wearing a red jumpsuit with brass buttons and wore a pair of thick steampunk goggles around her neck. The Time Cube was hovering over one shoulder, turning into various different shapes. She was also fiddling with a 40th century computer.

Beside her was a brown skinned teenage girl with a thick pony tail, wearing a gray hooded sweatshirt with a pair of blue-jeans. The sweatshirt had the Ultragoddess symbol on it and looked like it had been bought in a mall. Her eyes glowed with the Ultra-Force. I also saw Gizmo child Leia standing beside adult Leia which made me wonder if Death had left her with herself.

Mind...blown.

"I really hope I didn't miss your entire childhoods," I said, looking over at them.

"You didn't," Leia said. "However, I've got some bad news for you."

I covered my face. "Let me guess, I have to save the world, again."

Mindy, at least I presumed that was her, looked at Gabrielle then me. "Actually, no, papa, we need you to screw it up."

Merciless will return in:
THE FUTURE OF SUPERVILLAINY
Book Six of The Supervillainy Saga

About the Author

C.T. Phipps is a lifelong student of horror, science fiction, and fantasy. An avid tabletop gamer, he discovered this passion led him to write and turned him into a lifelong geek. He is a regular blogger and also a reviewer for The Bookie Monster.

Bibliography

The Rules of Supervillainy (Supervillainy Saga #1)
The Games of Supervillainy (Supervillainy Saga #2)
The Secrets of Supervillainy (Supervillainy Saga #3)
The Kingdom of Supervillany (Supervillainy Saga #4)

I Was a Teenage Weredeer (The Bright Falls Mysteries, Book 1)
An American Weredeer in Michigan (The Bright Falls Mysteries, Book 2)

Esoterrorism (Red Room, Vol. 1)
Eldritch Ops (Red Room, Vol. 2)

Agent G: Infiltrator (Agent G, Vol. 1)
Agent G: Saboteur (Agent G, Vol. 2)
Agent G: Assassin (Agent G, Vol. 3)

Cthulhu Armageddon (Cthulhu Armageddon, Vol. 1)
The Tower of Zhaal (Cthulhu Armageddon, Vol. 2)

Lucifer's Star (Lucifer's Star, Vol. 1)
Lucifer's Nebula (Lucifer's Star, Vol. 2)

Straight Outta Fangton (Straight Outta Fangton, Vol. 1)
100 Miles and Vampin' (Straight Outta Fangton, Vol. 2)

Wraith Knight (Wraith Knight, Vol. 1)
Wraith Lord (Wraith Knight, Vol. 2)

Curious about other Crossroad Press books?
Stop by our site:
http://www.crossroadpress.com
We offer quality writing
in digital, audio, and print formats.

Made in the USA
San Bernardino, CA
19 April 2019